Love
by
Design

Love by Design

MADDIE EVANS

Philangelus Press
Boston, MA

Love by Design, Copyright © 2025, Maddie Evans.

ISBN: 978-1-942133-58-2
Cover design by Once Upon a Cover
Editing by Charity Horniek
Section art by HailMarii Art

CHAPTER ONE

Brooke held her breath whenever a customer paused at the "local crafts and gifts" section to look at one of Jonathan Levesque's hand-turned wooden bowls. *Buy it, buy it, buy it.*

Although every instinct told her to sidle up to the customer and talk up the glossy bowls, Brooke's instincts were most often wrong. Therefore, she stood at the yarn store's counter, hoping the customer would see the bowls as they truly were, accept them, and then want to keep them. *Look at how well they're polished, and how the curve of the bowl matches the grain of the wood.*

It would be nice to have mind-control powers. Or mind-reading, for that matter, because people made no sense.

Lilah, who might actually have mind-reading abilities, slipped up alongside Brooke. "Tell Jonathan to make a couple of yarn bowls. I'll dye a skein to complement the sample bowl, and maybe someone will buy them both."

Brooke nodded. "He'd love that."

"It's a natural pairing. He should have thought about it long ago."

Brooke wove her fingers together. "He doesn't put things

together that way. You're right, though. It should have been obvious."

The trouble was, after everything Jonathan had gone through in the past six months, placing one more demand on him felt obnoxious. First, Jonathan had lost his favorite great-aunt, and second, he'd lost his dream of becoming a Catholic priest, and then he'd moved back to his parents' house in Brighthead. He'd started making those wooden bowls as something to focus him while he figured out his life, and then his mother had run out of both space and patience. Hence, Jonathan was selling them. One stormy day in August, he'd called them therapy bowls.

Also, he'd gotten a carpentry job with a cabinet-maker, so in effect his entire life had gone from prayer or whatever pre-priests do, to woodworking all day. Then, for his hobby, he did more woodworking.

Which, come to think of it, was like Brooke's life, too, except substitute "wood" with "wool."

The customer came to the counter, bringing not one of Jonathan's bowls but instead a stained-glass maple leaf in fall colors. Its orange and red glinted against a blue background. "That's darling." Brooke rang her out while Lilah returned to the Sit and Stitch table—most likely working on the Brighthead Crafters Guild. "It looks a lot like the actual scene out the window right now."

The customer said, "I have to say, I'm surprised that you have a gift corner for crafts that aren't yarn-based."

Brooke nodded. "It's because we've started a crafters guild. If all the local artists, artisans, and crafters band together, we can put our work in front of more people. We trade ideas and publicity, and we support one another." She pulled out some tissue to wrap the window hanger. "This stained glass was made by an artist in Juniper. Those hand-turned wooden bowls are made by a lifelong Brighthead resident."

Lilah looked up, smirking, but Brooke ignored her. The customer said, "And I would hope they're selling yarn for you at their shops?"

Jonathan didn't have a shop. Most of the members sold at craft fairs and summertime town spirit days, but he didn't do even that. Bright Stitches didn't benefit from this arrangement. In fact, in some ways, they were losing out. "Lilah's hand-dyed yarn is in a few shops, but mostly, they just hand out our business cards."

The woman said, "I guess it would be hard to sell yarn to people who don't knit or crochet."

Brooke said, "And it doesn't work to sell finished objects. No one wants to pay what they're really worth."

The woman half-rolled her eyes. "You don't have to tell me. People think they can hand me a dollar and poof! Out pops a hat. They barely want to cover the cost of the yarn."

Brooke tucked the stained glass into a plastic bag. "That's not even considering the value of your skill and your time. So for now, we'll just feature other people's work." She passed over the bag. "Have a great day."

The woman didn't take it. "Those fingerless gloves are gorgeous!"

Brooke glanced at her hands. "These came out nice, didn't they?" She'd knitted these gloves from her own pattern two Valentine's Days ago. They had a lace panel down the outside of the hand, and nestled into the lace were a series of interlocked hearts. Brooke had used one of Lilah's speckled yarns, and she'd picked these hand-warmers today because the speckles matched the maroon on her handknit sweater.

The customer looked closer. "That must have taken seven hours to knit, right? But no one would spend minimum wage times seven hours plus the cost of the yarn for a pair of gloves. Even I wouldn't, and I know what they're worth."

Brooke said, "Plus three dollars for the pattern. But... you've got magic. You can buy a copy of the pattern here and then make them yourself."

The woman's eyes widened. "You sell the pattern?"

Brooke turned. "Lilah, do you have any more tonal sport weight?"

It took five minutes to run the customer's card a second time for the pattern plus a skein of Lilah's yarn, although the yarn was harder to push. "This is the yarn I used," Brooke said, "and you *might* have sport weight yarn in stash, but if you buy the same yarn for this project, you know it will work well. Plus, you can cast on right away without looking through your stash."

The customer tucked the new yarn and the pattern into her bag. "I know how I'm spending my evening."

Brooke said, "Come back to show off the gloves when you're done. Then in two months, come back to the craft corner, and do all the rest of your Christmas shopping!"

The woman laughed. "You know, I just might. Have a great day!"

To Brooke, seeing her own patterns come back to her, or encountering them "in the wild," was always a thrill. Invariably, a knitter would modify the pattern to suit her own preferences. Those subtle changes made all the difference, and some were so clever.

As Brooke went to straighten the inventory, Lilah said, "You're going to sell all of Jonathan's bowls for him, aren't you?"

Brooke sighed. "I wish. I stink at handselling items to customers."

Lilah's eyes widened. "Did you miss how you just moved a pattern and the skein of yarn for it?"

"She saw the pattern worked up, and that's why she wanted it." Brooke shrugged. "I wish I could make his bowls sell themselves the same way. It might make him happy."

Jonathan never looked happy any longer. During middle school and high school, he'd been so confident as to what his future held. Now, he was tense and sullen. When she told him a bowl had sold, he wasn't happy. When nothing sold, he wasn't happy with that, either.

It was a shame because he had a terrific smile, and Jonathan deserved some happiness.

Lilah said, "Tell me again why Jonathan left the

seminary. You said it wasn't so he could get married."

"I don't understand it, either." Brooke pulled a Madelinetosh skein out of a Cascade bin where a customer had abandoned it. "He said he 'discerned out,' whatever that means. I looked it up, and it doesn't mean that he failed out or got thrown out. I guess he and his superiors decided God didn't want him to be a priest after all."

Lilah's nose wrinkled. "Do they have God's email address?"

Brooke had wondered the same. "I told you, I don't understand."

If God had a direct line to tell people what they should and shouldn't be doing, wouldn't more people be calling it? Last summer, wouldn't Lilah have called God to say, "Help me set up Brooke with Emerson Charles, the fantastic, handsome painter?" Then God could have replied, "No, you silly goose. *You* should be dating him."

Lilah turned back to her computer screen. "Maybe Jonathan ditched the seminary because Catholic priests don't get married, and he realized not getting married was going to stink."

Brooke snorted. "Just what any woman would want: a guy on the rebound from getting rejected by God Almighty." When Lilah giggled, Brooke added, "Jonathan used to brag about not having to get married even back in middle school. Pretty sure he didn't wake up one day and think, 'Wait, I'm going to miss out on splitting holidays with my in-laws. And what about the tax deductions?"

Lilah sighed. "Those missed tax deductions would have haunted the guy forever. Although, do priests pay income tax?"

"You nailed it. He *wanted* to file income tax, and the priesthood might have denied him the chance." Brooke finished with the yarn cubbies and turned back to Lilah. "Whatever it was, he's not talking about it, and I hate that for him. I can't figure out his facial expression, but it's not quite sad, and it's not quite angry. It's almost neutral. But his voice is tense."

Back in high school, Lilah had made Brooke a poster of facial expressions, and she'd labeled them so Brooke could decipher faces on the fly. When she'd gotten a smart phone, Lilah had done the same with emojis, identifying the expressions and defining each one's proper use.

Lilah sighed. "If Jonathan's going to get angry, can we turn him loose on the Historical Society? Did I show you this?" She pulled an envelope out of her computer bag. "Our friends from the Historical Society already tried, and failed, to file an injunction to keep us from buying any kind of property within Brighthead, and now they're trying to challenge our incorporation as a nonprofit because they think we don't fit the description."

Brooke said, "Can we sue them for harassment?"

"I'd love to, but the thing about being a nonprofit is that we have no profits with which to hire a competent attorney." She pursed her lips. "I'm so fed up. They've got a vendetta, and all I wanted was a place to have meetings."

Art and history should have been natural companions. It made no sense that the Historical Society should pitch this much of a fit over the Brighthead Crafters Guild. In the last few months, though, Brooke had learned (specifically, learned from the Historical Society,) that artists were *iconoclasts* who would travel to Brighthead, Maine, from all over the world merely to offend an innocent citizenry who longed to live quiet lives of nostalgia. Oh, the horror. If only Brooke had some pearls to clutch, and perhaps a couch on which to faint.

Brooke said, "The library has been good to us for the past couple of meetings." The librarians had put up coffee for them and set out snacks, which was unnecessary but made everyone feel welcome. Most of the meeting was just mingling and talking, but Lilah had actually brought up business at the gathering, which technically made it more than a BCG social.

"After which, the Historical Society went after them for daring to allow Brighthead residents to use the Brighthead Public Library." Lilah huffed. "Although one of the librarians shut them right down."

Brooke took a seat at the table. "We'll keep using their room for now."

Lilah scowled. "It's not useful for any of the other things I want to do! Exhibits, classes for the public, readings, and an artist-in-residency program—all that needs a space of our own. Especially the artist-in-residency program. For that, we need a building with an apartment. That's why the Main Street church was so perfect."

The Main Street church was the reason the Historical Society had gotten up in arms in the first place. If Lilah had tried to resurrect another building, they might not have flipped out as hard. Brooke had been over that with Lilah a half dozen times, though—four times before Lilah had even started the process of acquiring the church—so there'd be no use in explaining again. Not as if it would be any use, anyhow. Of all the things Brooke could do, she couldn't turn back the clock.

She glanced at the gift section. She also couldn't turn over Jonathan's bowls. Sure, some of them had sold, but it should be more. Everybody ought to have one.

For that matter, she should have bought one, but her studio apartment had no room for a decorative bowl, even one made by Jonathan.

Oh, Jonathan. He'd struck out in a quest for the best thing he thought he could ever have. Right at the edge, he'd been turned away, and now he was resigning himself to a life of everything being second-best.

Maybe that was the expression on his face: resignation.

It was a feeling Brooke could identify all too well, although she didn't make the facial expression Jonathan had been making. *I never wanted that for anyone, but especially not for him.*

Jonathan was made for great things. He'd just need to regroup and come up with a new best-case scenario. Until then, Brooke would be here, finding homes for his collection of therapy bowls.

CHAPTER TWO

It was full dark by the time Jonathan Levesque pulled into the driveway of the home he shouldn't be living in anymore.

With a sigh, he shut off the engine and grabbed his battered backpack from the passenger seat of his pickup truck. Which he also shouldn't be driving. Except that made him sound bitter, and he wasn't going to be bitter about this. He'd met enough bitter people that he didn't want to become one.

Still, he wasn't quite ready to go inside, so he checked his phone. There on the lockscreen was an alert that Brooke Evart had messaged. Had one of his bowls sold? Hooray.

Instead, it was a photo of a ceramic bowl with a curly cut down the side, almost all the way to the bottom, with a wide circle at the edge like a keyhole. This bowl was useless, no? Anything you put into it would fall back out again.

Brooke's message followed: "I was wondering if you could make something like this. It's a yarn bowl."

Couldn't yarn sit in a regular bowl?

Next message: "The user sets the cake in the bowl. The yarn end feeds through the groove, which keeps it in place. As the user works up the yarn, the cake turns in the bowl, and the yarn doesn't roll away."

This sounded pointless, but it would be easy to make one for Brooke.

"I think they'd sell well. Lilah offered to dye a skein to coordinate with your sample bowl."

Ah. So Brooke didn't want it, either. She just thought maybe it would be easier to sell than the ones he'd already made.

He should have realized right off the bat. Brooke never asked for anything. For as long as Jonathan had known her, Brooke had been the quiet one, smart and appreciative and unassuming until the moment she had to act, when she became direct and clear-headed. She must have realized today that yarn bowls would sell better than bitterness bowls, and she'd taken steps to correct the oversight.

Jonathan texted back, "I assume that groove needs to be very smooth so as not to snag the yarn."

Brooke was smooth that way, too. Nothing snagged on her. She went with the flow, a fixture among his friends ever since middle school.

Her reply came right away. "Thanks. Yes, maybe half an inch wide, and smooth like glass."

It was good to see Brooke installed at the yarn store. As much as she tended to diminish herself, he'd been half-afraid he'd come home to Brighthead to find her being piled on by an entitled employer, or saddled with a spouse who never paid attention. Instead, she'd made that yarn shop her own domain, set up a pattern business, and gone head-to-head with the Historical Society over co-opting a decommissioned church.

Which, to be honest, Jonathan wasn't sure how he felt about. All he knew was that his mother had seen video clips on the "Bright Hearts in Brighthead" social media group, after which she'd walked into the kitchen saying,

"Remember that girl you brought to the prom? She and her friends nearly took the mean girls of the Historical Society to the woodshed."

Inside the house, the scent of Mom's cooking greeted Jonathan like a wave of nostalgia, and that—well, Jonathan couldn't be bitter about that. Mom's cooking had been something he'd have lost when he entered the priesthood, but getting it back didn't hurt because it was good. "I'm back and covered in sawdust," he called.

Mom replied, "You've got time. Your dad's not home yet."

Even so, the scent of the cooking led Jonathan into the kitchen, where he found Mom making chicken piccata. "Did you forget it's not my birthday?"

"Wow, I totally forgot it's not your birthday." She sounded nervous, though. "I wanted to make you something nice."

"You baked cookies, too." He tilted his head. "Is someone coming for dinner?"

"My two favorite men, and they deserve a good meal." Mom kissed his cheek. "Get your shower. Dinner will wait for you."

Under the hot stream, Jonathan reflected that none of this sounded good. Mom used food to soften bad news, and after the year they'd already had, more bad news was not welcome. Great-Aunt Millie had died in January. Jonathan had left seminary in May. Now it was October, and—what?

Neither Mom nor Dad let anything slip during dinner, but with both on edge, Jonathan had no idea what to expect. Was Dad sick? Were they selling the house? They'd joked about moving once he became a priest and his sister finished grad school, seeking out a warmer climate where Dad didn't have to dig out quite so much. Except Dad wasn't ready to retire, and Mom loved her job at the grammar school.

Well, Jonathan loved chicken piccata, so if this was his last meal, he should at least enjoy it.

After they cleaned up, Mom put the cookies on the table, and she and Dad both sat. Here it came.

Dad said, "We have something to tell you."

Yes, please, drag it out longer.

Mom folded her hands and looked down. "I'm the executor of Aunt Millie's estate, and we had told you she'd left you some money."

What that it? Was there no money left in the estate, and the terrible thing they'd tell him was he didn't get any cash? Thank heaven!

He'd felt so uneasy when they said she'd left him money. Aunt Millie had been fun and kind, and Jonathan preferred to remember her as the woman who let him summer over in the granny flat rather than the woman who'd bequeathed him five thousand dollars. In a way, losing the inheritance would be like getting her back. He missed her terribly, not her money.

Mom's mouth twitched, and she wove her fingers together. "That wasn't all she left you."

Jonathan went cold. "What?"

Why all this tension about something else in the will? But then again, why hadn't they told him early on? As the executor, Mom would have known all this from last January.

Dad waved him down. "Don't get angry. I'm sure Aunt Millie meant well."

Jonathan looked from one to the other. Dad should have said that to Mom, because Mom looked ready to kill. As in, if Aunt Millie rose from the grave right now, Mom would be putting her back.

Worse, no one ever said someone "meant well" when the person actually meant well. They only said it after someone pulled something underhanded.

"Aunt Millie left you her house." Mom's fists clenched on the tabletop. "She left it to you on the stipulation that you could only have it if you got married."

Jonathan's throat closed up.

"She rewrote the will three months before she died,

when the doctors told her it was terminal. She knew darned well what she was doing," Mom added. "She knew she'd die before your ordination, and she wanted you to abandon your calling so you could claim the house."

Jonathan stood from the table and walked to the window.

Mom's voice was flat. "She set up a trust for the house, including a stipend. She put me and your father in charge of maintaining the property for ten years, with everything going to you as long as you got married in that timeframe. Once you're married a full year, you become the trustee, and the house becomes yours. Until then, we have to keep the house livable."

Jonathan whirled from the window. "I didn't want her house!" His voice cracked, but was it disbelief or rage?

Dad shook his head. "We know."

"She thought she could bribe me to leave my vocation?" Jonathan strode back to the table. "She thought I'd look in the mirror and say, 'Gee, God is awesome, but that big house on Sky Ridge Drive? Now that's even more awesome'?"

Mom's mouth tightened. "That's why we didn't say anything in January. You and she were buddies. Why would we wreck your memories over something that would never happen?"

Dad said, "But you've had a lot of time to think since leaving seminary, and since you're not returning, you needed to know."

Jonathan gripped the back of his chair so hard his hands hurt. "I don't want her house. I didn't even want her money."

He certainly didn't want her betrayal—didn't want her last action to have been an attempt to undermine something Jonathan had aimed toward ever since he was a kid. Sure, Aunt Millie wasn't Catholic herself, and maybe a few times she'd shut him down with, "Enough religion, okay?" but that wasn't the same as offering a bribe with the intent of changing him.

Mom said, "Honey, sit down."

It was taking all Jonathan's self-control to stand in place and not stomp into the back yard to split wood. "Sell the house. Challenge the will."

Dad sighed. "We've had lawyers look over it. It's solid."

Mom shook her head. "I talked to the lawyer who drew it up, and before you ask, Aunt Millie was of sound mind when she crafted this scheme."

Head dropped, Jonathan leaned hard into his shoulder blades, letting the fury roil through his body.

He'd loved Aunt Millie. He'd spent summers with her in that awesome house overlooking Brighthead Bay. As an older teen, he'd lived in her guest cottage. He'd used his great-uncle's woodworking tools and hung out with his friends, and all that time, he'd thought she loved him. When she'd gotten sick, he'd prayed for her every day. Every blasted day. And now this.

Mom drummed her fingers on the table. "That's where things stand. We planned to let the clock run out so as not to tarnish your memories. Since now it might come into play, you need to know. If you get married in the next ten years, the house is yours."

Jonathan's voice was small. "I don't want it."

Dad said, "It's a nice house."

"I know it's a nice house!" Sky Ridge Drive was home to Brighthead's most expensive property, and Aunt Millie's was not the most shameful of the lineup. It even stood on the better side of the street, with an entire wall of windows facing the bay. The property didn't back down onto the water, but from highest elevation in Brighthead, it had an unimpeded view. It had a carriage house, which Jonathan had used for a workshop, and the guest cottage with a single bedroom, bathroom, and kitchenette. Inside, Aunt Millie's house had a gorgeous library, three bedrooms, and wainscoting on the walls. It even had quarters for a live-in servant. The finished basement was wide open and perfect for large-scale entertaining. She'd hosted his graduation party.

So many awesome memories, ruined in one blow. Aunt Millie had tried to sabotage his vocation.

Dad's hands landed on Jonathan's shoulders, and he tensed because he hadn't even realized Dad had gotten up.

Dad said, "Try not to be too hard on her."

Jonathan scowled. "I'm not interested. The last thing she did to me was so...disrespectful. Anything you say is going to make it worse."

Dad sighed. "She loved you and probably thought she was looking out for you."

"If she'd been looking out for me, she'd have sat me down and said, 'You know, I'd prefer if you didn't become a priest."

Mom said, "In all fairness, I think she did. You told her it wasn't her decision."

Right, because it wasn't Aunt Millie's decision. Except in the end, it hadn't been Jonathan's decision, either.

"Look, I can't." Jonathan flexed his hands. "I don't want the house. I'll relinquish my inheritance, and then you can sell it and split it up among all the other heirs. Give it to my sister. You go live in it. I'll return the five thousand, too. I don't want Aunt Millie's money. Let it all go."

Let Aunt Millie be dead to him. All of that time, and she'd never said any of what she really felt. He was just a puppet to her, someone to be tied up with obligations and the tantalizing gift of more money than he imagined having. And that, after he'd resolved himself to a life of chastity and obedience as a diocesan priest.

Mom pushed the cookie plate toward him, but Jonathan couldn't imagine eating anything right now. "Sweetie, we'll figure this out."

Jonathan fought to keep his voice under control. "If I did meet a woman who wanted to marry me, I'd have to tell her to wait eleven years, just so we don't get saddled with a tainted house."

Dad snorted a laugh, and Mom shot him a look.

"I'm sorry. I'm not in a good frame of mind to continue this conversation." Jonathan got up from the table. "If I keep talking, I'm going to say something I'll regret."

He retreated to his bedroom and stared into the mirror.

More than half his lifetime ago, a religious education teacher had told the class about Saint Jean Vianney, a French man who'd worked hard to become a priest. That hadn't made any sense, so Jonathan had visited the library over at Saint Lucy's to get a biography. It was barely ninety pages and written for fifth graders, but halfway through, it was as though the sky opened and inspiration poured down. Jonathan had never read anything half this fascinating, like stepping through the entrance of a world that sparkled and shone, where every moment vibrated with meaning..

He'd checked out another biography from the public library, this one twice as thick and with fifteen pages of citations. Long before he'd finished, he'd committed to becoming a priest.

From that second, every decision had been made with one aim in mind: the priesthood. For high school, Jonathan chose the regional vo-tech because it made better sense to graduate with some kind of technical know-how. He'd specialized in carpentry because Jesus was a carpenter. Jonathan had picked his college so he wouldn't have any debt to hinder his plans, and the month after graduation, he'd left for major seminary.

Then, three years in, God had said, "Actually, no."

Through all those years, Aunt Millie had offered Jonathan a home away from home. She'd been a mentor and a friend and a provider. She'd never had children, so she'd become the Cool Aunt to him the same way she'd been a Cool Aunt to his father. She'd become a staple with his friends, too, showing up for baseball games and school plays, and even his Confirmation. No, she wasn't Catholic, but he'd thought she understood.

Why were all the guiding lights in his life so... unsupportive?

He watched himself in the mirror and waited for his own image to resolve into something that made sense, a person with a purpose now that his purpose had vanished.

It wasn't fair to say his guiding lights were all letting him down. God must have reasons for cutting him off, and when Jonathan took stock, his parents had always been supportive. By keeping this information from him until he'd already decided not to become a priest, they'd shown exactly how supportive they were. Father Tim from Saint Lucy's was also supportive. Finally, when Jonathan had returned to Brighthead, he'd reached out to the man he'd co-opped for in high school, and he'd been offered a job on the spot.

It was just Aunt Millie. That betrayal stung, and it stung hard. An hour ago, Jonathan had wished she hadn't left him any money because he wanted to remember her as she was—bright and funny and kind. Now he wished she hadn't died at all. Not because he wanted to talk to her again, but because if he'd never heard about her will, he'd have been able to keep thinking of her the same way.

Jonathan returned to the kitchen to find his parents talking softly, with the television on in the corner.

Mom looked up, concerned, but Jonathan only shrugged as he reached for the plastic container with the cookies. "I've got an idea for the house." He took two, not looking her in the eyes. "You're going to hate this, but I know someone who can use it."

CHAPTER THREE

Natalie sighed as Brooke drove toward 28 Sky Ridge Drive. "These houses are gorgeous. I'm so jealous that you attended a graduation party here."

Lilah snickered. "I was surprised that they even let me set foot in the place, but *Father Jonathan* never cared about social status. His aunt was wicked chill with having two dozen teenagers invade her home."

Brooke smiled. That party had been what she imagined Heaven would be like, with firepits, a DJ with a dance floor under a rented tent, and a delicious catering spread. When Brooke had fled indoors to have a low-key introvert meltdown (in addition to the aforementioned teens, there'd been an equal number of adults) she'd ended up in a spacious kitchen with Jonathan's great-aunt. The woman had taken one look at Brooke and escorted her onto the balcony to get herself together. "Stay as long as you like," she'd said, followed by, "You're the sweet young lady Jonathan escorted to the prom, right?"

Agog at the massive house, Brooke had only stammered, "That was nice of him. He didn't have to."

Jonathan had taken her to the prom out of pity. Her

entire friend group was coupled up at the time. Of course Brooke could go with her friends, but Jonathan had figured out they'd make an odd number. Therefore, he'd asked if he could escort her. Jonathan was able to have the no-strings-attached experience of a prom (not his own school's prom, but even so) and Brooke got to walk into the ballroom holding the arm of a handsome guy wearing a tuxedo. With a future priest, she'd had no fear that he'd try to get under her skirt. Whenever she wanted to dance, Jonathan had been willing to. Then, when she'd had enough of human beings (the same way she would later at his graduation party), he'd taken her onto the balcony where it was quieter.

He'd removed his tuxedo jacket and laid it across her shoulders because it was chilly. That kind of observation and thoughtfulness was going to make him an excellent priest.

Aunt Millie had fetched Jonathan to her own balcony during the graduation party. "Are you okay?" he asked.

Brooke managed to say, "Overwhelmed."

He'd chuckled. "Me, too." And then they'd stood side-by-side, enjoying whatever peace they could while watching the bay and the lighthouse and the waves.

It was a moment of stillness in the chaos. Sometimes, all you need is a moment.

As the car labored uphill, Lilah said, "I still don't understand why'd he want all three of us here today. His aunt died in January, right?"

Natalie sighed. "She must have been really young."

Brooke shook her head. "His great-aunt. He just called her Aunt Millie. We all did." As you'd expect from a rich neighborhood, Sky Ridge had an artificially low speed limit. "He wouldn't clarify why he wanted all three of us, even when I told him that for all three, it had to be a Sunday."

Natalie groaned. "Don't tell me she had a yarn stash, and he wants us to appraise it?"

Brooke flinched. "That would be unfortunate. Unless she

had a hermetically sealed cedar room."

Moths in the yarn shop would be a disaster. Saying that to Jonathan would hurt his feelings, so Brooke would have to let a tactful Natalie handle that.

At number 28, two other cars sat in the driveway: a tan SUV and a black sedan. The man who stepped out of the sedan wore a suit and tie and a humorless expression. So —this was not about a yarn stash.

Jonathan exited the house, less well-dressed but similarly grim, followed by his parents, who seemed uneasy.

Brooke's hands tightened on the wheel. "Should I throw the car in reverse and break the speed limit?"

Natalie sighed. "Let's see what's about to happen."

Lilah added, "I'm intrigued."

Brooke turned off the engine.

Lots of handshakes followed, and the grim-faced, black-suited man introduced himself as Theodore Hodges. Brooke hugged Mrs. Levesque and shook hands with Mr. Levesque, and they at least seemed pleased to see her. *How've you been? I was so happy to hear you two had bought Ellie's yarn shop! We've been following the Crafters Guild. Thank you so much for selling Jonathan's bowls.*

Brooke had never been certain how to take his parents' solicitude. Natalie and Lilah didn't think it was unusual, but both Natalie's and Lilah's parents had also been disarmingly nice, so maybe they couldn't understand.

Jonathan glanced around. "Before we talk, I wanted to give you a tour, since Natalie's never seen the property."

It had been so many years, but the grounds were sweet. Brooke exclaimed, "Oh, Aunt Millie added a rose garden! And she updated the fire pit." She turned to Natalie. "These towers on either side were propane heaters, so in addition to the fire, you had heat at your back. Out here on New Year's Eve, we had snow, but it was toasty." She turned to the Levesques, adding, "Aunt Millie was so generous. I wish we'd told her that more often."

Jonathan didn't respond with the fondness Brooke

expected, just, "Come on."

The carriage house no longer housed carriages but still had some woodworking tools. Beyond that was an orchard of thirty trees, heavy with apples. Jonathan picked a few for them, and they munched on apples while walking.

Back again toward the front of the property, there was the guest house where Jonathan had lived during the summers. Brooke had always wondered if Aunt Millie was lonely and wanted the company, or maybe she'd needed some help as she was getting older. The guest house was sealed, but Jonathan had his parents unlock it. It was dusty.

Then they climbed the slope to the main house, with two stories facing the road and three facing the bay. The main entrance had a small covered porch dwarfed by columns.

Just past the mudroom, the house opened into cathedral ceilings the way Brooke remembered, with a massive gathering space and a curved wooden staircase facing the entry. Above was the second-floor hallway, exposed behind a stair railing. Despite it being eight months since Aunt Millie's death, the house felt clean. Without most of its furniture and decorations, the place echoed.

And yes, the murals were still here! Using a technique called *trompe l'oeil,* Aunt Millie herself had painted murals in most of the rooms. The dining room walls had transformed into arches dripping with wisteria, and beyond those, a view of distant ruins. In the sitting room, vines crawled up the corners, and one wall looked as if it, too, gazed over the bay.

The first floor had an expansive sitting room, an equally impressive dining room, a library behind a glass wall, and beyond that, the balcony.

To the side was a kitchen that left Natalie speechless, and a smaller entrance with its own screened-in porch. Painted roses climbed the kitchen walls. Jonathan pointed out the six-burner stove with a center griddle and a dual oven, the updated fridge and dishwasher, and the modern cabinets and counter space. Brooke was most impressed by the separate handwashing station on the granite-topped island.

Natalie clenched her hands. "Can you imagine Colin in a place like this?"

Brooke nudged her. "I imagine the restaurant has a better kitchen."

She snickered. "He'd put this one to the test."

Every time they entered a new room, Lilah would give a little whine, followed by, "Oh, that exposed woodwork!" or, "I adore those leadlight windows!" The library still had hundreds of books behind glass doors, although only one reading chair remained. Also in the library was a masterpiece: Aunt Millie's grand piano. Brooke stroked the wood, but she didn't uncover the keys.

Mrs. Levesque said, "Do you still play?"

Brooke shook her head. "Not since college."

Mr. Levesque said, "Didn't you used to play for Saint Lucy's?"

Brooke walked away from the instrument. "I played piano to appease my grandmother, and she volunteered me for the teen services so I wasn't wasting her money."

Today was the first time Brooke had ever seen the upstairs. The master suite was larger than Brooke's entire studio apartment, with a walk-in closet and an en suite bathroom with a separate shower stall and a sunken tub. On the wall opposite the bed was a mural of mountains in springtime. Affixed to the wall behind the king-sized bed was a wooden mosaic headboard, a castle with turrets and a door like a portcullis that centered directly over the bed.

Brooke side-eyed Jonathan. "Is there a space behind that? Does anything come out at night?"

Lilah giggled. "Oh, that would be cunning."

Mrs. Levesque said, "Aunt Millie designed all these herself."

A second bedroom was smaller, with a walk-in closet but no en suite bathroom. The mural here was a flower garden, and again attached to the wall, but without a bed, was a wooden headboard, this one shaped like a red barn with a silo. It, too, had a door.

The third bedroom, also palatial by Brooke's standards, featured a mural of a peach tree and a headboard like a country church.

Lilah said, "It would be fantastic if during the night, all the little doors opened at the same time."

Brooke was getting a headache from all the murals, although they were well-done and the colors subdued. Aunt Millie must have put so much work into them. What a shame that the family couldn't remove the art from the walls to keep her memory.

All three bedrooms faced the bay. Opposite them was a full bathroom facing the road. Also on the second floor was, as Jonathan referred to it, "the servant's quarters." This empty suite had its own kitchenette and a three-quarter bathroom. That was where Aunt Millie's home health attendant had lived during the final years of her life. Prior to that, had the family had a live-in maid? With windows on two sides, this room faced the guest cottage and the road. It was the only one without a mural or a headboard, so maybe Aunt Millie didn't think the servants worth uplifting with artwork, or else the servants wanted to decorate on their own.

They also took a trip to the fully finished basement, which had a partial kitchenette, rows of windows, and still more exposed woodwork. It opened into the back yard through an enclosed area beneath the first-floor balcony.

With the tour finished, Jonathan brought them back to the first floor kitchen, where four of them crowded the round table. Jonathan brought in a fifth chair from elsewhere, but Mr. Levesque and Theodore Hodges opted to stand.

Natalie said, "Thank you for the tour, but what is this about?"

Jonathan's mouth twitched in a facial expression Brooke would have labelled disgust. "My mom's been following your attempt to get a location for the Brighthead Crafters Guild, and how the Historical Society shut you down.

Would this house work for what you need?"

Lilah nearly jumped out of her skin. "Are you kidding? This is an artist's house! There's space, and a massive kitchen, and the downstairs even has its own bathroom so people wouldn't need to access the rest of the house during meetings. You've got plenty of rooms, and those headboards are fantastic, and don't get me started on the murals."

Natalie added, "We'd want to turn some of it into studio space, but overall, it's perfect."

Brooke drummed her fingers on the table. This was a waste of time. "Other than the cost. We can't afford to rent it, and there would be a lawsuit from our friends the historians the split-second we signed a purchase agreement."

Jonathan raised his hands. "We've got that wrapped up, but it's about to get complicated."

Brooke frowned at him. The situation had started out complicated.

Mrs. Levesque was shaking her head, but Mr. Levesque's face was unreadable. Jonathan pulled two manila envelopes out of his folder and opened the first one. "This is Millie Levesque's will. The will stipulates that the house be put into a trust, along with a fund for its maintenance, for ten years. My parents are the overseers of that trust. Before ten years pass, if I get married, the trust and the house become mine."

Brooke recoiled. "Why would she do that? You were in seminary!"

Mrs. Levesque lowered her voice. "Aunt Millie was a woman in possession of many opinions."

Was that fury? It was so subdued. Brooke had never heard anger from Jonathan's mother.

"If I get married, after one year, this comes into play." Jonathan opened the second envelope. "This is a prenup agreement protecting both parties' assets. One year after I marry someone, the trust passes to me. I then add my spouse as co-owner of the trust. If we get divorced, the trust becomes the sole property of my ex-spouse." His eyes narrowed. "I want to see the Historical Society try to challenge that—first off, because they won't know about it. And secondly, because they can't stop spouses from commingling their property. And they certainly can't interfere in a divorce where there's an iron-clad prenup stating who gets what when neither spouse is contesting it."

Lilah breathed, "No. This can't be serious."

Natalie said, "Find a way to contest the will."

Jonathan's eyes flashed. "Do you think we haven't?"

The dark-suited man said, "I've consulted everyone I know, including two separate judges. Millie Levesque was thorough."

Jonathan said, "My parents are the executors. Doing this would get the house out of their hair."

Mr. Levesque said, "We don't care about losing the house. What we don't want is to continue to pay property taxes and maintenance out of the estate for an additional nine years only to lose the property anyway."

Brooke wrung her hands together. "This is in effect giving a house to the Crafters Guild. That's not fair."

Jonathan glared out the kitchen window. "Nothing about this situation is fair. But maybe it can right a wrong."

Which wrong was he talking about? The wrong of Aunt Millie trying to bribe him away from his vocation? Or the wrong of the Historical Society's vendetta against the BCG?

The dark-suited man added, "Legally, this is a convenient way to resolve both issues."

"In the meantime, if we've been hosting resident artists for a full year, they'll have to admit we're not a threat." Brooke lowered her eyes. "But back up. The Catholic Church isn't going to go for this. Catholics can't get married with the intention of getting a divorce. You're going to ruin your life because you'd never be able to marry anyone else."

Mrs. Levesque said, "He's thought of that, too."

Her voice was flat, but based on her glare, she wasn't

specifically angry at Jonathan.

The spark in Jonathan's eyes drew Brooke up short. "I know all the rules. If I get married in a lawyer's office with a prenup in place and the intent to dissolve the marriage, that's not a sacramental marriage. As far as the Church is concerned, it's a slam-dunk annulment because in their eyes, it wasn't a marriage in the first place. I could still get married in the Church afterward if I wanted to. If I were to go through with this, my wife and I would live as roommates. Afterward, everything would be exactly the same as it was, except the guild would have possession of a house for their artist-in-residency program."

Brooke rested her elbows on the table and her head in her hands.

Natalie's voice sharpened. "What do you mean, 'it's not a real marriage'? Are you saying something isn't a real marriage if it doesn't happen inside a church? And I thought the Catholic Church hated divorce."

Brooke raised her head. "No, Nat, he didn't explain it right at all. Jonathan's saying that signing a marriage license means the government thinks people are married, but the church hierarchy won't consider them married. For the Catholic Church to consider a marriage valid, people need to get married according to their conscience system. Muslims signing a marital contract during a Nikah—valid. Wiccans having a handfasting ceremony—valid. If Lilah and Emerson write their vows on a stick and throw it into the sea—valid. But for Catholics, the Church says the wedding has to take place with a priest as the official witness, otherwise they aren't considered as having contracted a *Catholic* marriage. That's all he's saying."

Jonathan raised his eyebrows. "Writing your vows on a stick and throwing it into the sea?"

Squinting, Lilah tilted her head. "That's not a bad idea..."

Brooke said, "What Jonathan suggests will appease a probate court, and when he divorces, the Catholic Church won't see him as divorced because ecclesiastically, he was never married."

Theodore Hodges cleared his throat. "Theology aside, we can amend the paperwork however you want, but I've run the prenup by some of my colleagues. We think this is bulletproof."

She looked up. "You're not a realtor?"

For the first time, he smiled. "I'm the estate attorney. We want this settled."

Jonathan said, "Aunt Millie was devious. And to think, every day I was praying for her, and she was pulling this nonsense."

Brooke tilted her head. "Surely this isn't why you left the seminary."

Jonathan frowned. "My parents didn't tell me about Aunt Millie's attempted bribe until three months after I got home. I don't want the house. To me, this house represents betrayal. To you, it could represent a dream come true. I just need to get married."

Jonathan meant Brooke. It couldn't be Natalie, who was over the moon in love with Colin. It couldn't be Lilah, who adored Emerson with a breathtaking passion. Brooke, however, was just Brooke.

She liked Jonathan. He'd been a friend since middle school, and he was good to talk to. But he was wrecking his life, and for what? For a house?

Natalie sat, eyes downcast. Lilah shook her head. "You don't have to do this. What you're talking about... It's huge. Marriage should be because you're insanely in love and you can't imagine it getting better than it is. You and Emerson broke up because as a couple you were only 'okay.' Don't you want more than a roommate?"

Jonathan said, "We wouldn't pretend it was more than roommates. We'll sign a legal document, and after a year, we'll sign a second legal document undoing the first."

The lawyer said, "This prenup protects everything you have going into the marriage. Jonathan's assets likewise would remain his own. The only thing that would need to happen is you remain married for the full year. Jonathan then receives full access to the trust, of which the house is a part. After that, he'll immediately add you to the trust, you'll divorce, and then he'll remove himself. Once the ink dries, you'll be left with the house."

Brooke looked at Jonathan. "You won't hate me for this?"

Jonathan's eyes tightened, and his fists clenched. "Right now, it feels like I'm angry at everyone, but not at you. You'd be doing my family a favor by getting the estate settled. You'd be doing me personally a favor by taking the house question out of my hands. I'd be doing you a favor by staying out of your hair and living in the guest cottage. You can start the AIR program immediately, and the BCG will be shielded from further legal action."

Brooke closed her eyes.

Jonathan said, "The maintenance fund means you'd live rent-free, and it pays for a groundskeeper and a cleaner who come once a week. We'll divide the household tasks like roommates, and we won't join our finances. If it turns out the house doesn't work for you, then at the end of the year we can divorce, sell the house, and split the proceeds. In the end, you're free to go."

Practically speaking, this wasn't a terrible deal. One year of rent-free living would give Brooke a nice savings cushion, maybe enough to buy a small home of her own. If it got Jonathan's parents off the hook, they'd appreciate it. Jonathan's anger zinged through the air, though, and Brooke kept recoiling every time she picked up on it.

Maybe he'd calm down over time. He'd always been thoughtful and soft-spoken. During prom, he'd treated her so gently.

He'd lived on his own for a while, too, so in the guest cottage, he wouldn't expect her to clean up after him. It might work.

Jonathan said, "My only ask is, immediately after the divorce, we have to file for an annulment. We've got five witnesses around the table who can testify that we had no intention of contracting a sacramental marriage. If you ever wanted to get married in the Catholic Church, you'd be free to do so as well."

This was so mechanical. A set of conditions to be met, after which a specific reward would be achieved. It was like a knitting pattern, in that regard. Increase two stitches per row and create this shape. Then knit in pattern for ten inches and bind off, and you had the body of a sweater. Sign these two contracts and achieve this legal relationship. Then after a year, bind off, and you have a house.

Natalie said, "What would happen if Jonathan ran out the clock on the will and didn't get married?"

Mrs. Levesque said, "Other than us having to maintain the property for a decade? The trust would be given to a charity that Aunt Millie picked out."

Jonathan said, "That's why I feel justified in this scheme. She was a strong supporter of the arts, and she would have appreciated her money going to that kind of effort, especially since it's taking place locally."

Brooke frowned. "Are you saying you didn't design this scheme to go directly against her wishes because she so throughly went against yours?"

Mr. Levesque laughed, and Brooke started. Mrs. Levesque murmured, "Never mind him."

"Do mind me," Jonathan's dad said. "You've got spirit. I'd been wondering that myself, whether there was a way we could twist the will to make her sit up in Heaven glaring at us for what we'd done."

Jonathan shook his head. "I'd love to stick it to her as much as anyone else. But this feels like it helps everyone without changing too much. You get free rent for a year, and afterward, if you want to deed the entire trust over to the BCG, or sell the house and buy a commercial property for meetings, that's fine."

Natalie said, "Excuse me, though. I'm not having Brooke become the caretaker of the BCG property just because she lived here first. She's a lot more than the maidservant and the cook for whatever random artist we bring to town."

Lilah exclaimed, "We can work those details out! All that is solvable. The unsolvable problem is Brooke and Jonathan getting married for a legal obligation. I don't like that at all."

Brooke turned to Lilah. "Marriage started out as a legal contract. Most ancient cultures used it as a means of ensuring proper succession and transfer of wealth. The Catholic Church came up with its own rules about marriages during the Council of Trent to protect women who sometimes got trapped in 'secret marriages' that the men would later deny. If the couple had to have witnesses, the man couldn't escape his obligation to his wife and children by publicly marrying upward."

Lilah pursed her lips. "And while historical trivia is cool, it has no bearing here."

"It does because it still protects me and Jonathan. He has a legal problem, so he's suggesting a legal solution. Our problems with the Historical Society are legal problems, too, and this seems like a legal solution. While this house isn't zoned as a commercial property, as long as we're not being commercial, I don't think they can touch us. It's legal for a married couple to commingle property. It's legal to hold meetings in my living room. It's legal to invite an out-of-town guest to stay for a week."

Theodore Hodges said, "I can give you the names of a couple of attorneys if you want a quick consult."

Jonathan added, "And we'll pay for the consultations. I've got ten years, so take some time to think it over."

Brooke looked up. "I want to discuss it with Natalie and Lilah, but I think we should do this."

Jonathan tried to quell his nerves as they walked back outside. Brooke paused on the driveway, then turned to get a better look at Aunt Millie's house.

"Before you go, I have something for you." Jonathan pulled a bowl from the back seat of his parents' SUV. "Is this what you wanted?"

Brooke's eyes widened. "Yes!" She took the yarn bowl from his hands, her fingers brushing his. "I love it! You made it smaller than the other bowls, too, which is just right."

"I looked up the dimensions of commercial yarn bowls and made it steeper than the decorative ones."

She ran her fingertips over the cut side, all the way down through the curl and then back up again. "I'm not trying to be critical, but right here, it's sharp." She extended the bowl back to him, and he touched an edge that seemed rounded off enough. "Some of the finer yarns, or the overspun ones, are going to catch. Is there any way to smooth it out a bit more?"

Jonathan shrugged. "I can try, sure."

"Other than that, it's perfect." She cradled it in her hands. "Thank you for trying."

That sounded like what the director of the seminary said when he sent Jonathan back into the world. *Other than not having a real vocation, you were perfect for the priesthood. Thank you for trying.* Hah.

Brooke flinched. "Sorry. Did I make you angry? It is a nice bowl, and it would work for most yarns."

"No, it's fine. I'm wondering how much I can smooth this one out now that it's varnished."

He reached for the bowl, but she stepped backward. "Then I'll keep it."

He grinned. "It's not that big a deal."

"I don't want you to ruin it." She tilted her head. "You know, technically what you just did inside was a proposal."

His stomach tightened. "I guess."

"Then this is my engagement bowl." She stuck the tip of her fourth finger through the curl at the base of the cutout. "You are not allowed to wreck my engagement bowl by sanding it down."

Jonathan laughed. "An engagement bowl?"

"I think it's very becoming." She held out arm toward Natalie, supporting the bowl with her other hand. "Natalie, look at my engagement bling."

Natalie sighed. "You are entirely too glib about this."

Lilah said to Natalie, "Colin hasn't proposed to you yet. Maybe after he does, you'll be freaking out about an engagement bottle of apple cider vinegar."

Brooke turned back to Jonathan. "Thank you for thinking of us. I don't understand your Aunt Millie." She lowered her eyes. "I don't expect you do, either. It's awful when people make decisions that seem like they don't love you, only you still love them. She probably didn't want to hurt you."

It wasn't worth correcting Brooke about that. "Whatever you decide, enjoy your engagement bowl."

She smiled at him, then looked quickly away, but that instant was the first time Jonathan thought it might actually work out.

CHAPTER FOUR

When Brooke texted to ask if they could meet for lunch, Jonathan agreed right away, then wondered what time she thought lunch was, or where she intended to have it, and if this was it—her answer.

She'd already questioned him a number of times about details he should have gone over when they met at Aunt Millie's house. She'd had the oddest questions, like would they need a ceremony, should she tell her parents the real situation, was he planning to get rid of the piano, and how were they going to handle estate and property taxes? "No ceremony," Jonathan said, and she wrote back, "Thanks. If it was going to be a big to-do, I was going to tell you no."

He said, "I can buy you a white dress."

She replied, "For something old, something new, something borrowed, and something blue, I'm sure Natalie has a pair of patched-up jeans she can loan me. That fulfills all four criteria."

Brooke was probably joking. She'd always been understated.

No doubt Lilah had spent the past forty-eight hours convincing Brooke to say no, but one thing Jonathan had always found interesting about Brooke was that while she deferred to other people's opinions on a lot of things, once she made up her mind, she became oddly stubborn.

Also, oddly loyal.

Regardless, he and she did determine a place and time to meet for lunch on Wednesday (the Thai restaurant), and they agreed it had to be fast so she could start her job and he could get back to his.

He opened the menu. "Are you free every morning?"

"Natalie opens. Lilah comes through the mid-day. I close. Natalie and I overlap briefly, so around noon, you'll usually catch all three of us." She interrupted before he could protest that it was already noon. "We cover for one another. Today they gave me time to come meet you."

Jonathan said, "As part business owner, you could just order them to do it."

She deflated. "I fought so hard to establish myself as the ice queen, but then spring came and my throne thawed, so instead we learned to negotiate."

Jonathan laughed, and after that, Brooke giggled.

He said, "You've still got an incredible deadpan."

"It helps when I'm dealing with the customers." She folded her hands and made a perfectly blank face. "No, ma'am, we don't have that same sweater pattern, only in purple."

Jonathan paused. "Do you have to knit the pattern in a specific color?"

"A pumpkin hat had better be orange. Otherwise?" She opened her hands. "Sky's the limit. But yeah, enough of business talk. Let's talk business, instead."

He sighed. "I guess it is talking business."

Brooke looked earnest. "You said it yourself—contracts, and the letter of the law. That's business. My chief question for this lunch meeting is what you get out of the deal, because in order to be legal, contracts have to benefit both parties."

Jonathan sat back. "Why?"

She tilted her head. "Why does the law say what it does,

or why do I expect you to benefit?"

Jonathan said, "The latter. If I'm willing to do my duty by you, why are you questioning it?"

"Because it's not all supposed to be about duty and sacrifice." She made a face at him. "I know, you meant to become a priest and *that* was all about duty and sacrifice, but marriage shouldn't be duty and sacrifice."

Jonathan shrugged. "I think it should be."

She snorted at him. "Then I'm glad we won't be *really married.* My point is, there's very clear benefit to me and the BCG if I go through with this, but I'm seeing exactly no benefit to you."

He opened his hands. "You don't think I'll benefit from talking to you every day?"

She seemed skeptical. "Not six figures worth of benefit. More like three figures."

Jonathan laughed. "Give yourself some credit! At least four."

"You'll be getting the bargain-basement hours of the day, when I'm toast from working at Bright Stitches. I'm a hermit after closing. I want quiet, and I'm not going to be good company. Which leads to an issue."

Jonathan paused. "You have a boyfriend, and he'll want to stay over at the house even though your husband is camped out in the granny flat?"

Brooke made a snorting sound. "As if." Still, she backed away from the table, folded her hands, and didn't meet his eyes. "In full disclosure, I am a terrible roommate."

Jonathan squinted. "Really?"

She still wouldn't look right at him. "I'm fussy and picky. I want things exactly the way they're supposed to be. I spend a lot of time by myself. I like routines."

Jonathan shrugged. "That doesn't sound terrible."

"It doesn't sound terrible until the minute your routine clashes with my routine." She fiddled with her napkin. "I never did well with roommates or apartment-mates. It always felt tense, like they had expectations I couldn't live up to." She kept looking at her hands. "Lilah tried to convince me to move into the barn with her, but me and other people—nothing fits. They wonder why I do the things I do, and I never predict their unspoken expectations. If you marry me, you're going to have an annoyed woman watching everything you do."

Jonathan sipped his water. "If I stay in the guest cottage, and you live in the main house, that's plenty of room. You'll barely see me. There's even the kitchenette on the second floor if you find me so annoying that you need to be at a higher altitude."

Brooke laughed, but it was painful. "I never knew all the ways people could be annoying until they were in my apartment."

Jonathan said, "You're afraid I won't last the year?"

"I'm not sure *I'd* live with me a year if I had the choice." She finally looked up, then averted her eyes again.

He said, "Where do you live now?"

She smiled, and it startled him. "A studio apartment just off Dean Street. It's small, but everything is in its right place." Then she frowned. "You're going to move things. You'll watch TV and leave the remote on the arm of the couch. You're going to change the settings on the washing machine. And I'm going to notice every one of those changes."

How to decode this? But then again, no need to decode it. This was a business negotiation. "Are you worried about you, or about me?"

Brooke bit her lip. "Both of us. By the time we're done, you're never going to want to talk to me again."

Jonathan hesitated. "That's…drastic."

"You've been my friend for a long time." She shrank further into her seat. "You've always been easy to talk to. Plus, when you were Father Jonathan, you were off-limits. No one teased me when we talked or if we walked home from middle school together. I was with someone safe, and you felt pity for me, so it worked well enough."

Jonathan went cold. "What?"

Brooke looked up, concerned. "I worry that after this

year, that's going to change, and you won't want me as a friend anymore."

Jonathan raised his hands. "Wait, wait—back up."

Of course, then the server interrupted by bringing Brook's pad Thai and his stir-fried noodles, so he stopped. Brooke pulled off her fingerless gloves and set them to the side, then waited, watching him. Oh—she'd clicked back into high school mode, when she always waited for him to pray grace silently before starting to eat. She'd been the only one of his friends who did.

In effect, that meant God had interrupted them, too, but the moment after his silent "Amen," Jonathan said, "Back up. You said I felt pity for you. I didn't."

She waved her left hand as she got her chopsticks with her right. "Of course you did. You took me to the prom because no one else was going to. You were nice to me because you're a charitable person. That's why I thought you were going to make a stellar priest."

"I wasn't your friend as a corporal work of mercy. I thought you liked talking to me, and you were a part of the group."

She tilted her head and raised her eyebrows. "Would the group have accepted me if you hadn't been there to lead the way?"

"Yes, because you're an awesome person. And I'm not going to just ditch you as a friend because we happen to be divorced." He half-rolled his eyes. "Can we eat now, or do I need to swear on a Bible?"

She shrugged, and that was awesome. She still hadn't said yes or no.

Weren't proposals supposed to be a straightforward thing? You asked, your partner answered, and then you had some decisions to make—maybe good decisions, and maybe not-so-good ones. Instead, Brooke was cogitating and negotiating and warning him, and he couldn't get a read on her.

This is your fault, he thought to God. *I wouldn't be here if you'd just said, "You know what? You get to be a priest after all."*

Brooke focused on her food, which gave Jonathan's brain time to gear down. This dish was more complex than he'd anticipated when he'd ordered it: wide rice noodles with broccoli, shrimp, and egg, cooked in something like soy sauce except a bit sweeter. How awesome was that? He'd gone out for lunch and accidentally ordered a metaphor.

"Do you like your food?" he asked when Brooke had been quiet too long. "If we do get married, I should take you out somewhere afterward."

This time she did look horrified. "No."

"No?"

"No! Whatever we do, I don't want it to look like a wedding. We're not getting the Fruits de Mer function room for thirty people—or four people. I'm not dressing in white with a veil. You shouldn't even wear a suit, although obviously I have no say over your clothing choices. We don't have flowers." She straightened her shoulders. "We treat it like a business deal."

Jonathan raised his eyebrows. "Have you never heard of the *business lunch*?"

That drew her up short.

He added, "When you and Natalie bought the business from Natalie's mother, did all of you have dinner together afterward?"

Chastened, Brooke deflated. "Yes."

"Therefore I feel perfectly justified in having *asked* if you wanted to go to dinner. You've refused, so we won't, but business dinners are perfectly acceptable for networking and for sealing a deal. " He added tartly, "And therefore, I can wear a business suit."

"Wow. Aren't you driving a hard bargain?" She didn't meet his eyes, but she was smiling. "Do I, too, need to wear a business suit and heels? This whole deal may be off if heels are required."

He said, "That's the break point, is it?"

"I suppose not. I'd wear heels for you. For the house, I

41

mean. Also, no ring. I don't like diamonds, and I'm not wearing a wedding ring."

He held up his hand. "I can't wear a wedding ring. It's too dangerous with all the equipment I work with."

"Oh, right—I've read about degloving." She said that as though it weren't a horrible injury that Jonathan had always wished he'd never heard of, let alone seen a video about during safety lectures. But then she hesitated, looked aside. "Also, um...we need to have an uncomfortable discussion."

Jonathan fought unease. "If it's the same uncomfortable discussion I'm thinking about, the answer is no, we won't."

Brooke looked up, relieved. "Thank you. I know sex is a part of being married, but it's not something I'm comfortable with just because we signed some paperwork."

"As far as I'm concerned, we aren't married because the Catholic Church won't consider us married, and I'm still Catholic." She might still consider herself Catholic, too. Jonathan made a point of never prying into his friends' beliefs or practices. "There's something called a Josephite marriage where two married people live together as if they're brother and sister."

Brooke flinched. "I wouldn't live with my brother, either, thanks. It's not that you're not attractive," she added, as if she herself weren't attractive enough to turn heads. "It's that I don't react the way most people do. Lilah will see a guy and say, 'He's hot!' while I'm trying to puzzle out what brand of sneakers he's wearing. The last guy I dated, I never even kissed him."

Jonathan nodded. "Consent. It's a thing, and we're in agreement."

Brooke looked relieved. "I was joking about the heels, but compulsory sex would be a dealbreaker."

Jonathan flinched. "Would I ever do something like that?"

She shook her head. "You wouldn't, but most guys I've dated, they push and push and push and push. They concede when I say no, and two minutes later, they make me say no again."

Jonathan raised his hands. "No means no. I will never make you repeat yourself."

Brooke said, "I trust you. But about the whole contract marriage...I don't know what to think anymore. Lilah is horrified. Natalie has reservations. Then I called my mother, and she said it's fine, that I should go for it. Lots of women marry for money."

Jonathan choked. He managed to swallow while Brooke was staring at him in surprise, and he blurted out, "I never thought someone would marry me for money."

Her eyes narrowed. "You never thought someone would marry you for love, either, wise guy. This was your idea. Mom said there's nothing wrong with marrying for money as long as I don't expect to be happy. When I said I didn't expect you to make me happy, she told me to go for it."

Cold all at once, Jonathan said, "I was hoping you'd be happy anyhow."

"Not that you'd deliberately make me sad. Just that I should go into it with my eyes open. As long as the house is there, that's what this is for: the house. Treat it like a job. That's what we've been saying, isn't it?"

That didn't feel right, either. Brooke was a terrific person. It felt wrong making her uncomfortable just to unload a house and posthumously stick it to his meddling aunt. She knew what he was doing, though. With her eyes wide open, she wasn't being scammed. He'd given her a sheaf of legal paperwork to prove he meant everything he said.

It was just... He did want her to be happy. Not chained to someone by the ankle, a prisoner gazing every morning at her beautiful ocean view and yearning for freedom that loomed a year away.

"You deserve happiness." It sounded weak. Brooke deserved happiness, but the best he could give her was free rent, pad Thai, and a place to host her fellow artisans.

"We don't get what we deserve." Brooke shrugged as

though that statement didn't encompass ninety-nine percent of the tragedies of human existence. "I daresay you aren't getting what you deserve, either, living on the same property as me. But since you seem determined to do this, even though it doesn't in any way benefit you, then yes. I accept your proposal."

CHAPTER FIVE

Brooke agreed to the marriage on Wednesday. They got a marriage license and signed it on Thursday morning, after which she spent the rest of her off-work hours packing moving boxes and getting everything ready for the heavy lifting.

Sunday afternoon, it was Brooke and Natalie, Lilah and Emerson, and Jonathan and his parents—plus a rental truck that claimed it was $19.95 an hour, but which you never could get for $19.95 an hour. "You'd have to be some kind of rock star to hold them to the posted rate," Mr. Levesque said. "But what the heck: you're worth another ten dollars."

This whole arrangement was about money, so Brooke got out her wallet, but then everyone seemed horrified. People were weird. Like, did they want their sacrifices paid back? Or did they just want them acknowledged? Because Mr. Levesque also seemed uncomfortable when she thanked him for looking out for her and paying more for the truck.

Regardless, her apartment was tiny, and the truck, though also tiny, swallowed its contents. Her bed, her kitchen table, her dresser—all that went into the truck and then got covered in boxes of clothes, dishes, and books.

Mrs. Levesque got into Brooke's car with her. "The cab of that truck is so noisy, not to mention uncomfortable."

"Comfort isn't their primary consideration." Brooke chuckled. "The rental place wants you to return it."

Then she cut herself off because she'd entered into a temporary marriage with Mrs. Levesque's son and was planning to return him. It was rude to remind the woman her son was going to spend an entire year in discomfort.

At the house, the men hauled her boxes upstairs. Brooke followed up into the primary bedroom—and stopped in the doorway.

"Wait." She stopped Jonathan and Mr. Levesque before they got anything else. "This is all wrong."

The shape of the room—the size, the feeling, the view of the ocean— Wrong. All wrong.

She'd just said temporary things shouldn't get comfortable. But this...?

Jonathan said, "What's wrong with it?"

The king-sized bed was wrong. Also wrong: a triple dresser so heavy no one could move it. Another wrong: a walk-in closet big enough that she needed a map like a shopping mall.

Mr. Levesque said, "If it feels like Aunt Millie's spirit is here, remind her she made all this happen. If she'd bequeathed her house to the National Council of the Arts, you'd be back on Dean Street."

Mrs. Levesque arrived with a box of clothes. "You still feel her here, too?"

Jonathan said, "Brooke's a bit unnerved."

Not by ghost stories. More by the wrongness and the speed at which the wrongness had come at her. A week ago, she'd toured the house wondering if the Levesques would ask the trio of spinsters what to do with a cedar chest full of cashmere. Almost exactly a week ago to the hour, she'd been propositioned, and today, she was four days married.

She didn't have to live here, did she? She could keep paying rent to her landlord and have the occasional budget meeting with Jonathan, then pay him out for any bowls they'd sold. That seemed like a reasonable, wifely thing to do. No need to live on the same property.

Except here she was, with a truck full of furniture and a bunch of friends to unload it.

Stepping back, she let them move her in.

They had no idea what to do with her furniture. They put her bed and dresser into the second bedroom, empty now of the antique furniture which Mrs. Levesque, as executor, had been instructed to sell. Brooke's couch stayed downstairs. They left her drafting table in the sitting room, uncertain where it ought to go. Her bookcase didn't belong in the library with its built-in floor to ceiling shelves, so they stuck it in the primary bedroom. Her cooking equipment went into that fantastic kitchen, and yet there was still an entire kitchen to fill.

Her food disappeared into a corner of the fridge, but at least that was kind of normal. The freezer was just a freezer.

Natalie came into the kitchen. "Where should we put your bike?"

At home, Brooke had used a wall mount. There wasn't a mount inside the house, of course, and a bicycle didn't belong inside a home this upscale anyhow.

"I'll chain it on the porch." She should be able to get the cable around the porch post, right?

Mrs. Levesque said, "Don't be silly. No one's going to steal it."

Brooke paused. "People steal bicycles."

"Not up here."

Brooke said, "If I were a bicycle thief, I'd come to Sky Ridge Drive to steal better bicycles."

Mrs. Levesque tilted her head as though trying to look at Brooke from an angle that made sense. "This is a very safe neighborhood."

Brooke said, "Aunt Millie had a security system on the

house. I'm going to trust her judgment and lock up the bicycle."

Jonathan entered the kitchen holding a box as his mother said, "That's ridiculous."

You know, one statement from Brooke should have been enough. "Why are you arguing with me about locking up my own bicycle? If I don't have to lock it—if no one would steal it anyhow—then who am I inconveniencing? Not you. Not Jonathan. Just me."

She said, "But honey—"

Brooke took a deep breath, but then Jonathan stepped in. "Mom, let her lock up her bike. It's not like a bike lock brings down the property values. Also, Dad wants to ask you something outside. By the truck."

Brooke had learned a long time ago that statements of this sort meant, "I'm giving you a graceful way out," and not, "Dad actually has a question for you."

Jonathan pushed Brooke's box onto the kitchen table, then motioned at his mother with his head and his eyes, and his mother followed him out of the kitchen. Seconds later, Lilah came up to her with a hug. "You need to sit. Breathe."

Brooke cupped her hands over her face. "It's too many people."

"I've got it. You're going to crash. Let's sit."

"Not here." The kitchen was chaos central. "Where's my couch?"

Lilah guided her to the couch in the sitting room, and Brooke hunched forward over herself. Beside her, Lilah waved off anyone who wanted to talk to her. Silence. Well, silence other than the whispering from other people in this big echoing house that should never have belonged to her.

The floor creaked. Lilah tensed alongside Brooke, but then it was quiet again, and whoever had joined them (Natalie?) didn't speak. Brooke focused on her body, focused her thoughts away from the space around herself. Go deep. Go inside. Focus.

When she looked up, it was Jonathan on the floor in

front of her, looking sad. At least, that seemed like a sad face. He said, "Is it okay to talk?"

He'd pitched his voice low, but the problem wasn't the talking—the problem was all the questions, all the decisions, and how out-of-place everything was. Brooke nodded.

Jonathan said, "I'm heading out with my dad to return the truck. Mom and Natalie are shifting stuff around upstairs. If you need anything, I'll keep my phone on."

Brooke murmured, "I'll be all right. This is like when I needed space at your graduation party."

Jonathan brightened up. "Oh! Then come with me."

Lilah said, "Maybe let her rest?"

Jonathan said, "Trust me."

He brought Brooke to the balcony where they'd stood the night of his party. "Stay out here a bit. You did a lot of work today."

"It's not the work. It was all the decisions and the changes. I appreciate that everyone's trying to help, but you all keep asking me questions. *Where does this go? How about that?* Well, I don't know the right answers, and it's too much."

He gestured at the hills. "Stand here and remember the quiet. Then you can go back inside and lock up your bicycle, and lock up the fridge and the piano. Say the word, and I'll stop at the hardware store on the way home for another ten locks. I'm a carpenter, and I own a drill to install them."

She giggled. "Thank you."

"I mean it." He stepped away. "Text me if you need me."

As he left, she watched his back. Need him...to do what? But still, it was nice that he was looking out for her.

He was right, though. The quiet and the breeze and the motion of the water was settling her.

When Jonathan and his father returned, they brought pizzas. See, now that was correct and right. Pizza was the only acceptable moving-day meal. Here was a touchpoint. Some things could still be predictable.

(Although, then she had to hunt up a knife and fork because she was the only one who used those. Which also was, in its own way, predictable.)

Afterward, they fiddled with the computers and Brooke's tiny TV until they managed to play a movie (the internet wouldn't get hooked up until Tuesday) and that was a lot of people, too—but at least they were focused on the movie. Without enough furniture, Jonathan sat on the floor against the couch, his back between Brooke's leg and Lilah's. They were crammed in close, but that was all right. Outside was getting chilly, but inside was warm.

One by one, everyone gathered themselves to leave. Natalie and Lilah congratulated Brooke on her new house, and Mr. and Mrs. Levesque made sure Brooke had their numbers in case anything went wrong. At the same time, Jonathan retreated to the guest cottage.

Brooke was alone, alone in a huge house where nothing fit where it should—least of all herself.

Brooke spent the rest of the evening reading in Aunt Millie's way-too-large bed, flanked by the mural on the far wall and the wooden castle behind. She'd ordered this book yesterday, the last package she'd ever accept at Dean Street: a same-day delivery of *The Modern Guide to Your Arranged Marriage.*

Technically, she'd arranged her own marriage, but most of the book fit her circumstances. A man had married her for practical reasons without a courtship period (unless you counted going out for Thai food, which Brooke didn't —that had been negotiation) and now they were making the best of it.

At least they had separate residences. Most of the situations covered in the book weren't going to apply because she didn't need to work around his schedule. Likewise, the book advised putting off having sex until they both felt comfortable, and Jonathan had said he would never feel comfortable.

At least Jonathan wouldn't have to worry about having an overbearing mother-in-law. When they got divorced, he'd never even have met Brooke's parents.

When she'd read herself into a bleary-eyed state, she took a shower in the overly complicated shower stall (that was nice) and changed into fuzzy pajamas. It took a while to plan how to get the lights off and herself into the bed when the lamp was all the way over there and the room was dark and everything still didn't fit.

Why had Aunt Millie owned a monstrously huge house in the first place? It felt like a gaping maw around Brooke, with too many entrances and exits, too much empty space, and her belongings scattered. She made it into the bed using her phone as a flashlight, then laid there hearing the world wrong. The bed beneath her wasn't right. Over her head was a castle with a door, and even though the door didn't open (she'd tried it, and so had Lilah) she kept wondering what Aunt Millie had locked up inside.

Finally she sat up, hugging her knees. Time to solve this problem. If she was going to live in this house, she had to learn to sleep in it. But with the shadows and the echoes and everything she owned being who-knows-where, security was nowhere to be found.

Speaking of nowhere to be found, where was her weighted blanket?

Brooke navigated out of bed and clicked the lights back on. In the second bedroom, she found the box of bedding on her old twin-sized bed. That yielded her weighted blanket. Maybe using that, she could sleep.

Although nothing was to stop her from using the bed she already had.

Once she'd made up her bed, she went back down the hall for her lamp and set that where it should be, too.

With those two pieces together, she tucked herself in

and passed right out.

The next morning, she awoke oriented but then became rapidly disoriented. Her coffee maker was in that opulent kitchen, and so were her bagels. She had to trek back to Aunt Millie's room to locate her clothes (huddled together at the back end of a closet big enough to fit a pool table) and why was her toaster so far from the fridge, and who'd put the coffee maker on yet another counter entirely? She pushed them together. Brooke was one person, for crying out loud. Why should she do laps around the kitchen to make breakfast?

Come to think of it, she only ever used her coffee maker and toaster in the morning, so why not move them upstairs to the kitchenette? Technically, that was the servant's quarters, but the house didn't come with a servant.

Once she did that, it made sense to disassemble her kitchen table, remove it from where it looked hilariously tiny in the dining room, and assign that to the kitchenette as well. And the chairs. Oh, and the butter, the bagels, and the bagel-cutter.

While eating breakfast, Brooke stood abruptly and paced the servant's quarters. Paced it back again. Side to side. Forward to backward. The layout was *almost* right. Having windows on two sides made it a bit wrong. Still...

Brooke tracked down the furniture sliders and pushed her twin bed into the servant's quarters, in the same relative position it would have inhabited in her studio apartment. Next she set the sliders under the corners of her dresser, and she pushed that down the hall to set it at the foot of the bed the way it had been in the studio apartment, framing off her sleeping area.

Time to re-create her whole apartment. Her clothes came out of Aunt Millie's closet and into this reasonably sized one. She plugged in the kitchenette fridge so she could bring all her food upstairs.

Her bookcase came into the room next, into the "living room" zone, followed by her books. She disassembled her drafting table in the sitting room and carried it up in pieces for reassembly in her micro-apartment. The light would fall differently, but that was okay: she still had her two crafting lamps aimed over it.

It took exactly two seconds to determine she couldn't move the couch on her own. Tonight after work, she could ask Jonathan to help.

Brooke pivoted in the center of her new apartment. The layout wasn't quite right. The en suite bathroom took up less space, and the kitchenette was a bit wrong, but she could work with this. Something was still missing, though. Oh! She went diving through the box with her yarn supplies, and there she found Jonathan's engagement bowl.

He'd given it to her the day he'd suggested this arrangement, so it belonged on display. She set it on her nightstand without any yarn in it. It gleamed in the light, so pretty.

Speaking of pretty, though, she had art. Without a landlord or a grandmother to complain about holes in the walls, she could hang all her art.

The wall was a blank canvas, but alas, now she had to head to work.

She got on her bike. Sky Ridge Drive was further from the shop than Dean Street had been. She'd need to leave herself extra time, although that massive hill at the bottom of Sky Ridge might take time off the outbound trip. Inbound...? She'd have to hope her legs could deal with it.

In a week, everything had changed, but she could retain some sameness. Jonathan would barely have to see her at all. She didn't have to use that fantastic kitchen to cook solitary meals. She could come home as usual, use the tiny oven or her microwave in the kitchenette, and stay ensconced with her computer or her knitting until it was time for bed. She shouldn't bring her bike upstairs and mount it on the wall, but Brooke could wheel it into the house and park it in the mudroom. Or was it the dooryard? A house this grand probably called it a foyer.

Whatever. In the mornings, she'd have access to her coffee maker and her toaster oven, and by the time she was moving about the rest of the house, Jonathan would have left for work.

In other words, perfection. She wouldn't lose his friendship over roommate issues if they never encountered one another. She'd rather see Jonathan every day, but it was better for him—for their friendship—if they didn't. He was giving her a house. She could give him his space.

CHAPTER SIX

Alone in the guest cottage, Jonathan made dinner while occasionally glancing out the window to see if the lights had come on in the main house. He'd forgotten about that, how when he lived at Aunt Millie's, he'd be in "the guest house" and she was in "the main house." There was also the carriage house, which hadn't been used for much for as long as Jonathan had been visiting. Well, other than stringing orange lights inside it and having a savage Halloween party. He'd turned it into his woodworking shop.

So many awesome memories, and with one stroke of her pen, Aunt Millie had immolated them all.

Brooke's car was here, so she must have taken her bicycle. Biking in the pitch black seemed unwise, didn't it? None of these streets had lights, and some of them were both narrow and curvy, not to mention the hills. Even less to mention the cold. Surely she didn't bike in the snow, too? Should he get in his car and look for her?

Or, and this was likely the better option, should he get a grip and leave Brooke to live her own life, which she had managed just fine until now?

He'd thrown her into this situation, though. He had a wife, for pity's sake. They were going to file taxes together. Brooke had even texted him about whether they should start a joint account for household purchases. Yes, he'd taken a class on marriage and family dynamics, but only from a theoretical perspective. When distraught couples came to their priest for counseling, he'd need to know how to counsel them. Instead he was living it, and how would he counsel a man who came to him with exactly this set of parameters?

Jonathan could paraphrase Father Tim from Saint Lucy's, at least. "That's going to be a lot harder than you think it will be."

Jonathan had replied, "Brooke's a good person. I'm sure she'll be fair, and it's only for a year."

Father Tim had said, "I mean the 'living like brother and sister' part."

Well, brothers worried about their sisters. Jonathan had a sister off doing a graduate degree in Burlington, Vermont, and he'd certainly worried about her.

Then it turned out he should have worried about himself: when he went to wash the dishes, he realized something he'd forgotten. On the shopping list magneted to the refrigerator, he wrote, "Dish soap," then headed to the main house. Brooke wouldn't mind if he borrowed some. There might even be a leftover bottle from Aunt Millie, so he wouldn't have to bother Brooke for, what, five cents worth of bubbles?

He could leave a quarter on the counter. He could already predict the blank look on her face if he did that, followed by her solemnly sending back two dimes.

The house loomed over him with a pervasive emptiness, and unexpectedly, he missed Aunt Millie. She'd always greeted him with an effusion of questions followed by a hug and a machine-gunned series of offers of every single thing a teenage male could want to eat.

He flipped on the lights, and that was odd—the drafting desk was gone. Had Brooke moved it?

So was the end table.

In the kitchen, the place seemed even emptier. He'd plugged in the coffee maker on that counter, which was now clear, and the toaster oven was gone, too. Not only was the fridge empty, but the light didn't turn on.

Had she moved out? Already?

He pulled out his phone. "You left?"

Who else could he ask? The message said it had been delivered, so she didn't seem to have blocked him. But why else would her belongings be gone? If he didn't remember moving her in yesterday, he'd have no way to prove now that she had ever been here.

He flipped on the lights for the stairs and headed up, and yes, the primary bedroom was empty.

That made no sense. How would she have gotten furniture out of the house? Although not the couch—that was here. Had Natalie helped her move? But why?

The phone buzzed in his hand before he could ask Natalie where Brooke was, and it was Brooke's reply. "I left work late, but I just got back."

He rushed downstairs in time to hear the door unlock, and Brooke wheeled her bicycle inside. Her cheeks were shiny pink and her eyes bright beneath her helmet.

Relief flushed through him, along with confusion. Followed by more confusion, because why was she here with all her stuff gone?

"I didn't mean to worry you. I get back at odd times if there are things to take care of at the shop, and I'm further away than before." She studied his face. "Were you waiting for me?"

"I needed something from the house, and all your things are gone."

Unzipping her jacket, she perked up. "Oh! I need to show you!"

She led him back upstairs, straight past the primary suite and around the bend in the hall to the servant's quarters. She flipped up the lights in triumph. "See? I haven't moved at all! My whole apartment fits in here!"

He took a step back. "Why would you do that?"

"The house is too big." Then she spun out a whole tale (which she found funny for some reason) about being too uncomfortable to sleep and then retreating to the room that was most like her old room, moving the bed, moving her furniture, moving her kitchen appliances—and basically establishing her empire in the far corner of the house.

Thank goodness there wasn't an external stairway with a servant's entrance, otherwise Jonathan would never have seen her again.

She looked so pleased. He said, "This isn't a pretty room. All the others are artistic and creative. I thought you'd like them."

She shrugged. "They haven't gone anywhere. I can still look at them."

Struggling to get his bearings, Jonathan added, "And you're more comfortable this way...?"

Her head pumped up and down. "I've never needed a lot of space. Only, I hate to bother you, but could you help me move my couch?"

Mom was going to lose it. This was no way to treat his wife, legal or otherwise. On the other hand, having a wife meant respecting her decisions, so Jonathan said, "Now, or after you've had dinner?"

They got the couch up the stairs. Then Brooke showed him how to use the couch to create a division in the room to offset her "bedroom" from the "living room," and all Jonathan could think of was Brooke putting herself in a cage when she deserved to be free.

She said, "When they install the internet, can you make sure the Wi-Fi reaches my room?"

Her room. She should have the whole house.

She followed him back downstairs. "What did you need from the kitchen?"

"I was hoping there was some dish soap left from Aunt Millie." He opened the cabinet, and there was. "Are you really not going to cook in here? It's a lot nicer than the one upstairs."

"I need two burners and a microwave." She shrugged. "But that means you can cook in here all you like because the kitchen in the granny flat is pretty lackluster."

He recoiled. "Hey! That stove put heat into my food tonight!"

She gestured at the gas range Aunt Millie had installed during her remodel five years ago. "Surely it's not stylish heat with a center griddle and cast-iron burners? Amazing heat surrounded by granite countertops?"

He laughed. "Heat is heat."

"Said by someone who never baked cookies with designer heat." Her eyes crinkled as she smiled. "You need to try harder."

He said, "I'm not sure cookies are my thing."

She flexed her fingers. "Baking bread, then? My grandmother taught me a bunch of stuff, but I never baked once I was on my own because the oven was too small for a cookie sheet."

"And then you moved upstairs where the oven is even smaller?"

She ducked her head and avoided his eyes, but she was laughing. "Yeah, but that's cooking for special. Cooking for everyday, it works."

"Then I'll thank you not to mock my generic heat."

She said, "Given the age of the guest cottage stove, it's probably 'geriatric' heat." He dissolved into laughter, and she looked up briefly, then ducked away again. "Plus, one of these is the high BTU burner that can boil water in fifteen seconds, so if you ever want to make pasta, this is the place to cook it. And before you say it, I'm fine cooking on the lame upstairs stove because I've got it all timed out with how long it takes my sauce to heat."

He folded his arms. "You drive a hard bargain. But thank you, maybe I'll cook in the house when I'm ready for name-brand BTUs."

She looked at him again, and he shifted his weight, saying, "Well, I guess that's all I needed to do. Find dish soap and verify that you haven't left the state."

She opened her hands. "Behold. Here I am. And there's your soap."

He should say something else, right? Farewell? Goodnight, sweetheart? Except you don't say those things to your friend or to your sister, so instead he said, "Thanks. I'll return the bottle tomorrow," which was lame, but at least it freed her up to do whatever she did at night. Whatever she did alone in that little room that mimicked her apartment.

Tuesday afternoon, Jonathan returned from a few hours at his job so Brooke could go to hers while he waited for the internet installation.

Inside the house, he heard hammering. He headed upstairs in case she'd lost patience with Aunt Millie's castle headboards and was prying open the doors with a claw hammer. Instead, he found Brooke in her room, nailing artwork to the walls.

"Whoa!" He halted in the doorway, face to face with a wall of colors. "I mean, knock-knock."

"Who's there?" She giggled. "Cart. Cart who? Cartoon!"

Jonathan's brain whirled as he beheld colorful chaos, and yet it was all in order. Although many of the pieces were different sizes and shapes, Brooke had laid dozens of pictures out so they all interlocked on the wall, balanced in form and color. All of them were bright, brilliant animation images, and every one of them was an image from the movies of Paxley Studios.

Her smile was brilliant. "I haven't had any of these up since college, and even then, I made sure to put the nails in the holes left behind by the other tenants. Since I don't have a landlord other than your great-aunt's angry ghost, this is the first time I could lay them out however I wanted." She stepped back to regard an interior wall covered with prints, animation cells, hand-drawn sketches, watercolors, and fabric posters. "What do you think?"

Jonathan beheld character after character caught in a beautiful moment, a smile of rapture or a gaze of devotion. "This is incredible. You did a great job."

"I learned to frame prints in college because I wasn't allowed to just tack things up, and later I learned it was better not to stick pins through posters anyhow." She had far more than posters, though. She had framed postcards, canvases, and animation cells. Were those actual production cells? And then there were hand-drawn pieces, watercolors, and one letterboxed collage. Fan art? Had she gone to conventions?

Brooke ran a hand through her hair. "I said I wanted everything the same as home, but when I asked my heart what it desired, it turned out, I wanted these where I could see them."

Jonathan inspected them closer. "You must have needed an entire extra suitcase to fly back from Orlando."

"Oh, I've never been to the Paxley theme park. I cannot imagine what would happen if you turned me loose in their gift shop." She rubbed her hands together, still in fingerless gloves. "Most of these came from online sellers or lucky finds in stores."

Jonathan was about to ask if she ever planned to take a trip there when her yarn bowl caught his eye. His yarn bowl—sitting on her nightstand.

Most of her belongings were still packed, and chaos was everywhere—but while putting up the artwork she loved, she'd also found and set out his bowl. It didn't even have yarn in it. She'd just wanted it near.

That was—well, unexpected.

Brooke checked her phone. "I need to get going. Natalie's going to accuse me of being a starry-eyed newlywed and forgetting the time."

Jonathan walked in Brooke's wake as she raced down

the stairs. "You do have stars in your eyes. Only it's for your artwork."

She grabbed her backpack and wheeled her bike out the door, and that was all the contact they'd have on their sixth day of married life.

He headed back to her room. So many bright and pretty images, but why hadn't he known about her Paxley obsession back in school? She'd never worn character merchandise, but shouldn't she have mentioned something she loved this much? She certainly talked about knitting and yarn.

He picked up the bowl. Could he sand down that edge without ruining it? He should. Brooke deserved to knit with equipment that didn't snag.

As he replaced the bowl on the nightstand, he noticed the book in the compartment beneath. *Arranged marriages?*

A bookmark peeked up from the spine, about halfway through. He left that in place and checked the table of contents. How to start your new life together when you know little about each other. How to negotiate. When to compromise. When not to compromise. How to deal with your partner's family. How to make important decisions. How to deal with one another's imperfections. Deciding what you want your relationship to be like.

Did Brooke consider herself in an arranged marriage? While it was indisputably "an arrangement," she'd been part of arranging it.

Sitting on her bed, he skimmed the early chapters, his heart in his throat. "Marrying for money is fine as long as you don't expect to be happy," she'd quoted to him, and here this book wasn't even about the money. Was she this miserable? Clearly she expected him to make her unhappy, and then at the end, she expected him have been just as unhappy and never talk to her again.

That couldn't happen—shouldn't. He'd known Brooke for ages. All through seminary, she'd mailed him care packages. She'd kept him posted on the goings-on in

Brighthead, and he considered her a staple in his life. Most of the reason to marry her and give her the house was because she'd always been there. He'd never thought it would leave her despondent.

Unsettled, Jonathan walked the property while keeping an eye out for the internet installer. For late October, it wasn't all that chilly, but still he hunched down in his jacket. Brooke—unhappy. Unhappy with him.

Now he was unhappy with himself, too.

He didn't walk through the apple orchard at the back of the property because that would take him out of sight of the driveway, but he did open up the carriage house, and there he paused to let the air rush through.

He flipped a switch, and half the lights went on. Most of the bulbs must be dead. The edges of the building were dotted with cast-offs. The responsible thing to do would be to call for a junk haul before Brooke assumed ownership.

Until then, though, why not use it? Brooke had claimed the servant's quarters as her own, and there was no reason Jonathan couldn't turn the carriage house back into a woodworking shop.

He moved things, made sure the outlets still worked, and then had to walk away because the internet installer arrived.

Hours later, once he'd verified that Brooke's brilliant cartoon kingdom and the guest house and the carriage house all had a decent Wi-Fi signal, he decided it was late enough to cook dinner. And that was where he made his first real mistake.

Hence, when Brooke opened the door well after dark, windblown and exhausted, he greeted her at the door. "I kind of have a favor to ask."

He held it open as she wheeled the bike inside. "Ask away, most esteemed spouse."

Was that something she'd read about in the book—using honorifics? "Really?"

She snickered. "What part are you questioning? Of

course you can ask a favor, and you know I hold you in high esteem."

"You might question the esteem part after you see what happened in the kitchen."

Her eyes widened. "Do I need to call the fire department or the Environmental Protection Agency?"

"Neither, unless it's worse than I thought."

"Wait, give me a moment to get my bearings." She unbuckled her helmet, removed her jacket and gloves, then inexplicably pulled her wool fingerless gloves on in their place. She picked up her backpack and flinched. "That hill onto Sky Ridge Drive is either going to kill me or give me the best legs in Brighthead."

He said, "Well, you don't have that far to go," and she started. "Um, I didn't mean I've been checking out your legs. I meant, the hill part isn't that much of a distance."

She smirked at him. "Sure you did. Also, 'that much' distance is kind of relative."

Heat crept up his cheeks. "I hope it doesn't hurt your legs too much to walk into the kitchen."

She followed him. "Are you insulting my legs?"

He huffed. "Your legs weren't even supposed to be part of this conversation."

"Wow, disregarding my legs. What a terrible man."

Eyebrows raised, he faced her at the entrance of the kitchen. "Are you done raking me over the coals?"

"Are coals a more stylish form of heat? I was thinking of raking you over the high BTU burner because you're cute when you're flustered." She tried to see around him. "No, really, it's killing me not knowing what you've done to Aunt Millie's kitchen, and whether her outraged phantasm will open one of those wooden doors tonight to avenge her appliances."

"Nothing quite so drastic." Jonathan stepped aside to reveal the mostly clean, untrashed kitchen. "It's more of an embarrassment. I made dinner, but I had a slight portion-size accident."

He led her to the stove, and when he opened the lid on a

Dutch oven, Brooke burst into laughter.

"It's not that funny," he muttered.

"Yeah, everyone starts chicken and dumplings with... five entire chickens?"

"Nowhere near five chickens, thank you." Jonathan sighed. "I learned to cook in seminary, so I only know how to make dinner for fifteen people."

She smothered a laugh. "And when you came home, your mom cooked for everyone, so you kept seeing huge serving bowls. You, esteemed spouse, have no sense of scale. This is both awesome and hilarious, and I want to post a picture to my social media."

Jonathan shifted. "Please don't. I'd prefer to get rid of the evidence, and the fastest way to do that is if you eat dinner with me."

She made her eyes huge. "Really? You need help from li'l ol' me, and that help would be eating a meal I didn't have to cook for myself?"

Those huge eyes combined with her disarming smile made the bottom fall out of Jonathan's world. He didn't want her to look sad, even if she was faking it, but at the same time, that smile was why. Did her book on arranged marriages assume the couple ate together? Was there a chapter on when it was acceptable to start?

He should write his own book. *Too Many Questions, No Answers: The Memoir of Jonathan's Last Six Months.* In this section, the author accidentally intensifies his bride's melancholy with something as minor as dinner.

Still, she didn't look miserable. She seemed to enjoy the teasing.

He'd already set the table because he'd figured Brooke wouldn't mind sharing a meal. Maybe that was another faux pas. They'd eaten together before, though, so this wasn't a horrific ask.

"Although yeah," he added, "you told me you usually want alone-time after you get home from work."

"You said that as though we were having an actual verbal conversation that you were continuing." Brooke looked concerned. "Will you laugh at me if I try to use the water dispenser in the fridge and it's not hooked up?"

"No, for two reasons, the second reason being that the water dispenser is, in fact, hooked up. I plugged the fridge back in."

"In that case, I feel doubly safe." Brooke filled a pair of glasses while he set bowls of chicken and dumplings on the table. "These were Aunt Millie's everyday bowls?"

"Mom rehomed anything that looked like a set. These are the leftovers."

Brooke paused. "You and I are like that: leftovers that we cobbled together into a set."

He took a seat. "Except you're not unwanted."

He bowed his head while she maintained silence, but she didn't speak again when he looked up at her. He said, "You can start."

She poked at her food. "I'm not sure I'm not unwanted. I didn't think about it until you said that."

A twinge shot through Jonathan's heart. "I want you here. I asked you to eat with me."

"I mean, if I'm wanted in general. I don't fit anywhere, not very well. At the yarn shop, yes. But at school, I didn't fit in. I did make some geeky friends in college." She took a bite of the chicken stew. "This is delicious. I didn't realize they taught priests to cook."

"We have no choice. It's not as if priests live together in gangs with a housekeeper to prep the meals."

"Whoever taught you did a good job, other than the portion sizes. But I'll tell you a secret: I cook that way deliberately. Then I freeze it in pieces so I can eat without having to cook the whole thing over again." She laid a hand over her heart. "I've consumed this dumpling under false pretenses."

Jonathan made a grave face. "Do you want another one, so you can consume it under true pretenses?"

"Yeah, I may end up with seconds, if you don't mind." She wasn't looking miserable. "Do we have internet now?"

He nodded. "As my esteemed spouse requested, I

verified the signal strength in her room."

"Your esteemed spouse thanks you, as does her entourage of electronic devices. Do you get it in the guest cottage?"

"After we verified your signal strength, we went and checked mine. I have a repeater."

She fluttered her eyes. "That's so sweet, making sure your wife has Wi-Fi before making sure you have it."

He inclined his head. "I promise you, it was entirely self-serving because I want to save my data for when I'm not home. Also, I have a great idea for the carriage house."

She sat forward, but he raised a hand. "Not until after dinner. I want to show you."

He and Brooke washed up together, although there wasn't much washing up to do. Then she showed him how much to set aside in innumerable freezer bags so he'd have leftovers for months. (Not *months*, she corrected. He wouldn't stop eating chicken and dumplings *just* in time to start the Thanksgiving leftovers.) With those all in the freezer, they ventured to the carriage house.

The chill bit into him, so Jonathan hurried forward with a flashlight, but Brooke lagged behind. She stood with her neck craned, inspecting the stars.

He returned to her. "Click off the flashlight," she whispered. "I want to see."

Momentarily, they stood alone together in the darkness.

"That's the Milky Way." Her voice was soft as starlight, gentle as cosmic dust. "I never figured out how to name the stars, but if you see that smear of light, that's us looking side-on into the barred spiral of matter that makes up our galaxy."

She backed up a step and bumped into him, but he didn't step away.

She breathed, "All of that, surrounding us. Are we alone?"

Jonathan kept looking up. "Of course we aren't. We're surrounded by saints and angels and God Himself. There may be life on other worlds, and there may be aliens, too."

Brooke's head rested against his shoulder. "Sometimes, I feel like an alien."

Jonathan laid his hands on arms. "You're not an alien. This is where you belong."

"I've never belonged. I've been tolerated." She turned to him. "But you were going to show me the carriage house."

He turned. "You talk yourself down too much. You're none of these things."

She tilted her head. "I'm not tolerated?"

"More like, you had trouble fitting in as a kid, and you think that's still the truth. You fit in now."

As he pushed open the carriage house door, Brooke said, "Maybe I know better how to fake fitting in."

"Maybe everyone's faking it, and you're the only one smart enough to realize it's a game." He turned on the lights. "Okay, I need your imagination online here. When I used to stay for summers, I kept all my woodworking materials in this space."

Brooke said, "The lathe and the wood-turner. Right."

"But here's my better thought. What if we find a way to transform the whole carriage house into a studio for the artists in residence?"

Brooke gasped. "That way they don't drop paint all over the hardwood floors. Yes!" She strode into the middle of the building and pivoted. "We'd need better lighting, and probably better insulation." She stamped. "This has to go. The floor needs to be something we can clean."

Jonathan pulled out his phone. "I'm taking notes. Just shout out any idea you have, and pretend we've got an infinite budget."

"I like that! We have a utility sink already, but write me a check for a counter next to the sink, plus a mini fridge because some crafting gear needs refrigeration. A microwave because yarn dyers need that. That means we also need to update the electrical system." She looked at the overhead, at the loft, at the shelving. "We need to update or at least clean the shelves. A bathroom. Corkboards or a whiteboard or something for planning.

Tables and tables and more tables. Adjustable-height tables. And a table with a sewing machine, too."

Jonathan laughed. "Wait!"

Brooke exclaimed, "Have I already spent our infinite budget?"

"No, but I can't type that fast." He poked at his phone until he caught up. "Okay, ready."

"Painting easels. A storage closet for drop cloths. No, better, a roller on the wall for those gigantic spools of plastic sheeting so we can cover the place against art that makes a mess."

Jonathan said, "Some kind of wheels to move things around. I used to roll the woodworking stuff to the front of the carriage house so we had natural light."

Brooke gasped. "You're a carpenter!" Before Jonathan could point out that this wasn't a surprise, she gestured at the ceiling. "You can install a skylight so we can have natural light!"

He laughed. "In addition to infinite money, you're assuming infinite skill."

"Please?" She made exaggerated big eyes that wrung Jonathan's heart. "I'd love a skylight."

Nevertheless. "Do you love to get dripped on? Because those seals fail, and I've never done one before."

She faked a trembly lower lip. "But— But— Real light changes how colors work together."

Jonathan drew back. "Does it?"

She dropped the wounded fawn act. "The full spectrum of light evokes all the colors, so you see an object as it really is. Then you can make better decisions. Spending a lot of time with an object in unnatural light doesn't make up for quality time in real light." She put her hands on his arm to look at his phone screen. "When do we start?"

As close as she was, Jonathan tensed, but then relaxed. She wasn't focused on him, only on the studio space. "After we figure out what's affordable."

"I'll bring it up on the BCG forums. We're due for a meeting, and it can be our first meeting at the new house."

Jonathan nodded. "Just let me know when to vacate."

She frowned. "Absolutely not. You're an artisan, too, and the nominal homeowner. You need to hear everyone gushing about Aunt Millie's murals and the beautiful windows and the sweet sitting room." She hugged him, and Jonathan went warm despite the chill. "You have to see the joy you've made possible."

CHAPTER SEVEN

The November meeting of the BCG did take place in Aunt Millie's house.

This is a mistake. This was all a huge mistake. Brooke's hands trembled while laying out napkins and cutlery and plates, setting the drinks on the buffet tables, and arranging catering stands. Natalie and Lilah were cooking —a huge help—with an occasional foray to the basement kitchen to keep something warm in its oven.

The members were loud. The hardwood floors did nothing to absorb the echoes of so many people, and some of them, Brooke didn't even know.

Some of them, she did—like Emerson, who walked in the door with a smile and a tray of fruit. He hugged her. "Congratulations, Mrs. Levesque."

"Still Evart." She tried to relax at his touch because here was an ally. "And no need to congratulate me. It's the BCG that's winning."

"You're the reason it's happening."

"Jonathan is the reason it's happening." She looked around. "I need to find him."

She took the fruit tray to the kitchen, but found only

Natalie and Lilah and a couple of quilters, so Brooke left it and headed upstairs. He wasn't there, either, but upstairs was quiet, so Brooke stepped into her room and closed the door.

Aah. Silence.

With the commotion at bay, she texted Jonathan. "Where are you?"

"Basement," he replied. "These thirty-two rented folding chairs refused to unfold themselves."

Blast. "I'll come down and help."

"No need. Nearly done."

Victory! She got brownie points for offering, but she didn't have to interact with anyone.

Brooke regarded her bright artwork, and she smiled. These characters were freedom and triumph, and if they could get through all their respective struggles, so could she. In a few hours, this meeting would be over, and she'd have quiet again. Even if she never exited the room until it happened. Eventually, the people would have to leave.

Her brain kept ticking down the list of things to do. Chair and table rental: done and delivered. Food: getting done. Notices posted online: done. Meeting agenda: written and disseminated. But at every turn, there was always more. Like, ice had to be put in the ice bucket, and that meant she needed to dig in the kitchen for ice tongs. Should she have locked people out of the library? What if they tried to play the grand piano? But what if the piano wasn't even in tune?

A light knock sounded at the door, and there she found Jonathan. He said, "Mind if I come in?"

She stepped back to admit him, and he closed it behind him. A little concerned, he said, "Are you already peopled-out?"

"I'm pacing myself." She looked aside. "I wanted to ask a question, but I don't even remember it any longer. And now I need to find ice tongs."

"I'll help you look. If worse comes to worst, I have pliers in my toolbox."

She snickered. "Yes, that's a great idea. I've got a leather punch we can stab into the heart of an ice cube."

He hugged her. "There you go," he said, not noticing how she stiffened in his arms. "But before we start stabbing, let's open a few drawers."

As she followed him out into the noise wafting up the stairs, he looked over his shoulder at her. "Any time you feel like bailing, reassure yourself that there's going to be a lot of leftovers."

She studied him, brow furrowed.

He prompted, "That way you aren't relying on my cooking."

Oh. "Your cooking isn't bad."

He brightened. "Thank you! But please, back off with the praise or I'm going to become insufferably arrogant."

She half-rolled her eyes as she followed him down. "Brighthead's chosen one? Arrogant?"

Brooke hadn't eaten many dinners alone since moving here. Breakfast and lunch, sure—Jonathan wasn't home, so she'd eat upstairs, sometimes sitting on her bed while tackling a chapter out of her second how-to arranged marriage book. Every night when she'd gotten home, though, he'd been in the kitchen. He'd invited her to stay because once again, he'd cooked in excess of one meal. A stack of individually sized leftovers inhabited the freezer, but lately he'd been cooking large batches and doubling up the leftover portions. "In case we eat together," he'd say, but then he wouldn't leave any singles so he could eat solo —which was ostensibly the reason to make extra portions. Wasn't it?

People were confusing. Nevertheless, Brooke enjoyed dining with him. After they cleaned up, sometimes she'd sit in the kitchen to design because she could still feel his presence, but usually she'd lock up and retreat to the micro-apartment to knit or read.

In the kitchen, Jonathan announced to Natalie and Lilah, "Good news! Brooke has proclaimed that my food isn't disgusting."

"Brooke!" Lilah exclaimed.

Brooke started. "That's not at all what I said!"

Jonathan made a face. "You mean it *is* disgusting?"

"I didn't say that, either. You're reading entirely too much into the subtext." He shouldn't feel that way about her. She wasn't criticizing him. It was generous to cook for her, even though he insisted she was being generous by sharing her post-work alone-time. He'd even gotten unnerved when she'd ciphered out her portion of his grocery bill and cash-apped him the money.

Natalie looked up from making a salad. "Jonathan does the cooking? Didn't you move your kitchen upstairs to cook there?"

Brooke said, "Jonathan provoked this whole conversation by saying I could keep today's leftovers to spare myself the pain of eating his food. I never said anything of the sort, and if it's all the same to you, everyone else should take home the leftovers."

Brooke loved leftovers: her own leftovers. Food out of buffet trays was less her speed. If it all went home with the BCG members, she would be very happy. In fact, she'd picked up a package of quart-sized Chinese food containers at the same time she'd picked up the catering trays and stands, just to ensure the food's disappearance.

She added, "I could cook for Jonathan. He just pre-empts me before I get home, and on Sunday he eats with his family."

Since they weren't really her in-laws, it didn't seem right to pop herself into the front seat of his truck and say, "Now your parents can feed me, too."

Jonathan put a hand on her shoulder, but she sidled out of the way. "I need to find ice tongs."

After a quick house tour (by Lilah, which Brooke spent taking deep breaths on the kitchen porch) the BCG members filed into the basement for their November meeting. Satisfied they'd herded down the last of the stragglers, Brooke went last with a clipboard, making sure everyone signed in and gave their contact information. She didn't recognize all the names, so after the first row, she added a column for screen names. That increased the number of recognizable members. The very quiet white-haired woman at the end of the third row was, in fact, a common-sense internet presence who had a way of shutting down fights with one paragraph.

Brooke stood to the side while Lilah ran the show. "Isn't this house amazing? We're going to need help bootstrapping this place as a headquarters, though. You saw there wasn't a lot of furniture."

"But all the books!" someone called out.

"The books are off-limits. The point is, we're putting out an open call. If anyone here is getting rid of furniture, please message me first."

Natalie added, "If anyone happens to have thirty-two folding chairs and six portable tables, we'll save a bundle. Even with us picking up the rentals, it's not cheap."

Lilah said, "I've put in for three separate grants to outfit the carriage house as a studio, but I haven't heard back. I'm worried we might not get that because technically the house isn't ours, yet."

One of the women raised her hand. "What's the situation with this house? It's clearly a residential property."

"The house belonged to Jonathan Levesque's aunt. She deeded it to him in her will with some other stipulations about donating to charity." Lilah was clever. From a vocabulary list in seventh grade, Brooke had learned that this conversational tactic was called *paltering*: saying something entirely true in all its parts, and yet didn't add up to the conclusion the listener was going to draw. "The Levesque family has graciously allowed us to use their property to host all our meetings and our artist-in-residency program."

When a number of people turned to look at Jonathan, Brooke's skin crawled. Brighthead had expected him to become a priest. Lilah's brief explanation wasn't going to hold water with them, no matter what Lilah assured her.

The woman said, "Will you be selling art out of this

house?"

Lilah shook her head. "This house will be for meeting and eating, and for hosting out of town artists. We might host the occasional exhibit, but there'd never be any sales."

Natalie stood. "What you're suggesting would violate zoning laws. It's one thing if Jonathan does woodwork out of the carriage house and consigns it to area stores, but operating an actual storefront out of a residential property...? None of us wants that."

The woman said, "Will this house be our official address?"

All the hair stood up on the back of Brooke's neck. On the sign-in sheet, she counted backward from the last name she recognized. This woman was Anita, self-identified as a hand-quilter, and she didn't have a screen name.

Natalie said, "The paperwork we filed with the state gives the Bright Stitches address as our official address, and that's where the BCG receives mail. You can be confident we've made sure everything is legal. It's not a commercial activity to host a meeting in one's house, and it's not a commercial activity to host a guest."

Anita huffed. "It seems as if the neighbors on Sky Ridge Drive would have something to say about several dozen cars clogging up the street once a month."

Did this woman live on Sky Ridge?

A fabric restoration expert said, "My aunt lives up the block, and parties are frequent. I assure you, no one is inconvenienced by a few cars parked in a driveway for a couple of hours once a month."

Anita fell silent, but Brooke edged around to the stairway at the back.

Lilah said, "If the neighbors complain, we're more than happy to talk to them. But, on the subject of the house, let's talk about what we've all been waiting for: the artist-in-residency program."

Lilah was a magnificent marketer because really, the AIR

program was what *she'd* been waiting for since the day she'd conceived of the BCG. No one else had thought about it until she'd hand-sold it to everyone.

"First off, we've won a grant to get our program started!" Everyone applauded, and Lilah beamed. "Secondly, I'd like the chair of our AIR committee to explain what we've done."

While Adrian was heading to the front, Jonathan came up behind Brooke. He whispered, "What's that woman's problem?"

Brooke had run Anita's words backward and forward in her mind, and every time, she'd identified anger. On tiptoes, she breathed into Jonathan's ear, "Historical Society."

He straightened away from her and looked right at the woman, who was glaring fire at Adrian. He turned back to Brooke, then took her hand and squeezed.

At the front, Adrian was saying, "We're running the first residency as a test. The artist understands that we're in effect using her to work out any potential snags in the system, but she's also very easy-going and flexible. She promises to report back on areas of improvement when she gives her presentation at the end of her stay. We'll start taking applications for the general AIR programs in mid-December, and then start accepting artists for short-term residencies beginning in late January."

Anita called out, "How long would each artist stay?"

Brooke's skin crawled, and when Jonathan stepped closer, Brooke tensed even more. She wasn't asking for Jonathan's physical protection. She just wanted that woman to leave them alone.

Adrian said, "That's the beauty of our program. We have the flexibility to discuss with each artist how long they require."

Given how long it had taken Lilah to design the program, Brooke was glad not to be the one figuring it out. When Lilah joined the Economic Planning Board, she'd taken to grant applications like a jellyfish to the ocean.

With that skill, she'd obtained what looked like a steady stream of both income to care for their resident artists and sources for potential AIR applicants.

The woman said, "Will they stay for months at a time?"

Brooke stepped forward. "Anita?" When the woman turned to face her at the back, Brooke continued, "You have a lot of questions about the program that would be better answered during a long conversation. After the presentation, you and I should chat. Come sit with me during the dinner, and I can address all your questions at length."

Natalie looked worried, and Lilah off-balance. Yes, this happened at the store, too. Natalie and Lilah never wanted to shut anyone down. But when it had to happen, it had to happen—so Brooke did it.

Anita said, "When did Jonathan take possession of the house?"

"That's another conversation topic for our meal." Brooke signaled to Adrian. "You can continue. Tell them about our first resident."

Brooke wasn't sure if that would have been Adrian's next point, but it got Anita to clam up.

Jonathan folded his arms and leaned against the stairway. "Excellent work."

Brooke muttered, "I hate rude customers."

Unfortunately, Anita's silence for the rest of the meeting came at the price of Anita's presence during the meal. She pushed her paper plate into position across from Brooke while Brooke tried to compare her facial expression to Lilah's chart. Outrage?

Brooke had known this wouldn't be easy. "I'm sorry to hear the AIR program has you so worried. But now that you've heard our first resident is a bead artist from Manchester, New Hampshire, and she'll only be staying five days, I hope we've eased your concerns."

The woman regarded Brooke. "I thought Jonathan Levesque was becoming a priest."

"I thought so too, and it's a pleasant surprise that he moved back to Brighthead." Maybe not pleasant—but also not unpleasant. More like, shocking? Unprecedented? She could feel sad that he'd lost his dream, but comfortd in that at least his hometown could offer a safe harbor while he figured out what to do with his life.

Anita said, "What changed his mind?"

Brooke narrowed her eyes. "It's so complicated, but you're concerned about the artist-in-residency program, and I don't want to become 'that girl' who gossips about other people when everyone would rather she shut up. Let's talk more about artists."

Anita said, "I don't mind."

Brooke didn't change tone. "You're so kind to say so. Do you have an artist you'd like to recommend for the AIR program? I can send them an application."

Grandma used to scold Brooke for sounding like she was reading the phone book. Lilah tried to smooth that over by saying Brooke had a useful deadpan. It certainly came in useful now. Shut this woman down like an irate customer. Don't show your feelings. Don't give an opening.

Which was also how Brooke had shut down the mean kids in high school and the pretentious professors in college. With a blank face, blank eyes, and flat voice, keep everything actual-factual.

Anita said, "If you house a guest for an entire month, that means they've established residency. After that, you can't throw them out."

Brooke pulled out her phone. "I will definitely make a note to ask our attorney about that."

Not that she would ask. Only that she would make a note. Which she did.

Jonathan joined them, and Brooke fought a groan.

Because Jonathan would *talk* to this woman. He'd give away more information than Brooke ever wanted her to have.

Brooke said loudly, "It's our host, the founder of the feast," taking Jonathan's hand as he settled into the chair at her side. He started, and she squeezed hard. "Stop me if I begin gushing about your generosity to anyone who will listen. Anita has been very tolerant, but I need you to keep me on track so we talk only about the artist-in-residency program."

Understanding came to his eyes. "That shouldn't be hard. I'm excited for it, myself." He turned to Anita. "Isn't this a fantastic opportunity? It's clearly an artist's house."

Anita said, "I used to be friends with Millie, so I know it's an artist's house. I noticed during the tour that no one's using her bedroom."

This jerk was completely digging for information. "We decided to leave the primary suite available for the Artist in Residence, at least for the time being. That may change after the first residency, but we want the artist to feel at home. She should feel free to do whatever she needs in the home, not like a guest."

Anita smirked. "You keep calling the Artist in Residence a guest, but if you're not here, hosting, then it's not a guest. It's a tenant."

Jonathan softened his eyes so he looked charming. More than that, he looked innocent. Probably because he was. "Do you remember how I used to stay in the guest cottage? I loved those summers, so it was natural to move right back in there."

Brooke turned to Anita and decided to channel Natalie's objection. "We don't want to turn Jonathan into the BCG's de-facto groundskeeper and clean-up crew. Whenever we talk about the BCG, though, he's so accommodating. He's the one who suggested we use this house for the AIR program, and he suggested having meetings here. Aunt Millie loved the arts so much."

Jonathan said, "I cannot imagine what she would say if

she knew about everything that's happened."

Brooke's deadpan was a good thing right about now. She followed up with, "Aunt Millie always did have such strong opinions."

Anita glared at Jonathan. "Why did you leave the priesthood? Was it because Millie left you the house?"

Brooke straightened her spine. "Wow, such an intrusive question."

Natalie joined them with her tray. "Did you try the carnitas? Colin gave me his own personal recipe, and they're amazing." Then she turned to Anita. "I'm glad you're talking about the residency program with Brooke and Jonathan. Jonathan's been a gracious host."

Lilah arrived right behind Natalie. "Oh, good, I hope we can answer all your questions now, since we couldn't during the main meeting."

Surrounded by the BCG core group, Anita seemed to have lost her appetite. "Yes, you've answered all of my questions."

Brooke said, "In that case, I have a question. Why does the Historical Society keep pursuing their vendetta against the BCG, considering that you won your sortie about the Main Street church, and considering that this property isn't historic in any way?"

Anita scowled. "What on earth are you on about?"

"Come on, everyone at this table knows you infiltrated tonight to get dirt for your Historical Society overlords. That's why you were asking questions about commercial versus residential zoning, why you wanted to know about tenancy in the house, and why you want details about where Jonathan is staying and Jonathan's relationship with Aunt Millie." Brooke leaned forward. "Since you've learned that nothing we're doing is illegal, immoral, or otherwise something your attorney can write a Cease and Desist letter about, I figure it's fair game to ask why you tried."

Lilah said, "If anyone's causing issues here, it's you disrupting one of our meetings. Sounds like harassment to me."

Natalie added, "Plus, you've made us curious as to why you just won't let it go."

Brooke said, "Except now you *are* going to let it go, since we're not defacing the property, not selling paintings, and enjoying fair use of a residential home."

Jonathan had her hand tight beneath the table, and Brooke drew strength from him. Jonathan had her back.

Brooke tilted her head and smiled. "Also, on your way out, please be sure stop at the dessert table. Jonathan made cookies, and they're mouth-watering even though the stove isn't an antique."

CHAPTER EIGHT

Beader-in-Residence Casey Castanella had bright eyes, curly black hair, and an absolute awe for Aunt Millie's murals. While Jonathan led her from room to room, she never stopped gasping: at the murals, at the sitting room with its hardwood floors, at the balcony overseeing the ocean, at the library with its grand piano and hundreds of books. Then, upstairs: "No! This is my room? For real?" She laughed and then went back into the hallway where she could see over the railing. "Brooke, this house is amazing!" After which, she needed to see the other two bedrooms, but Aunt Millie's was her favorite. "I love the wooden castle! I want to crawl through that tiny door and live in the castle, but then I won't be able to enjoy this amazing house."

That was going to be their experience with the first Artist in Residence, then: nonstop talking. Jonathan sent Brooke a hopeful smile because she'd already been dealing with Casey's extraversion for a couple of hours.

"I met up with Lilah at Bright Stitches, which is just the most amazing shop, but they don't have a lot of beads." She sat at the table narrating her day to Jonathan while

Brooke cooked dinner. "Actually, I met up with all three of them, like the Three Fates, but then Lilah took me on a tour, and we ended up in Juniper at a bead store called Bead and Breakfast, and that woman even makes her own beads!"

Jonathan said, "Brooke, do you need me to do anything?"

She didn't even turn her head. "I'm fine."

Ah! She was getting space by letting Casey talk to him while keeping her back to them and not even being rude about it. Obviously she had to look at the food she was cooking. Clever.

Well, clever or desperate. How often had he missed Brooke using escape tactics?

After dinner, Brooke made sure the crafting lamps put enough light on the desk in Casey's room (Brooke's lamps and a desk lamp one of the guild members had pulled from her garage). Jonathan didn't want to hover, but he stuck close, keeping the conversation going (although Casey didn't need help in that regard). When Brooke returned downstairs, Casey followed with a hard-sided case. "This house is beyond amazing. You guys are so generous to be hosting artist retreats."

Brooke said, "You know, we could host three at a time..."

Jonathan said, "You're getting ahead of yourself."

She laughed. "I could never get ahead of Lilah. Lilah initially started by wanting to build an artists' colony. If she'd had her way, we'd already have fifteen tiny houses on this property."

Jonathan muttered, "And fifteen less-than-tiny lawsuits."

Brooke said, "I like the way you think—because that's exactly what I said."

When Jonathan laughed, Casey said, "You two are far too comfortable with one another."

Both of them turned, but Casey was opening up her beading case without paying them any attention. "You said Jonathan only moved back to Brighthead this year, but the way you act, you've been married forever."

Brooke said, "We've known each other forever."

Casey looked up, smiling. "That's sweet. I'd like to think there's a soul out there who's known my soul forever, too."

Jonathan caught the twitch of Brooke's head, but she didn't object. Instead she picked up her knitting, settled on the couch, and got to work.

Comfortable with one another. Huh.

Tentative, Jonathan sat on the other end of the couch and pulled up the ebook reader on his phone.

He and Brooke didn't do this. After their dinner clean-up, he always went to the guest cottage so she could have her alone-time. Tonight, he tested the waters. Would she ask him to leave? Would she herself leave?

She didn't. Jonathan would read for a while, then gaze over his phone at her, and she never caught him.

Brooke didn't believe it, but she was disarmingly beautiful.

For her, the world had vanished. In this moment, she was hyperfixated on whatever she was designing on that graph paper. She knitted, made markings, worked it up, ripped it back. Why would she throw Jonathan out when she wasn't aware he existed? Right now, her world was a series of mathematical notations—zeros and ones like knits and purls, images traveling up and down whatever pattern she was creating. The universe was her pair of needles, and the yarn that wound into and out of itself every time she moved them.

At the table, the bead-crafter was doing the same, but murmuring to herself. Meanwhile the night darkened outside, and their house was an oasis of light on Sky Ridge Drive—a beacon full of art and not just brilliance.

Then Brooke put away her graph paper, and she gave the tiniest of starts when she realized Jonathan was still with her. But she only announced that she was exhausted and heading upstairs, and Casey decided that she, too, was going to bed.

Silence descended over the house. Jonathan closed up

the downstairs, locked the house, and returned to the guest cottage.

Brooke's lights were on in her micro-apartment, so he texted her. "You're still awake?"

"Processing," she replied. "Thank you for staying up with us tonight."

"No problem." That didn't feel like enough, though. "It did feel comfortable reading together."

Brooke hadn't been reading, though. If she had, she'd have been reading that book about how to tolerate your contractual spouse.

She didn't reply, so he texted, "Good night, esteemed wife," and she replied with, "Good night to you, too."

At three o'clock in the morning, Jonathan awoke and used the bathroom, then got some water—and noticed Brooke's lights still on.

He retrieved his phone from the charger, but she hadn't texted. He sent, "Are you still awake? Your lights are on."

Her status immediately changed to read, followed by the typing indicator, and then, "Sorry."

Sorry? "Is something wrong?"

The typing indicator stayed on for so long that Jonathan had changed out of his pajamas and was tying on his boots by the time she replied. Her text was only, "Yes."

He ran across the property, right to the door, unlocked it with shaking hands, and then dashed upstairs without scuffing the dirt from his boots. Casey's lights were off.

He reached Brooke's door and knocked, and when she didn't answer, he texted, "It's me."

She opened the door, pale, her eyes bloodshot. He stepped inside her micro-apartment and shut the door behind. His low voice didn't hide the strain. "What's wrong?"

Her lip trembled. "I can't sleep. It's nothing wrong. It's just—" Her breath caught. "It's stupid. I'm sorry."

"Hey." He hugged her, and she pressed up against his jacket even though his jacket must be chilly and she was warm in her pajamas. "Whatever's going on, let me help.

Are you sick?" She shook her head. "You're scared?"

Her breath caught again, and she nodded.

He guided her to her bed because it was the nearest place to sit, and she just kept holding onto him, her fingers clenching his jacket. He hugged her and smoothed her hair and wondered what on earth you do with someone so scared they can't even speak.

She'd been joking about things climbing out of the woodwork doors, and so had Casey (actually, no, Casey had joked about climbing into the door) but there wasn't even a tiny door in this room. Had she seen a ghost?

Brooke choked out, "I'm not dealing with this."

Jonathan said, "'This' being...?"

Brooke pointed toward the only other occupied room in the house.

Jonathan went cold. "You're anxious? Because someone is here?"

She nodded.

"Okay. We can solve this." He paused. "But not by throwing her out onto the lawn."

Tucked up against his chest, Brooke laughed, but it was silent. It was a start. If he could make her laugh, he could make her relax. He added, "For one thing, her beads might spill."

Her shoulders shook again, and he squeezed her tighter as he continued, "Also, that might affect our ability to invite future Artists in Residence."

She pressed closer.

He said, "I could threaten her, but that also seems like a horrible idea."

Brooke swallowed hard and tried to steady her voice. "I'm being irrational."

"Who cares? Irrational fears are real just like rational ones." But now, he had a plan. "The two good options are, either you go stay in the guest house, or I stay here and guard you while you sleep."

She wrapped her arms around his waist. "Did you bring your gun?"

Jonathan didn't even own a gun. "I have a ring of cannons surrounding the house, ready to fire on my orders."

Brooke sat away from him and made a circle with her hands, then little darting motions toward the center. "They'll all end up firing on each other."

Jonathan offered, "I didn't say it was a great strategy."

She bit her lip, then looked up at him for about two-tenths of a second before averting her gaze again. She had dark circles under her eyes. She hadn't been crying, but she looked wrung-out.

He said, "Take your pick. You need sleep, so either you stay in the cottage, or you stay here, and either way, I'll stay here."

She glanced around at the room, and he saw the moment when she felt safe. Everything looked familiar in this mock-up of her home. Yes, there was someone in the building, but in the comfort of her micro-apartment, and with another person to guard against the unfamiliar, she felt safe.

Jonathan's arms ached to pull her closer to him once more, so he edged away. "Now would be the time to disclose that from the first moment I saw your couch, I had an irresistible urge to sleep on it."

Brooke said, "You'll need a pillow. Hang on."

She slid a plastic bin from beneath the bed and gave him a blanket. She had her pillows arranged in a U-shape that looked cozy, but she broke up the nest by giving one to him. Between the wall of pillows and the weighted blanket, she must be sleeping in a fortress. Except she still looked unnerved.

Jonathan said, "I have a better idea," and he spread out his blanket on the floor in front of the door. "Extra security."

Her mouth trembled again. "You're going to be uncomfortable."

Given his height and the length of that couch, discomfort was a given. "I don't mind. You wouldn't ask if you didn't need help."

She hadn't asked, was the problem. She'd been prepared to face five sleepless nights in a row because she wasn't going to ask. But there was no need for this extreme independence, not when he was around to help her. They weren't really married, but shouldn't a woman feel able to ask her husband for something small to help her feel safer?

Jonathan shut the light and wrapped up in the blanket. Brooke's scent surrounded him as he laid his head on the pillow she'd been cuddling.

In the dark, she whispered, "Thank you."

Her voice sounded small, but less scared. Jonathan whispered back, "You're welcome, most esteemed wife."

After three hours asleep on Brooke's floor, Jonathan awoke to his phone alarm and silenced it as quickly as he could. Brooke didn't move.

Using the phone flashlight, he got the blanket folded and onto the couch, and he replaced the pillow on her bed. He didn't want to shine the light on her face, but he thought she seemed tense. Who knew, though? She'd replaced whatever curtains were in here with light-blocking drapes (he'd have done that for her if she'd asked) and the place was dark like a sepulcher.

At her drafting desk, he found paper and a pencil. This would have to suffice.

"Brooke, I don't want to wake you up because you finally got some sleep, but I hope it's okay that I'm going to work. Text or call me if you need anything. I've set the phone to notify me for you even if I've got notifications off. I'll be back at 5:30. Call off work if you're feeling draggy. Later! -J"

He hesitated because he'd always closed his letters to her with, *"Later! -Jonathan"* but amidst the darkness and the exhaustion, he'd gotten to the L and nearly written, "Love, Jonathan."

That's not love. That's protectiveness. She'd been so scared last night, and if he put it back on what Father Tim had said—of course a big brother would have done exactly what Jonathan did for his little sister. You step in, address the fear, and protect her. Technically, he'd spent the night with a woman, but *technically,* he was married to her. There wasn't anything sinful about his behavior. If the pope himself had been standing in that room, Jonathan would have done exactly the same.

He grinned as he slipped out of Brooke's room into the hallway. No, if the pope himself had been standing in that room, Jonathan would most assuredly have not behaved the same way. For one thing, he'd have started with, "No wonder you're nervous, Brooke. The pope is here!" and then he'd have grabbed his Bible for the pope to bless before he flew back to the Vatican.

What would the pope even be doing in Brighthead? Should the BCG phone the Vatican and offer them a space for one of their musicians to claim a residency? Even more importantly, was Jonathan out of his mind with exhaustion to have gone down this trail of thought?

Fortunately, he hadn't lost much sleep. Back in the guest cottage, he turned on the coffee maker, got himself presentable in time to pour coffee into his thermal mug, and out the door he went.

Brooke texted him at nine. "Thank you. I'm sorry I worried you."

He replied, "Are you all right?"

"I'm fine. I was always fine. I panicked and got caught in a feedback loop."

These clinical texts were not the same woman who'd been curled like an egg under her weighted blanket. How embarrassed was she feeling? But worse, why did she think he'd shame her for panicking because there was a stranger sleeping right down the hall? For all Brooke knew, she'd awaken in the middle of the night to find their Artist in Residence creating a new form of art by pinning thousands of beads to her body. *I call it living acupuncture. Please hold still so I can make all your pressure points glittery and beautiful.*

He replied, "Thank you for trusting me."

Given her skittishness, he didn't want to keep poking her through the day with an endless barrage of, "Are you okay?" and "How about now?" so he came up with other questions. "I forgot to check the fridge—do we need more milk?" She did go to work on time, which he hoped was a good sign.

Except when he got home, he realized she'd biked to work. Worse, she'd be returning well after dark. Exhausted.

No.

Casey met him at the entrance of the living room. "Please don't take this the wrong way, but I have fifteen thousand beads on that table, so would you mind not breathing in here?"

Jonathan laughed, then covered his mouth.

"Well, I guess you can breathe. I'm breathing. But if you wanted to set up a trampoline, maybe do that in the library? That library is gorgeous, by the way..."

Casey's chatter was just what he needed after a day of measuring a kitchen for cabinets and then standing on the lawn with a portable table saw to cut molding to exactly the right length. It always made him feel like the best carpenter in the world when he used a saw out on someone's lawn to cut all the pieces to fit, then walked into the house and got them very nearly set up...and then, bam. One tap of the hammer, and everything slid into place.

I bet you did that, Jonathan thought to God. *But now I need to do something a little less form-fitting.*

First he headed to Brooke's room (careful not to tread too hard past all those beads) with a care package. It was a matter of five minutes to replace her doorknob with one that locked. Following that, it took another twenty minutes to install a deadbolt.

This was no longer Brooke's micro apartment. Henceforth, it was Brooke's fortress, mighty defense against any and all artists except those with excellent lock-picking skills and a mean kick to the doorframe. But to be honest, she'd have been vulnerable to that no matter what he did. Maybe he could have installed a safety plate against crow bars, but he knew exactly what Brooke's face would look like if he did. She'd think he was making fun of her. He'd do just enough to ensure she felt safe. If thirty dollars in hardware could give her a good night's sleep, that was worthwhile.

He went to start dinner and instead discovered a note on the fridge.

"Most Esteemed Jonathan: Dinner awaits in the crock pot. Sincerely, Brooke"

The crock pot contained a mushroom and barley stew, along with a note explaining that rolls were chilling in the fridge (just put them in the oven for fifteen minutes) along with a salad, and they could eat whenever.

Technically, the Artist in Residence wasn't someone they should be feeding. They'd fed Casey last night to welcome her, but it shouldn't be required every night. Also, Jonathan was going to go out on a limb and assume the menu meant Casey was vegetarian. He hadn't thought anything of it last night when Lilah had left them with a veggie lasagna and garlic bread, but he detected a pattern.

He found Casey. "Can I speak if I don't talk too loud?"

She looked up from what looked like a map of the universe with more beads than stars in the sky, her eyes unfocused, and her brain in another time zone. "Sure."

"Whenever you're hungry, Brooke left food. She'll be home around eight if you don't want to wait that long, but otherwise, that's when we'll plan to eat." He glanced at the fully covered dining room table. "And I guess that'll be in the kitchen."

Casey glanced at her universe of beads. "I guess so."

Jonathan was keeping a tickle file of things to change for future AIRs. "Larger table, dedicated space" fit nicely on the list.

At seven-fifty, with Maine pitch black all around, Jonathan set the table, then looked at the clock, looked at the meal Brooke had assembled before heading to work, and picked up his keys.

At seven fifty-five, the Bright Stitches bells jangled as Jonathan walked into the shop. Brooke looked up with a smile, and then her smile changed. "Hey! What are you doing here?"

That change in her smile jolted him. "I was looking for a yarn bowl," he said, struggling to decode what had just happened. She'd looked up with a smile, and then—had it gotten realer? Her eyes had gone from neutral to crinkled. The angle of her head had changed. Her shoulders had straightened.

She'd turned to greet a customer—but then she'd recognized and greeted Jonathan.

Brooke swept over to the gift corner. "Most esteemed sir, we do indeed carry yarn bowls."

The only other customer in the store was at the Sit and Stitch table. "Most esteemed sir? Isn't that Jonathan Levesque, the Catholic boy wonder?"

Brooke rested a hand on Jonathan's arm, sending electricity through him. "Of course he is. Jonathan, this is Lavender Paul, one of our regular customers."

Lavender Paul sniffed at him. "Feminism means we don't have to treat random men like lordlings."

Jonathan said, "Feminism means women can call random men anything they want to, and she chooses to tease me without remorse."

Lavender pursed her lips. "Well, then, go right ahead and tease him."

"Thank you. I will." Brooke turned to Jonathan. "Why are you here? I assume not just to see how well your yarn bowls are selling."

They had been selling—chalk up one for Brooke on that

score. "I'm here because I have a pickup truck, and you have a bicycle, and your bicycle would fit nicely in the bed of my pickup truck."

Lavender muttered, "You two need to get a room."

Brooke's cheeks went red. "He didn't mean it that way at all," and then Jonathan parsed it the way Brooke might have meant, and—

Now it was his turn to feel flustered. "No! What I meant is—"

"What you meant is, you wanted to give me a lift rather than having me strap on my light-up gear and pedal up that huge narrow winding hill in the dark." She smiled, again with her eyes crinkled up and her head tilted, looking cute. "That was thoughtful, but entirely unnecessary."

Lavender Paul started gathering her things. "Well, doll, I've got this Estonian lace sorted out, so you two can keep making eyes at each other." Lavender fixed her stare on Jonathan. "You take good care of her, and maybe she'll knit you a sweater."

"Duly noted."

Brooke said, "What about the Sweater Curse?"

Lavender buttoned her long wool coat. "Marry him, and then knit him a sweater."

Brooke followed her to the door. "I'll keep that in mind, Mrs. Paul. It was great seeing you." Then she locked the door behind her and flipped the sign to CLOSED.

Jonathan started pushing the chairs back at the Sit and Stitch table. "What's the Sweater Curse?"

"If you knit your beloved a sweater before you're married, you'll break up." She went to the register area. "It's a longtime yarn superstition, but I suspect it started because knitters were tired of getting pestered by their boyfriends for wool sweaters that would take twenty hours to knit."

Jonathan prompted, "Is that a euphemism for guys not wanting the cow if they can get the milk for free?" He nearly said, "A euphemism for putting a bike in the truck bed when you can just pedal home," but that was getting into a weird area, and they'd only end up embarrassing each other.

Brooke still wouldn't look at him. "I think it's a cautionary tale about wasting effort on a sweater someone's not going to appreciate, so make sure you're keeping the person in your life before dedicating those kinds of resources."

She wasn't being explicit, but they both knew they'd be divorcing next November. Why knit him a sweater she wouldn't have the pleasure of seeing him wear?

"I'm not asking for a sweater," he reassured.

She turned to him, hands and eyebrows raised. "Lavender Paul suggested it, not you."

Today's fingerless gloves were a chocolate brown with tan flecks, and they disappeared up her sweater sleeves. He teased, "You knit the sweater you're wearing."

"A calculated risk. It's hard to break up with oneself."

Leaving the seminary had felt like Jonathan breaking up with Jonathan. Although it also felt like God breaking up with Jonathan. What did it all even mean any longer? Everyone had assured Jonathan that leaving meant the process was working, that he'd discerned in earnest and heard God's direction. If it had been Jonathan's will alone, next summer he'd be getting ordained. Except it hadn't been, and instead he would be getting divorced.

Rather than following that train of thought, he picked up a wooden spindle, then spun the top part. It whirled on ball bearings. "And this is?"

"A yarn buddy. Why does everyone always want me to explain these?" Brooke took a cake of yarn and stuck it on the spindle, then showed him how with every stitch, the spindle would turn. "It's a higher-tech version of a yarn bowl, but I prefer what you made."

Brooke's bicycle did, indeed, fit neatly into the bed of his truck (no euphemisms involved) and Brooke fit neatly into his passenger seat, and he drove home in silence. Not an uncomfortable silence. He was just lost in thought, and when he realized he'd been lost in thought, he also realized she'd been comfortably silent herself.

She was easy to be silent around. Some people demanded an explanation for silence. Not Brooke.

At home, Casey was once again full of surprise that they had come back (Jonathan had left?) and that time had passed. Brooke asked questions about the beadwork. It was gorgeous, a million minuscule spheres woven into one another in a rippling fabric, following a chart that Brooke studied until suddenly saying, "Oh!" and then seeming to get the whole concept.

They ate at the round kitchen table, Casey regaling them with tales of the artistic scene in New Hampshire. "I'm fortunate to be so close to University of New Hampshire, Southern New Hampshire University, and Saint Anselm College. It's only a couple hours to Burlington, and that's got just as much life."

After dinner, Casey helped clean up even though as their guest she shouldn't, and then she had another request: "Can we work in the library tonight? I hope you don't mind, but I explored it today, and merely being surrounded by so many books, I felt inspired."

Jonathan said, "I always loved that room," and not until they were setting up in there did he realize Brooke had never agreed to this. She seemed content, though, and settled down on the couch with her graph paper and the tube she was knitting. Jonathan asked, "Socks?"

She raised it for his inspection, and now he could see something of a design on it. "I think I have the pattern figured out, so I'm just repeating the chart down the leg to make sure I did it right the first time."

Casey walked over to the piano. "Which of you plays?"

"That would be Brooke." Jonathan chuckled. "I can't do anything with a piano."

"It's Aunt Millie's piano. I haven't played in years." Brooke didn't look up. "We don't even know if it's in tune."

"Try to play," Casey said. "A library this grand deserves music."

Brooke kept her eyes on her work. "If it deserves music, we ought to turn on the stereo."

Still, at the end of the row, she took a seat at the piano bench. Jonathan looked up from his book (he'd made sure to carry a paper book in case they repeated last night's evening) and watched Brooke pick through a scale. "It's not *terrible,*" she pronounced. "It needs a coffee date with a piano tuner, though. I wonder if I remember anything?"

She sat in total silence for so long. Was Jonathan supposed to offer suggestions? He couldn't remember what songs she used to play, but was that because she'd never played for her friends, or just because he couldn't remember? Had she ever invited them to her recitals?

Finally she began a song Jonathan remembered from beginner band, plunking it out more than playing it, along with lots of wrong notes. "I'm sorry. I'm no good without sheet music."

Jonathan got up. "This is a library with a piano. There's got to be music."

"Not the caliber I'd be playing." Brooke snorted as she raised the piano bench lid to reveal a compartment. "Ah, yes, the *'Moonlight Sonata'*. And *'Fur Elise'*. Definitely what to play after not touching an instrument for years."

"Keep digging. Maybe there's something further down."

"Perhaps a *Brandenburg Concerto*?" She hunted. "Please tell me you used to take piano lessons, and your original books are in here."

He shook his head. "Uncle Roger was the pianist. Aunt Millie did play sometimes, I think Christmas music at Christmas, but I'm not sure what else."

"Oh! Hymns. Let me see if I remember any." She looked at Casey. "Do you mind if I play hymns?"

She shrugged. "Just don't sing about hating me."

"I assure you, our hymns were basic. God loves you, and God loves me, and God is awesome, and..." She looked around. "Did Aunt Millie have a hymn book?"

"Maybe, but they wouldn't be the ones our church played. Remember...?"

Brooke's eyes flared. "I'm sorry! I forgot."

Casey snorted. "That sounds like a story."

Brooke said, "It's our thing, Jonathan and me against the world."

On the shelf nearest the piano, Jonathan found books of piano music, and Brooke scanned for anything close to her skill level. Or what her skill level had been. "Hymns are usually simple, or at least, ours were. Which is a good thing right now because sight-reading is a use-it-or-lose-it, and I guarantee, it's lost."

After frowning at the book for a bit, she started playing —very, very slowly—a version of, "How Great Thou Art." Which, considering it was a slow hymn anyhow, rendered it agonizing.

Brooke laughed. "Casey's feedback form is going to stipulate that future Resident Artists not hear the host family playing piano."

Casey exclaimed, "I'll say no such thing!" except what Jonathan heard was, "We're a family."

He and Brooke...? A family?

Until this moment, he hadn't considered that. They were roommates, and they were friends, and they shared a tiny bank account into which they transferred money for household expenses and out of which they paid household bills. They ate dinner together. And yet, she'd just called him and her a family.

He stared at his book without the words making sense.

Jonathan wasn't supposed to have a family—not in this direction. His family was supposed to be upward on the family tree, not lateral and certainly not downward. Except here he was with a family.

Brooke looked tired as she played, and eventually she slid the cover back over the keys. "I should keep doing that," she murmured to herself. She picked her knitting back up, then looked at it, then just stared at it.

Jonathan said, "Maybe get to bed early tonight?"

She bit her lip.

He said, "Actually, can you come with me a minute?"

and led her out of the library.

She followed him upstairs. "I'm putting you through all this trouble, and it's nothing. Maybe if I take melatonin and turn on a fan for white noise—"

Jonathan said, "Or maybe if you give me a minute to show you something, it'll be okay?"

At her door, he gestured to the lock, and her eyes widened. He brought her inside to where he'd left two keys attached to their flimsy ring, and then he showed her the deadbolt.

Biting her lip, Brooke clenched her hands. "I feel ridiculous."

"I installed locks because I don't think you're ridiculous."

She stepped into his arms and buried her face in his chest.

He couldn't breathe, but he tried to hug her and smooth her hair. He had to close his eyes because the feelings rushed through him like water through the gates of a dam.

She bent down her head so just her forehead was touching his chest. "Thank you. That's so sweet after the trouble I caused."

Jonathan found his voice. "Also, I brought up a sleeping bag and a pillow. If you want me here again tonight, say the word."

Brooke looked at the door, looked at him (well, looked at his knees) and then back at the door, and then hunched her shoulders.

She felt ashamed. She didn't want to ask, but she didn't want to say no, either.

Jonathan said, "You know what? I'm not even giving you the choice. I'm the rude man who plans to spend the night sleeping on your floor. If you want me not to, you'll have to lock the door when you turn in for the night, at which point, I'm going to slink out to the guest cottage and sleep there, instead."

Brooke's mouth twitched. "There are two keys."

"Both of which are in your hands, and neither of which

operates the dead bolt slider."

She unwound one of the keys from the ring. "You should have access, regardless. That's just a safety concern, like if a fire starts in my room, and I'm not here."

If a fire started in her room and she *was* here, wouldn't that be even more of a concern? Regardless, he took the key. "You're nervous about Casey having access to your room, but not me."

"Having her in the house feels wrong. I wasn't afraid of her. I was just—constantly aware of how wrong it was."

Jonathan tilted his head. "And having me here felt right?"

Her mouth trembled. "You belong here."

He belonged in seminary, washing dinner pots for fifteen priests and seminarians while listening to his fellow clean-up crew members making jokes about whether Saint Charles Borromeo would approve of reading the Liturgy of the Hours on your phone screen. (Which Jonathan had done often enough. The books with the ribbons were nice, but in his opinion, it was a lot of page-flipping to very little good end.)

He only said, "I'll leave it up to you whether I come in. If the door's locked, I'll go."

She shook her head. "The door will be locked. But if the deadbolt is on, then you go."

"Agreed." He moved toward the door, but it didn't feel right just to walk out, so he stepped back inside and hugged her. "Thank you. It means a lot that you trust me."

CHAPTER NINE

Chaos in the kitchen, but the good kind of chaos. The kind of chaos Brooke hadn't experienced often, and which would be over by the end of the day.

To wit: Thanksgiving.

Or, rather, the day after Thanksgiving, because a twenty-four-hour delay meant Colin and Austin could come, too.

Did Aunt Millie's house really have enough seating? This was going to require every single chair and table. She and Jonathan. Emerson and Lilah. Natalie and Colin, and also Austin. Jonathan's parents were coming, too, because yesterday they'd spent the afternoon at Saint Lucy's making and delivering meals to several dozen homebound seniors. Which also meant they had invited their pastor, Father Tim.

Ten people. Brooke might not be peopled-out before the end of the evening, but by the end, she'd drift up the stairs like an autumn leaf on the wind, lock her door, and knit for three hours while wearing ear protection.

Lilah arrived first, and she brought a folding table plus some chairs. (Who knew you could have potluck furniture?) Natalie arrived soon after, and Colin and Austin arrived together. "Make way!" Austin announced, taking up the entirety of the kitchen with his tremendous presence and brilliant smile. "Colin has brought the masterpiece."

Colin was carrying a covered roaster by the handles, and he shot a look at Austin. "Holding the door would be better than trumpeting me like the town crier."

"You'll be fine." Austin stepped back so Colin could set the roaster on the counter. "Show them. Show them so they can all be astounded."

Brooke stepped back to let the chaos erupt on its own. Colin muttered, "How about I take off my jacket first?"

Austin sighed. "You're drawing this out for no reason."

Colin paused. "I thought you were all into showmanship."

"I'm the twin with the good sense of timing."

"You're also the twin with the annoying mouth."

Austin mocked defeat. He dropped his backpack near the table and went to hang up his jacket in the mudroom.

Natalie took Colin's jacket and coat. "Thanks. Yesterday was unbelievable. Twenty-two thousand dollars in sales, and a full house from opening until practically close. I turned away a family of seven that tried to walk in without a reservation at four minutes to ten. By then, we had no turkey, no prime rib, no pork loin, and we'd long since 86'd anything that looked like a potato. The servers were running on fumes, and the back of house was dead on their feet."

Lilah's eyebrows raised. "You could have slept in today. We'd have managed the turkey without you."

Colin made a face. "Of course I wouldn't force you to do that. I'll sleep on my day off."

Which, technically, this should have been. Fruits de Mer was closed for Black Friday precisely so everyone could recover.

Austin returned to the kitchen. "The talkative twin is delaying his great reveal."

Colin approached the roaster. "Behold," and he raised the lid.

Lilah gasped as Brooke struggled to figure out what she was seeing. It looked like a pink, marbled basket-weave, but it had the legs and wings of a turkey.

Austin said, "Yes, ladies and gentlemen. That man wrapped an entire bird in bacon."

Natalie's eyes were huge. "I thought you were joking!"

"Bacon?" Brooke exclaimed. "You can do that?"

Colin raised his eyebrows. "I did do that, so yes, I can."

"And he has in the past, so I know it's going to be spectacular." Austin rubbed his hands together. "Now, for the rest of the work."

The turkey went into the oven at way too high a temperature, and Colin set a timer. Austin hefted a bag onto the counter. "Guess what you can do if you have regular access to restaurant suppliers?" A moment later, fruit covered all of one counter, and from his backpack, he pulled out his own cutting board and knife roll. Brooke stepped back as he removed a steel rod, and then he swiped a forearm-long knife over the rod with bold strokes and a metallic vibration that set her teeth on edge.

Natalie shivered. "I'm going to get used to that. Someday."

Jonathan entered the kitchen, cheeks pink from the outside, and Brooke stepped closer to him. Jonathan said to Austin, "Kindly stop scaring my wife."

Austin said, "I'm the scary twin." He pulled a sheet of paper off the pad magneted to the refrigerator, and with his right hand, he dangled it by the corner. "Think it's sharp enough?" Then, slowly, he brought the knife down and sliced right through the paper.

Brooke backed up another step into Jonathan's chest.

Austin winked at her. "I learned this trick back in high school."

Leaning against the counter, Colin rolled his eyes. "And then our grandfather would bark at us, '*What are you cutting paper with that for? Knives are for food!*'"

Austin sliced a second strip off the paper. "Gosh, I miss the man. He had a point, and a temper, but I still miss him."

Austin got to work slicing fruit, and Brooke went to the dining room.

Jonathan followed her out. "Any time you need a break, you get out of here."

"Austin alone is like having fifteen people." She spread a tablecloth on the table. "Our guests brought four different sets of dishes, random cutlery, and I don't even know about the glassware. Everyone had better leave with as much as they brought."

Jonathan took the other end, and they straightened it across the table. "No addition, no subtraction."

"No kidding." They had two tables set end-to-end in the dining room to create one long table, one half not the same width as the other. That was the only way they could make it work. "I always saw big family dinners in movies, and I wondered how they did it."

Jonathan said, "And you're still wondering?"

She giggled. "Yes."

He lowered his voice. "So am I."

By one o'clock, the house was full and the volume at a roar. Jonathan's parents arrived with a salad, cranberry sauce, and a pie. Father Tim pulled up minutes later with a second pie and a can of whipped cream. Emerson joined with a tray of baked mac and cheese (which went right into the warming oven) and rolls. Colin and Austin were in charge, so Brooke avoided the kitchen, but the pair of them were a mixture of irreverently funny and deadly serious. They called "Behind!" when walking past someone, and "Corner!" when they went out to the dining room. Colin knocked before opening the refrigerator door, for which Austin mocked him relentlessly, and then, ten minutes later, did it himself.

The turkey came out of the oven and now, Colin declared, it had to rest. Everything else went into the ovens to warm back up. They had food in the upstairs and the downstairs, plus the microwave was reheating the butternut squash.

Mrs. Levesque hugged Brooke before the dinner. "You were so busy that I didn't get a chance to see you when I walked in, but everything's lovely."

Brooke struggled to stay on top of the urge to crawl out of her skin. "Thank you. I'm just hoping it all works."

Mrs. Levesque said, "It should either be an amazing meal or else a memorable story."

Brooke looked away. "I'm hoping for amazing."

Father Tim joined them, a bright-eyed man in his late fifties. "It's great to see you again, Brooke." He handed her a spiral-bound book. "Jonathan said you've resumed playing, and you wanted a copy of our old hymn book."

Brooke accepted it. "Thanks. It's been a while, but Aunt Millie's piano is right here, so it's been nice."

A piano tuner had gotten the instrument back into shape, after which, she'd begun playing in the morning before work, but after Jonathan had left. How'd he even know?

Although, after Casey had left, they'd continued spending evenings in the library. He'd read or pray his evening prayers, and she'd knit or read or work on her patterns.

They didn't talk while doing that, other than sometimes when she came across something interesting. Then she'd read aloud, and he'd listen. It was nice being together. She'd messed around with the piano in front of him a few times. When he told her she could play more, she'd demurred: "I need to get one of those old books so I can remember what I've forgotten."

She hadn't realized Jonathan was paying attention. No one ever paid attention.

When it was time to eat, Mr. Levesque asked Father Tim for a blessing, which he gave, and then Colin carried the turkey to the table.

Platters were flying in every direction. Brooke did her best to nab things as they moved around, but the noise and the chaos blindsided her. It was easier to observe rather than to stay on top of it. And then, strangely, everything she needed started coming right to her, and all of it was coming from Jonathan's direction. He'd ask for whatever wasn't on her plate, take a bit for himself, and then hand the serving dish directly to Brooke.

Emerson informed Colin, "You're evil. I'm never going to want a turkey any other way ever again."

Father Tim said, "Perhaps he's trying to make us come to his restaurant."

Austin snorted. "You think we did this for the paying customers? This was entirely Colin's doing, in his own apartment."

"I stand corrected." Father laughed. "What did you do for the customers?"

Colin shot Austin a look. "You make it sound as if our diners got sandpaper and sawdust. We brined the turkeys. I just didn't wrap them in two pounds of bacon."

Mrs. Levesque asked the twins, "How did you keep the gravy from getting too salty?"

Austin said, "Industry secret, but it involves a lot of butter."

Colin said, "Every industry secret involves a lot of butter."

Jonathan asked for the rolls, and when they arrived, he put one on Brooke's plate. She nudged him, and when he looked at her with a smile, she leaned in close. "I can feed myself."

Mrs. Levesque said, "Emerson, I don't think I've ever had mac and cheese at a Thanksgiving dinner. This is fantastic."

"I was on the phone yesterday with my grandma getting her recipe while she made it." Emerson half-rolled his eyes. "The directions were things like, 'A big handful of cheddar, and then you know that cheese mix I like, the one at the Mexican grocery? No, not that one, the other one? A smaller handful of that, but not too small.'"

Colin sat bolt upright. "You wrote it down? Tell me you wrote it down," and Austin sunk into his chair with his head back. "Oh, come on—you know I collect family recipes."

Mrs. Levesque said to Brooke, "Did you have any special family recipes?"

That must be how classy hostesses operated when not everyone knew everyone else: ask targeted questions of anyone who isn't speaking so you can make them feel involved. Brooke wasn't doing it, so as the matriarch, Mrs. Levesque was demonstrating to Brooke how it ought to be done. But how do you come up with questions like that for everyone, enough to get them talking but not make them feel intruded-upon?

Brooke said, "Grandma and I always went to Natalie's family for Thanksgiving."

Natalie said, "Your parents were supposed to come that one year, but then they backed out on Wednesday evening."

Mrs. Levesque tensed. "Oh, I'm sorry. I forgot about your family."

Brooke shrugged. "You don't have to say that like they're dead. We were just in two states. And traffic was bad."

Natalie huffed. "Mom always said your mother didn't want to do the drive."

It could have been. Brooke wouldn't have called them out about it

Mrs. Levesque pivoted to, "How is your brother doing?"

See, right there, Jonathan's mom had danced over the line from "conversation starter" to "intrusive questioner." "He's been fine. I called last night, and they said they had a nice dinner."

Natalie said, "Gavin's still working part-time at the game store?"

Brooke tensed. "He didn't like the hours, so he quit."

Jonathan said, "Colin, if you're looking for family recipes, my mother has my great-grandmother's Depression-era recipe cards."

Colin's eyes bugged. "Mrs. Levesque, I would give you a kidney."

Everyone laughed, leaving Brooke's head reeling. Had Jonathan just changed the subject to protect her? Or was he short-circuiting his mother's certain next question, whether Gavin was so disabled that he couldn't work a cash register for twenty hours a week?

Whatever the rules of the conversation game, Brooke wished they were written down like those Depression-era recipes. So far, she'd determined that Mrs. Levesque was the one who asked the leading questions. Mr. Levesque did it sometimes, too, but in general, he followed up on his wife's questions. Brooke should lob a question in his direction to give the illusion that she was talking (and therefore avoid another salvo from Mrs. Levesque) but what kind of question would that even be? "How is your job?" felt generic to the point of being rude, but she didn't know enough to ask something less generic.

Jonathan took her hand under the table. Leaning toward her, he murmured against her neck, "You okay?"

She was, oddly. The conversational rules were deeply puzzling, though. With just Natalie and Lilah, she'd have figured it out. Colin and Austin transformed the dynamic. (Emerson, not so much because she'd spent a lot of time with him.) The addition of Jonathan's parents and Father Tim turned the gathering from "casual, informal" into "a grand affair." Which, Brooke would be the first to admit, she wasn't in a class to handle. She'd need training, which Mrs. Levesque was providing by example.

Even stranger, they lingered over the table long after eating had ended. That also seemed the signal for Mrs. Levesque to stop enticing people to speak, maybe because by then conversation flowed freely. Brooke made a mental note of that. Finally, after some unspecified signal that everyone else seemed to notice, people started bringing their dishes to the kitchen. Jonathan took over the task of loading the dishwasher, and Colin seized a place at the sink. "I can wash dishes," Brooke protested, but Colin shook his head vigorously.

Natalie guided Brooke away. "The dishwasher at his

restaurant is a force of nature. He wants to wash a stack of platters without a hassle."

Brooke said, "Maybe I wanted to wash my own dishes." For one thing, doing dishes, you faced away from everyone.

Instead, shortly she was on the pair of mismatched couches with Jonathan's parents and Father Tim.

What would Jonathan's mother do? Brooke decided to test her conversational lessons on Father Tim. "Did you manage to get the heaters replaced at Saint Lucy's?"

He launched into a funny-but-not-funny story about the furnace giving up the ghost during Holy Week last year. During a segue about how the Holy Thursday incense had summoned the fire department, Jonathan slid into a seat opposite Brooke. "Pity me. I got exiled from the kitchen for putting something sharp in the dish pan."

Brooke said, "Poor you."

Father Tim said, "Remember the Holy Thursday fiasco? You were the one I sent out to tell the Fire Department to go home."

"Wow, were they ever unamused." Jonathan flinched. "I had no idea we were supposed to call the fire marshal ahead of time."

"Entirely my fault. I was the one who forgot to tell you." Father Tim rubbed his temples. "So many things going on during Holy Week, and of course the one thing we forget, it arrives with sirens."

Darkness clouded Jonathan's face all at once. That was...anger? Irritation? Or was it regret? He glanced back at the kitchen and was about to get up when Father Tim said, "Jonathan, have you thought more about leading the bereavement support group?"

Brooke tilted her head. Jonathan said, "I have, and I don't think that's something I should handle."

Brooke said, "Well, you did just lose your Aunt Millie."

Again that same look flashed over his face, and again she couldn't identify it. Jonathan's hand clenched in his lap. "I'm not a therapist. I don't have any wisdom or authority."

He'd put a subtle emphasis on "authority." In other words, he wasn't a priest. Still, Father Tim was only one person, so most of St. Lucy's groups *weren't* run by a priest, nor even by someone credentialed. The youth group wasn't run by a teenager. From what Brooke remembered, the religious education classes weren't taught by teachers, just parents and volunteers.

Father Tim said, "It would help me a lot."

Jonathan stood. "Speaking of helping, I'm going to try my luck again in the kitchen," which again Brooke recognized as the polite fiction of, "I'm going to leave without being rude."

Mr. Levesque watched him depart, then said in a low voice, "I'm worried."

With a glance at Brooke, Father Tim said, "Whenever he wants to get involved in parish life again, we'll be happy to have him."

Mrs. Levesque said to Brooke, "Do you two ever go to the parish couples' nights?"

Never had Jonathan mentioned such a thing existed. Why would he? They weren't a couple. Seeing the look on Brooke's face, Mrs. Levesque continued, "It's dinner and a talk."

"If it's before eight-thirty, I'm never home to do it. The shop closes at eight." Then Jonathan came back, which meant the Young brothers were dead serious about his exile. "Do you need me for something?" she asked, in case this was her ticket out of an awkward conversation.

"I'm taking orders if everyone wants decaf coffee or regular."

"Or tea." Brooke scrambled out of her seat. "I should show them that trick with the coffee maker," and she cut herself loose.

In the kitchen, she just kept going straight through and out the back door, where she stood on the frigid porch to get her mind clear.

Jonathan stepped out after her. "This looks like an

escape. Did Father Tim just ask *you* to lead the bereavement group?"

"Your mother asked if you were taking me to couples' nights, but I thought everyone understood we're not a couple." Brooke rubbed her temples so maybe the counterpressure would slow her thoughts. "She knows you don't live in the house. We're not even dating."

Jonathan raised his hands. "It's okay. I'll talk to her."

"You don't need to tell her to back off. I'm just surprised." She paused. "Shouldn't she be going to couples' night with your father?"

"You ask the most fantastic questions, and my only answer is, who knows?" Jonathan folded his arms. "Aren't you freezing?"

"Not really." She lowered her voice. "When Father asked you about leading the bereavement group, what were you thinking?"

Jonathan rolled his eyes. "Thinking I don't want to head up the bereavement group. Was I unclear?"

"Your eyes. You were angry. Or maybe not angry, but annoyed."

Now his eyes looked annoyed. It was different. "If God's looking for someone to head up the parish groups, maybe God should send them a priest."

Brooke pursed her lips. "Got it."

"I'm not asking for more work right now if they don't want me."

She shrugged. "I mean, clearly, Father Tim does want you."

"That wasn't the deal. The deal was, I was willing to give my life to the Church, not just an hour on Thursday nights. God's omnipotent and omniscient, and since God's also omni-resourceful, God should look for someone else to brew the coffee and keep the discussion on track, especially if it doesn't have to be someone who's lost someone."

Brooke frowned. "But you did lose someone."

Jonathan snapped, "Aunt Millie doesn't count," and

reached for the doorknob.

Brooke said, "You lost Father Jonathan."

His hand came off the door, and he trained his gaze on her like a searchlight.

It looked like anger. Abruptly, Brooke felt all the November cold.

He said, "I don't think anyone's grieving that loss."

She swallowed hard. "What you lost meant everything to you, and now you're in a house full of people expecting you to be thankful for a life where everything is wrong. That's plenty to grieve about."

His breath came like little clouds. She met his eyes and held the gaze even though it was uncomfortable.

Finally he said, "What do you want from me?"

Brooke broke eye contact. "I wanted you to have a nice meal and a place to come home to. I don't care if you volunteer with the parish, but whatever happens, I want you to be happy."

The porch door opened, and they both started back from it. Austin said, "We're about ready for dessert."

Jonathan said, "I didn't tell you who wanted what."

"Everyone's getting decaf. Safer that way." Austin held open the door. "Come in. It's cold out here."

Jonathan met Brooke's eyes again, and this time it wasn't uncomfortable at all. Stepping inside, she said, "It's not as cold as it seems."

CHAPTER TEN

Jonathan followed the sounds of the after-dinner piano until he met up with Brooke in the library. She frowned at the music as she played, striking each note deliberately and with the same amount of force. Surely she'd remember her dynamics with time, but a week after getting the hymn book, she was still re-learning the motions.

When she paused for a moment to glare at the music with an even more profound scowl, Jonathan said, "The woman two houses up used to teach piano. Maybe she still does."

Brooke sighed. "With my luck, she'd be my former piano teacher and dope-slap me off Sky Ridge Drive." She made a striking motion with her hands. "Away from me, ye foul non-practicer of the keyboard!"

Jonathan paused before sitting on the couch. "Is that what piano teachers do? All my clarinet teacher ever did was look disappointed and reach for the migraine meds."

"The backhands come during year four." She started over, and Jonathan recognized "We Gather Together" from Father Tim's hymnal.

Jonathan settled in the corner of the couch and opened his Liturgy of the Hours book for evening prayer. The book was so new the pages creaked. He'd gotten it last year, the whole leather-bound set, intending to use it for the duration of his priesthood. Which, in a terrible way, he had. He'd thought about leaving it behind in the seminary, but they were nice books, and he did still like praying in an ancient rhythm with so many others, both through time and around the world.

When he finished, he realized Brooke had stopped playing, and was in fact no longer in the library. He opened the book he planned to read, but then she reappeared, holding two large binders. Jonathan thought they were patterns until she sat with one on her lap, paging through. Photo albums.

He sat forward. "Mind if I look?"

Brooke tensed. "Well... I was an ugly, awkward kid, but you already knew that."

"You weren't ugly or awkward. I was there."

"I lived the awkward. I didn't have to look at myself, so I'll take your word on the ugly." She shifted so he could sit beside her, and she laid the photo album over both their laps. "Colin asked for pictures of Natalie because he's got some super-secret project for Christmas."

Jonathan groaned. "He's going to set the bar so high I can't meet it."

"You don't have to give me a Christmas present at all, most esteemed sir—but if you do, you can exceed anything Colin does by not having my photo on it." She stopped at a picture of Natalie sitting on a pony and holding a blue ribbon, then texted that to Colin. "Anything he wants, I'll scan it for real, but now I'm doing it quick."

"Makes sense." Jonathan watched as the pages turned. "That's your brother?"

The kid was scrawny and bald, his eyes sunken. Brooke said, "This was just after he got sick, when my parents moved us down to Boston." She kept turning pages. Despite warning Jonathan of her supposed awkwardness and ugliness, Brooke herself appeared in very few photos —probably because she was taking them. It amused him how many of the photos were taken looking upward at the adults. Of course. She'd been a child. Some of them, like Natalie with the horse, must have been taken by someone else and sent to her.

The scenery changed back to Maine. Now Jonathan recognized pictures of Brooke's grandmother, and there was Lilah as well. And then Brooke's class photo, with her eyes dark-circled, and her expression just a little off.

She sent Colin a few more pictures, but while she was taking a photo of a photo of Natalie holding a birthday cupcake, Jonathan focused on a different shot of Natalie and Brooke together at that same party. Natalie was beaming, and Brooke looked—flat? Not angry, but very carefully neutral.

She kept turning pages, and whenever he caught a picture of Brooke looking at the camera, he saw it again: that same tension, as if she were barely holding on.

She reached the end of the album and opened the next. "There's not many in here. At some point they gave me a digital camera, and after that they're all on my computer."

Jonathan braced himself. "Can I ask you a question? It's not the kind of thing a husband normally asks his wife, but are you autistic?"

"I don't know." Brooke kept flipping pages. "The school wanted permission to test me, but my mother declined. She already had one sick kid. She insisted there was nothing wrong with me, and I was just making trouble to get attention."

Jonathan recoiled. "You never got into trouble."

"Not that kind of trouble. But I was always stressed out, and I didn't have friends other than Lilah. I tended to obsess about details, and I was always reading, and I had a ridiculous vocabulary. The teacher suggested there were enough things 'off' that she'd like to refer."

Jonathan said, "One of the guys at seminary was autistic, and some of these photos remind me of him."

Brooke hesitated. Then, "Well, you're going to divorce me anyway. It doesn't matter."

"It matters because I want you to feel comfortable with yourself. The other seminarian said having a name for the ways he was weird made him feel more normal."

Brooke smiled. "I like being weird. I like it too much to play-tease you about how you just called me a weirdo."

He side-hugged her. "You know that's not what I'm saying."

"I get it." She leaned against him for a second. "I've wondered about it, but what am I going to do? It's not like there's a pill to make you un-autistic, and some of the things they say are autism are things I like about myself. Autists make good friends, and autists hold to their value systems even when it isn't to their benefit. They say autists are loyal and self-reliant. I remember special details about people, and if there's a system for something, like handling the shop or filing our taxes, I'm good at it. Why would I change those things?"

Jonathan shook his head. "I don't want you to change yourself."

Brooke said, "Other than getting overwhelmed in crowds."

Jonathan said, "But then I wouldn't have taken you out on the balcony during my graduation party and shown you all those stars."

She smiled. "That's a nice memory. I don't have a photograph of that because most of the important moments in your life, you don't think to take pictures. You have to save them in your heart."

There wasn't a photograph of the moment he'd married Brook. Sitting at Theodore Hodges' desk, they'd passed the paperwork between them, and then the notary had done her thing, and the attorney had shaken their hands. "Congratulations. I'll file this with the state."

Brooke turned a page, and there was a very familiar Florida theme park. She tried to close the album, but Jonathan stopped her. "You said you'd never been to

Paxley."

"I haven't." She opened it back up. "You know those charities that grant wishes to kids who have lethal illnesses? My brother came up on their list, so my parents took him to Paxley."

Jonathan went cold. "Without you?"

"The charity offered, but my parents wanted to make memories with Gavin."

Jonathan took the album off her lap, fighting rage. "And if the worst happened, didn't you deserve to have memories with Gavin, too?"

"They'd still have me later, so they could do those things again afterward." Brooke's voice had flattened out, as if reciting a speech memorized in grammar school and repeated on every holiday since. "Gavin needed their attention. They wanted him to enjoy his time there."

"Enjoyment isn't cake. It's not like you enjoying yourself would mean he enjoyed himself less." According to the photographic record, her parents had done the full gamut of activities with Gavin: character breakfasts and rides and parades and fireworks. But no Brooke.

That trip would have meant the world to her, only they didn't take her. Why? But then again, why had they shunted her back here to live alone with her grandmother? Why had they refused to let Brooke get neuropsych testing —refused to let her have any kind of "sickness" just because her brother was "the sick one"? According to Natalie, they'd never even come up for holidays. They'd had a life in Boston with their one and only child, and then on occasion, *oh, that's right,* they had another child, parked up in Maine.

Jonathan turned another page, and no more photos. The final three-quarters of the book was empty.

She reached for the book, but his hands clenched on it. "Why aren't you angry?"

Brooke tilted her head. "What?"

"What they did was inexcusable."

"Their child was dying. You can excuse a lot for that."

He shook his head. "Your brother needed them, but you needed them, too. It looks to me like your parents didn't feel like parenting you, so they gave you to your grandmother to raise. Only she didn't want to do it, either, did she?"

Brooke's grandmother had resented having another go-around at parenting. Even Mom had commented on that the one time they'd met. It was falling into place now: Brooke, walking to school in the snow because the school bus cost money. Brooke, biking to friends' houses and getting rides home after dark. She'd cobbled together a childhood with Lilah's friendship and her relationship with Natalie's family, but—

Jonathan turned back a few pages to a photo of the grandmother. The grandmother always looked sour, and in these pictures, Brooke seemed tense and scared.

As she ought to have been: her parents had jettisoned her because she was too much trouble. If she was too much trouble for her grandmother, who was left?

Brooke's voice was low. "You look angry."

"I haven't been this angry in about ten years." He paged backward through the photos, reversing the years and looking again at Brooke every time he could. "You weren't ugly and awkward. You were neglected."

"I had food and clothes and a roof."

"That's the legal minimum. Children also deserve adults who nurture them."

Brooke's voice got quieter. "That's not fair. My grandmother spent a lot of time with me. She taught me to cook and made me take piano lessons."

Jonathan looked up. "And?"

Brooke looked aside. "You're acting like they're monsters. They were doing the best they could. And I saw my parents every Christmas."

"Your grandmother put you on a train?"

"No, we did actually drive all the way to Boston." Brooke sighed. "It wasn't a terrible childhood. I didn't go to Paxley, but lots of children don't go to Paxley. You've never been to Paxley, and you don't hate your parents."

"I also wasn't a Paxley fan! I didn't spend my allowance on Paxley art."

Smirking, Brooke raised her eyebrows. "Have you ever been to the Vatican?"

"My parents were never offered a free trip to take me there." He huffed. "You honestly don't see that what they did was awful? I don't buy for a minute that they thought they were making higher-caliber memories if they brought only your brother. They forgot you."

Brooke recoiled.

"You wanted to know if I was angry, and that's why." He shut the photo album with a clap. "I had no idea this was going on."

"What would you have done?" Her voice was thin. "Found my mother's phone number and said, 'Mrs. Evart? You'd better take your daughter to Paxley'?"

"I'd have done more for you." He folded his arms and collapsed back on the couch. "I'd have done something."

"You did do something. You were my friend." She looked aside. "And now you're giving me a house, so that counts for something."

He could give her a house, but back then, she'd needed a family.

No wonder she'd called him and her a family. She had no idea what a family was. And in less than a year, he was going to take it away from her. He wasn't any better than her parents, and maybe worse because he'd known at the start what he was going to do.

She set aside the photo album and reached for her computer. "I appreciate you looking out for me, but neither of us knows what it's like to have a child with cancer, so I'm going to assume they did their best. They didn't have time for me because of my brother's treatments. They thought my grandmother would. They thought they had only one chance to take Gavin to Paxley, and now it's turned out they've had a lot of time."

"And have they taken you back to Paxley since then?"

"No. They said they've already been."

His hands clenched in his lap.

"You know how you said that wasn't a question a husband should ask his wife? Well, I've got one for you, too." She met his eyes very quickly before glancing away. "This is a question a wife should already know the answer to, but when you said you 'discerned out' of the seminary, what does that mean?"

A wide ache opened inside Jonathan's heart, like a sunburn that didn't sting until someone touched it. "It's so complicated."

She withdrew. "It's okay. I was just curious."

"No, you ought to know." He tried to dial back the feelings. "'Discernment' is the process of figuring out what you're supposed to do with your life, or with any multi-faceted question. Before you and Natalie bought the yarn store, I'm sure you did some discerning yourself. You probably thought about all your options, figured out whether owning a shop was a good fit for you, whether Natalie would be a good business partner, and so on. You may have prayed about it. You probably read a book on business ownership."

She certainly had read a book on arranged marriages.

She nodded. "You did all that. You knew during high school."

He said, "In seminary, it keeps going. There are formation directors and spiritual advisors. Vows are a big deal, so they're all over you about making sure this is exactly what God's calling you to do. Every day, we had a regular rotation of morning prayer, Mass, eating together, classwork, study sessions, free time, more classwork, holy hour and private prayer, evening prayer—all structured and in community. I loved that."

Brooke brightened. "I would love that, too! Plus, you had a uniform, so you didn't have to decide what to wear."

Jonathan laughed. "Yes, you would love that! Schedule changes were posted a week in advance, too."

She grinned. "Okay, so that's 'discerning in,' but none of

that sounds bad."

"None of it was. The further I went into the process, though, the less peace I felt with it. Everything was exactly the way I imagined it would be, but whenever I thought about going all the way, I felt uneasy. Things didn't fit. I was good at what I did, and my formation advisor said I'd be a wonderful priest, but the discomfort just wouldn't settle."

Brooke bit her lip. "You got cold feet?"

He shook his head. "You know how when you're assembling a puzzle, sometimes there's a piece that looks like it works, only it's just a bit off? You push it in anyhow, and then afterward, everything else is also a little off? And later you can't get anything to fit, like a piece will fit on one side but not on another?"

Brooke said, "So you have a whole section of the puzzle correctly assembled, only it's assembled in the wrong place?"

"Right. The further I went in the process, the more it felt everything was hanging off a piece that didn't fit. I wasn't peaceful, and I wasn't uncomfortable in the expected ways. My formation advisor asked me to imagine myself as Father Jonathan at Holy Cross Parish in some random town, and I could imagine it pretty well, but it didn't feel right. He asked me to imagine myself with a wife and kids, and that I couldn't imagine at all." His stomach burned. "But we couldn't ignore what my conscience was telling me. God didn't want me to be a priest."

"I don't understand. You're awesome for the priesthood." Frowning, she took his hand and wound her fingers through his, and he closed his eyes. She said nothing for a long moment, then rested her head on his shoulder and tightened her grip. "But maybe the things that would have made you an awesome priest are also the things that make you an awesome man. You're conscientious and a good listener, and you care about people. You're generous. Those are good traits, no matter what you do."

"I wanted to be doing *those* things. I wanted to have a parish and help people and see them through all those transitional points when they're vulnerable, like when they're born or when they die."

Or when they get married. No one had seen Jonathan through that moment.

She said, "After which, you could have called the fire marshal and worried about repairing the heating system."

He pulled away from her. "I'd have done that, too. Everyone else from my class got ordained to the transitional diaconate this summer, whereas I called back my former employer and asked if he needed someone to hang cabinets." He huffed. "People ask what I did wrong to get kicked out, only I didn't get kicked out. I went from knowing what every day was going to be like and where it was leading—and yes, what I'd be wearing—to having no idea about any of this. What did I do wrong that God gave me a vocation and then took it back? Why no second chance to make it right?"

Brooke said, "Do you think you're being punished?"

"It feels like it." He dropped his head back against the couch. "Yes, that's what it feels like. I got a glimpse of something I'd always wanted, and then God shut the door. Clearly, Brighthead's so-called chosen one messed up an amazing gift. I just can't figure out how, or how to set it right again."

In the silence of the library, Jonathan focused on his breathing. He needed to stuff this back into the box in his heart where he normally kept it. None of this was going away, so it was unfair to dump it all over Brooke—especially right after he'd asked her if she was autistic *and* lashed out at her parents. He wasn't being fair to her. None of this was hers to handle.

Brooke said softly, "A few minutes ago, when you were angry at my parents for not taking me to Paxley...do you think maybe it wasn't my parents you were angry at? You lost a lot more than a Paxley vacation."

Jonathan bristled. "I'm not angry at God."

"If I were God, I'd understand your anger."

The Paxley thing was different. Paxley wasn't a plan for someone's entire life. At no cost to themselves, the Evarts could have given Brooke all those happy memories and the excitement of being with her favorite characters. The priesthood meant your whole life. And while yes, God was a parent, it wasn't like Brooke's parents who'd chucked her aside when one kid needed attention and the other was seen as an obstacle.

Her voice was still soft. "I don't understand what you've lost. I just hope that if God did take it away, that it's a path to giving you something better."

Jonathan muttered, "Since I liked the structure and the community, maybe I should become a brother in a monastery."

Brooke perked up. "There's one a few hours from here where they hold retreats and raise sheep. Once a year, you can send me a fleece."

He tried to get a grip on his emotions because even floating that idea didn't feel peaceful—but nothing felt peaceful anymore. Jonathan shouldn't be in seminary, and Jonathan shouldn't be married.

He felt peaceful while working, at least. That was okay. He said, "Can you spin fleece into yarn?"

She chuckled. "Not even close. But I'd learn if you sent one."

Brooke opened her digital photos, which started in her early teens. The older she got, the less stress showed in her eyes. Jonathan recognized a lot of these. Most were with friends from this point onward: school theater productions, field trips, all of that. Brooke didn't do selfies, at least not alone. There were selfies of her and Lilah where Lilah's extended arm meant Lilah had taken the photo. And every so often, Brooke would text a photo of Natalie over to Colin.

She stopped when she reached their prom photos. "You were gorgeous in that tuxedo." She traced her finger over his image. "It was generous of you to take me. I hope you had a good time for real, and you weren't just saying that."

"Of course I had a good time. Remember Lilah joking around with the limo driver?" When Brooke laughed, he continued, "And then that weird food they served Blake, and no one could identify it because it wasn't one of the catered meals, just something special they claimed he'd requested?"

Brooke said, "I think he did request it and was embarrassed by whatever it was. Except he texted his older brother, and his brother delivered a pizza."

Jonathan laughed. "And then the after-party at Cindy's house?"

"Which would have been more fun if Cindy's parents had known she was doing it?"

Jonathan said, "Well, *we* all knew."

Laughing, Brooke leaned into his chest so she could angle the screen better. Now he was looking over her shoulder, so he put his other arm around her. "You looked great in that dress."

"I hated it. The color was awful, and my grandmother insisted I wear that stupid gold necklace that wouldn't in a thousand years go with a peach dress. I have no fashion sense, and even I realized that."

Jonathan said, "I thought you were gorgeous."

"That makes one person. At least I could dance in it. I felt bad for Cindy because that sheathe dress made her look like a million bucks, but she could barely move."

"Probably why she had the after-party at her house. That way, she could change into sweatpants and leave the rest of us in the good clothes. Why did you buy a dress you hated?"

"I made the mistake of dress shopping in Boston with my mother during Christmas, and my mother looks good in peach. Therefore I, too, must look good in peach."

Minutes ago, Brooke had tried to draw a direct correlation between her relationship to her parents and God's relationship to Jonathan, but at least God's uniform would have been a black shirt with a clerical collar.

She turned the page, and here were graduation photos, then lots of college pictures. (She skipped most of these because Natalie wouldn't be there, and ostensibly she was photo-hunting for Colin.) Then she was back again in Brighthead with photos from her grandmother's funeral. Photos from when she and Natalie bought Bright Stitches and had a re-opening party (even though it had never closed).

Brooke did have a family. She'd crafted a family over time, selecting and nurturing friends who valued her for who she was. Lilah and Natalie were at the core, and now she was expanding that family by including Colin and Emerson. Maybe according to that definition, she'd made Jonathan her family long before they married, sending care packages and emails keeping him on top of everything in Brighthead. At the time, he'd thought she was treating those letters like some kind of duty, the way women sent socks to World War II soldiers, effectively making him a soldier for the Church. Maybe instead, she'd considered him like a cousin. That's why it hadn't been outlandish to marry him: he was already family.

That's why she'd been so afraid she'd lose him afterward.

Meanwhile, he'd been building a family among the other seminarians and priests of the Diocese of Portland, and God had plucked him out of that. Maybe that was karma in reverse, if Jonathan had always been capable of detonating a family the way he was doing right now.

Brooke's photos had come up to the present. "The first BCG meeting. Lilah collected all the pictures and stuck them up on the group, so I grabbed the good ones." They reached the first photo of Colin with Natalie. Later, pictures of Emerson and Brooke. "You knew he dated me for a month, right?" She giggled. "I wasn't interesting enough for him, but he's perfect for Lilah."

Jonathan gave her a side-hug. "You're plenty interesting."

"But not interesting *to him*, which is the whole point of

dating. Discernment, right? You've got to find the people who aren't boring to you and whom you yourself don't bore."

Jonathan said, "Do I bore you?"

"Would you feel more secure if I stop calling you my most esteemed spouse and start calling you my endlessly fascinating spouse?" She clicked the button to shut off the computer even though she hadn't reached October, when they'd gotten married. "I'm sorry. You were about to read your book, and then I dragged you down memory lane."

"Yuck, all this road dust got into my clothes." Jonathan realized how close he was still sitting to Brooke, and he detangled from her. "What are you doing for Christmas?"

"I'll go to Boston." She said that as though he hadn't just called her parents myopic and neglectful. "Not buying a peach dress, though, thank you very much."

He said, "When are you going?"

"Christmas Eve. I'll work the store in the morning because that day is a madhouse with people coming in for last-minute yarns, gifts, and help with projects that aren't working. At about two, I'll hit the road and leave Lilah and Natalie to handle the mess. I'll come back on the evening of the 27th." She pivoted on the couch, and her knees ended up touching his leg. "How about you?"

"Christmas Eve with my parents, Midnight Mass, and then I'll spend the day with them and Gemma."

She grinned. "And will Santa have filled your stocking on Christmas morning?"

He recoiled. "Of course! Doesn't he fill yours?"

"He never knows where to find me because I'm bouncing around between Boston and Brighthead." Her phone buzzed. "Oh, joy, Colin is sending his photograph order."

Jonathan said, "Do you want a Christmas tree?"

She gestured vaguely around. "Where would we even put it?" Then, before Jonathan could point out that three thousand square feet of house was totally empty, she started laughing. "Would a tree make you happy? One in the living room, one in the guest cottage, my grandmother's ceramic tree in my room—? Let's have a forest."

Jonathan said, "Tomorrow, let's pick one up."

Brooke's phone buzzed again with more photo requests. "And lights. I don't care so much about ornaments, but whatever tree we have, I want it to have lights."

CHAPTER ELEVEN

On Christmas Eve, Jonathan walked into his parents' house directly from work. "Don't touch me! I'm covered in sawdust."

The house smelled of cookies and cinnamon and apples, and Jonathan paused in the kitchen to inhale it all. Mom shooed him. "Go get showered! You're late!"

"No kidding I'm late. Why does everyone need their kitchen remodeled right before every holiday?" He sighed. "I didn't think we'd get it done. Issues with the wall studs. I think the designer framed up a house and then removed every two-by-four he could without the thing collapsing."

Mom said, "Well, Dad will be back soon with Gemma, and she wants to go for a drive to see all the lights."

He snuck a cookie off the rack. Mom made an infuriated noise, so he ran for his old bedroom.

Christmas cookies. Always worth coming home for.

He showered. Had Brooke arrived at Boston? He should have checked the traffic, although realistically speaking, he didn't need to check the traffic to know it would be a nightmare getting through Portsmouth and then even worse on I-93. If she'd done this every year, then she knew it, too. And what was waiting at the end?

No, that wasn't fair. He was judging her parents based on a couple of incidents from years ago. Well, and one sentence from her mother about the marriage: *That's fine, just don't expect to be happy.*

That's fine? Even Natalie had been more cautious than that, and Natalie knew Jonathan. Lilah had been horrified. Lilah had been all over Brooke about only marrying for love.

Then her mom had been like, "Resign yourself to misery until you get a house." Had her mother even asked about the guy Brooke was marrying, or had she said, "Send me a copy of the real estate listing"?

With his hair still wet, Jonathan snuck back into the kitchen to steal another cookie. Mom exclaimed, "Scram!" and flicked the dish towel at him.

As he darted away, the door opened, and Gemma exclaimed, "Get him, Mom!"

Mom ran to give Gemma a hug, and Jonathan took the opportunity to steal a cookie. Gemma exclaimed, "Thief!" and he shot back, "Opportunist!" and then Gemma hugged him, too.

Jonathan always felt like the family was "tucked in" once the last person got into the house, but not tonight. Tonight, the four of them felt incomplete.

Gemma raised her eyebrows, so Jonathan slipped another cookie off the plate behind Mom's back, and when Mom turned, he passed it to Gemma. She didn't bother to hide eating it. "You're looking good, married man. When do I get to meet my erstwhile sister-in-law?"

Jonathan shook his head. "I told you, it's not like that. She went to visit her family for Christmas."

Gemma frowned. "Why didn't you go with her?"

Mom said, "Because they're not really married. They set up the paperwork to get the house off our hands. They don't even live together."

Gemma sighed. "Is she at least nice? Maybe she can blot the stain of Aunt Millie's perfidy off the physical structure so we don't have to burn the house to the ground."

Jonathan said, "That's a bit extreme, and yes, she's nice. I've known her since we were kids."

Gemma pouted. "Darn. I was hoping she was a wretched harpy who'd inflict the misery you deserve."

Jonathan snickered. "Sorry to disappoint. She's a good friend."

Gemma winked at him. "You never know. That could change."

Jonathan shook his head. "They told us in my marriage and family life class that marriage never changes people. They stay the same people they were beforehand."

Gemma glanced at Mom. "That wasn't what I meant," but then Dad came into the kitchen, and she didn't elaborate.

The family still felt incomplete. Gemma had gotten home safely, but had Brooke? Jonathan texted her. "Let me know when you get in, okay?"

As if he could do anything to help if she were broken down on the side of the road.

Some family friends held a Christmas Eve open house, so the Levesques stopped there for an hour. After that, they piled into Dad's SUV and cruised around Brighthead using a route Lilah had created for the Economic Planning Board website, highlighting the most decorated houses. (She'd said, "People are lighting up anyhow, so let's make it fun.") Dad put Gemma and Jonathan on the passenger side of the car so they'd be better able to see. Mom sat in back behind Dad.

Mid-drive, Jonathan's phone chirped. Brooke: "Traffic was brutal, but I'm here."

He sighed. "Glad you're okay." Then he told the rest of the car, "Brooke got in safely."

Dad said, "She should have left in the morning."

"They needed her at the yarn shop until the afternoon because she helps everyone with last-minute gifts." He laughed. "She said at around the end of October, they take all the sock yarn and laceweight yarn out of the prominent places, and out come the bulky and super-chunky yarns onto the display stands. She knits with needles as thick as hot dogs to make a few samples that people can work up in a couple of hours, and she hangs those all over the store."

In the front seat, Gemma laughed. "Does she do them in Christmas colors, too?"

"She does! She had her friend dye yarns in reds and greens and silvers, too, to subtly implant the idea that they could knit gifts for everyone. The problem comes," he added, "when it's Christmas Eve and someone's got dropped stitches or doesn't know how to cable forward, or how to make a pom-pom."

Gemma waved a hand. "Whoa, all the yarn vocabulary. Has she taught you to knit?"

He shook his head. "I've watched her working, though. She's doing all-out magic, with those sticks flying, and at the same time she's reading these arcane markings on graph paper, and then suddenly she's made a thumb."

Gemma giggled. "I've heard it takes a while to learn to read patterns."

Jonathan said, "Crochet patterns are even stranger! At least with knit patterns, they're on graph paper, so the stitches stack up over one another. Crochet patterns consist of Ts and cross-hatchings and arrows and slashes and chains. I have no idea how she follows that. But the mind-blowing thing is, she doesn't only read them—she designs them, too. I'll watch her sitting on the couch with a clipboard and a pencil, and she's whipping up something that looks like it might be a shape, and she'll take out her hook or her needles, and ten minutes later, she's holding a leaf, which she then rips out because it's not leafy enough."

Dad was chuckling and shaking his head, and Mom reached over the front seat to push him on the shoulder. What was that about? Mom said, "Here, on the right."

This house had a light-up Santa's sleigh with eight reindeer, all of which had one part moving—a hoof or a head or a tail. Brooke would have adored this. He pulled out his phone and got a five-second video, then texted it to her.

She sent back an emoji of a smiling face.

After that, Jonathan made sure to send photos of all the displays, and Brooke replied with things like, "We should have done the kitchen porch like that," or "I wonder how they're affording the electric bill?" and "I love what they did with the upstairs windows."

Then Brooke texted, "I will need to see a photo of the next one."

He sent, "Explain?"

"I'm following your progress on Lilah's list. The next house claims it has 30,000 lights."

Jonathan said, "Whoa." Said it out loud in the car.

Mom said, "Jonathan, honey, you're with us, not on the phone."

Gemma giggled. "Hush, Mom. Let him text his wife."

"Brooke says the next house has thirty thousand lights. She also wants me to send photos."

Jonathan texted her, "Look up at the sky. With thirty thousand lights, it's likely visible from Boston."

She replied, "Silly me, I thought that was the Aurora Borealis," and he laughed again.

Dad snorted. Jonathan looked up, but he couldn't see the place yet, so again, what was up with Dad?

Then they turned the corner, and—yeah.

"30,000 is an underestimate," he texted, then took a photo and sent that, then three more.

Brooke sent back, "Wow."

He texted, "A pedestrian just threw an empty soda can in their yard, and they ran outside to string lights on it."

She said, "Next year, I'm paying them to do Aunt Millie's house."

He replied, "No."

She sent, "You'll have divorced me by then. You get no say in the matter."

He replied, "Maybe I shouldn't divorce you."

"If I put up this many lights, you'll divorce me anyway."

"If you put up this many lights," he typed, "the Historical Society will get an injunction against you."

"Joke's on you," she replied. "The owner of this house is Vice President of the Historical Society."

Mom's hand landed on Jonathan's phone, and he looked up. She hadn't done that since he was twelve. "Sweetie, you're being rude. Put away the phone."

Gemma grinned. "Come on, Mom. His heart's in Boston."

Jonathan put away the phone. "You're right. I'm sorry. We got carried away laughing about the Bright House in Brighthead."

Then he pulled out his phone back out to text that line to Brooke, too. Along with, "But they want me to stop texting and pay attention."

She replied, "I'm sorry for distracting you."

Finally he put away the phone for real to look at the rest of the lights. But Dad kept wearing that unidentifiable smirk.

Midnight Mass was Jonathan's favorite hour of the liturgical year, with Christmas music, full darkness outside the church but lights within, beautiful readings and beautiful prayers, plus everyone brilliant and excited. Brooke might have enjoyed this. It wasn't too crowded, whereas the earlier Masses would have been standing room only as well as simulcast into the parish hall. Brooke also would have appreciated that all the responses were scripted. Stand, sit, stand, kneel. Sing the Gloria. Sing the Alleluia. Sing the Our Father.

They used to go to Mass together with the Saint Lucy's teen group, her playing piano and him volunteering as a lector. He wasn't sure when she'd stopped going, but maybe after her grandmother died.

Back at home, his family unwrapped one gift each, their traditional Christmas Eve pajamas. He texted Brooke a photo. "Does your family do Christmas pajamas?"

She replied, "No, but those look warm. Sleep tight."

On Christmas morning, Jonathan awoke to a mostly silent house. In the kitchen, his mother would be putting cinnamon rolls in the oven. He had so many Christmas traditions. What were Brooke's? Did they wake up and immediately open their stockings? Did she even have a stocking? He rolled over to grab his phone. "Merry Christmas, most esteemed wife."

Half an hour later, while Jonathan was enjoying cinnamon rolls with his family, also wearing new pajamas, Brooke replied, "Merry Christmas yourself, endlessly fascinating spouse."

Mom sighed "Are you going to start with the phone again?"

Jonathan said, "Brooke just texted me merry Christmas."

Gemma said, "What he means is, yes."

Jonathan huffed. "You act like you've never seen a phone before."

He didn't take out his phone while they opened presents. He kept it right there in his pajama pocket, and only afterward did he text Brooke with, "Santa got me new work gloves. Also two books from my favorite author, a documentary about the Dead Sea Scrolls, and two flannel shirts."

She replied, "Poor overloaded reindeer. I'm surprised the sleigh didn't fall from the sky."

He laughed. "At least the books were paperbacks. What are your plans for today?"

"Not much until dinner when we open gifts. My brother showed me his video game system. I'm knitting while watching *A Christmas Carol* with Mom."

Mid-afternoon, Father Tim joined them, looking exhausted. He had the grace not to complain about the sheer amount of work he'd done for the Christmas Eve and

Christmas Day Masses, plus Midnight Mass in the middle. It was taking everything for Jonathan not to snap at God, *You know, if you wanted younger guys who could stay up all night, there was one right here.* Instead, he helped Mom with the cooking.

Father Tim said, "Will we be seeing Brooke today?"

Jonathan shook his head. "She's in Boston, but I've been checking in with her in case she feels isolated. Her family is a bit...well, odd."

Father Tim nodded. "I remember thinking that."

Jonathan sighed. "She feels obligated to go down there, I guess because they think every year might be her brother's last year. But I'm trying to make sure she doesn't feel like it's been so long. She just needs to keep doing it, day by day, you know?"

Father Tim nodded. "I bet it feels strange without her around."

Amazing that Father Tim understood what his mother didn't. "The whole house felt emptier, and yeah, it's odd knowing she's not there." He hesitated. "I probably should do something for when she gets back, shouldn't I? But I have no idea what. She intends to come back late at night and just go back to work the next day."

When Father Tim nodded, Jonathan added, "It's going to be strange because I'll check out the window of the guest cottage and expect to see her lights on in the main house, only the whole house will be dark. That's not going to feel right. Or I'll go into the main house to get something, only it's going to be completely silent."

Dad prompted, "Ask when Brooke left."

Father Tim looked at Jonathan, who said, "Yesterday."

Father Tim choked on a laugh, and Dad walked away, shaking his head.

Jonathan looked from one to the other. "What?"

Dad called over his shoulder, "It's not even twenty-four hours. You're acting like she's been gone for weeks."

Jonathan blew out a breath. Father Tim was forcing himself not to have any facial expression whatsoever.

Dad came back with his glass of water. "*And* she's returning on the 27th. Two days. Not next May."

It felt longer than that. When she'd said the 27th, Jonathan hadn't calculated the time. But on the night of the 23rd right before he headed to the guest cottage, (which was actually the last time he'd seen her, *Dad,*) it had occurred to Jonathan just how many days stood between those bookends, and how it wasn't right that Brooke should be in Boston—because she ought to be here.

Christmas evening, Jonathan returned to the guest cottage, laden with leftovers and Christmas gifts, and feeling (*Yes, Dad,*) hollow inside because the only lights on in the main house were the ones set to timers.

The hollowness increased when he thought about two more days of a dark house. And it increased exponentially when he thought about Brooke feeling just as hollow in Boston.

Why'd you go back to them? We'd have included you in the holiday stuff. You'd have seen all those lights yourself, and you'd have hung out with my sister. Mom would have made sure you had whatever traditional food you wanted on the table.

Her family hadn't opened gifts until after dinner. She'd gotten a peach-colored sweater (she held back from saying she hated the color, but he knew) and a coffee table book about birds in the Galapagos. There was a pine-scented candle. Oh, and a set of cream-colored bath towels.

Do your parents know you at all?

He should have sent his gift to Boston with her, but he'd wanted to see her open it. That was selfish. He should have given up the pleasure of seeing her surprise so at least she'd have had a decent present to open.

Restless, he tried to read a book he'd gotten this morning, but the words wouldn't gel. Instead he made some decaf and turned on the tiny television, but that was just noise.

Why wouldn't her family have given her something personal? Even before marrying Brooke, he'd have known she'd love a gift of yarn. Or a biography of a famous knitter. Or a pattern book. He'd have plugged "gifts for knitters" into the nearest internet search engine and looked through the listings. Now, knowing her more, he'd done a lot better. At least, he'd tried to do better. Because that's what you do when you love someone.

Except her family didn't love her, did they? He'd said as much from the start, and she'd made excuses—but her brother had gotten video games and expensive sneakers and a new phone. Her parents did know how to show they cared when it was important to them. If those same people had needed to come up with a quick gift for Gemma, whom they'd never met, they could have given her exactly what they'd given Brooke.

Brooke's such a special person. Why wouldn't they treasure her? Jonathan paced his own house, but it was no good—this restless near-rage wanted something other than three rooms. He pulled on his heavy jacket and walked to the carriage house.

The stars weren't visible. In October, Brooke had stopped to gaze at the Milky Way, but under this overcast sky, it was just milky.

Brooke was smart and sensitive and funny. She observed everything, but then she had the softest touchpoints. Her heart reacted to even slight pressure, and it wouldn't have taken much for her family to have pleased her. They hadn't tried. They didn't love her like he did.

He stopped in place.

Wait, what?

Like he did?

Jonathan blew a cloud of vapor into the night.

He loved her?

He *loved* her. He'd come to enjoy the feeing of her presence, the expectation of her smile, the joy of making her laugh. He loved making her dinner and then washing the dishes together and then sitting in the library on the same couch. They didn't have to be talking. They were side by side, and that was enough.

Except now she wasn't by his side, and the world was flat.

How long had this been going on? Dad had been laughing all day. Was it obvious to everyone but Jonathan?

Jonathan shouldn't be in love. The plan for his life involved a vow of celibacy and a single bed in a rectory. His plan for this year had involved a roommate and a few high-ticket legal transactions. At no point had his plans involved bright eyes, a sweet smile, a demure tone of voice, and the whoosh of yarn slipping across wooden needles. He hadn't intended to miss Brooke when she was gone for twenty-four hours.

Was she trying to make him fall in love? Except most likely, she wasn't. Brooke was nothing if not straightforward. When he'd entrusted her with his dream of becoming a priest, she'd breathed brightness into the embers in his hands. At every turn, she'd accepted him exactly as he was and done what she could to ease his way through seminary. She'd made his dream her own. She wouldn't sabotage it now, not even after it was dust.

That was worse. He'd fallen entirely on his own.

What do you do if you've suddenly fallen in love with your wife? That wasn't in the plan. She was off-limits to him. They were supposed to be living like brother and sister. And you don't feel this way about your sister.

The chill stung his cheeks, so he kept walking.

At the carriage house, Jonathan turned on the space heaters. He might as well work off the emotions making bowls again. Therapy bowls. He'd slowed down production recently, but a bunch had sold right before Christmas. He got out the hand drill to set a log on the screw chuck, put on his new work gloves (*His parents paid attention, see?*)

then eye protection and ear protection, and turned on the wood turner.

Bowls were soothing. The lathe spun fast and hard, and shavings piled beneath as he used the bowl gouge to cut the wood down to the shape he wanted. He kept the bark rough for the top edges, and for the rest of it, he followed his own hand-drawn guide to make the right sizes.

Time stopped when he made these. It was part of why he'd made so many last June. Bowls gave him something to focus on. They braked the thoughts of failure. He could start and finish something, and that was success, though small. Even the sawdust and wood shavings were useful because afterward, he'd pack the wood-turned bowl into a paper bag with them so the shavings could draw out the moisture before he applied the finish.

He should make Brooke a better yarn bowl. All the yarn bowls had sold, but she still had the original and wouldn't let him fix it. Had she used it? He had no idea. But there was no reason she should be stuck with a useless bowl the same way she was stuck with a useless seminarian as her useless husband.

He loved her. He should make her something she could use.

Knitting needles.

Fifteen minutes later, after watching his third tutorial, he took a piece of scrap wood just to experiment, and he flipped on the machine.

CHAPTER TWELVE

An exhausted Brooke very nearly turned her car at Dean Street. Fortunately, she remembered about Sky Ridge Drive before parking and trying to fit her key in the apartment lock.

She wasn't all the way in Aunt Millie's driveway before Jonathan popped out onto the driveway, and she beamed. He opened her door, and she said, "You're here!"

He hugged her hard. "Merry Christmas! I'm so glad you're back."

He took her bags from the back seat, and she fished out the gigantic takeout coffee that had kept her awake through the drive home and would likely keep her awake quite a bit longer. Jonathan escorted her inside. "Did you drive straight through?"

"Yeah. Instead of a carrot on a stick, I motivated myself with the thought of one of your freezer meals."

He raised his hands. "I've got dinner taken care of. You get settled, then come back downstairs."

She bowed. "Thank you, fascinating husband."

He inclined his head. "No thanks necessary, esteemed wife."

He was in a good mood. Energetic, too. Had he had today off? Or maybe he was just more relaxed because the stressful kitchen remodel that had to be done before Christmas had come in under the wire. At least his stress wasn't worse. She'd figured someone would see that remodeled kitchen and decide they needed theirs done before New Year's.

She dropped her bag in her room and texted Natalie and Lilah. "I'm home. Jonathan is making dinner, and then I plan to collapse."

Lilah replied, "Glad you survived the trip."

What Lilah meant was, "I'm glad you survived your parents." Maybe Lilah knew someone who'd like that peach sweater, otherwise she'd pass it to Natalie for the family shelter. It wasn't even worth exchanging at the store because Mom had cut off the tags.

Then Natalie added a text: "Jonathan's cooking for you?"

Brooke replied, "I told him I'd eat a freezer meal, so I have no idea what he's making."

She got back downstairs to find Jonathan tending the microwave. "Nope. You come with me." In the living room, he'd pushed the little table in front of the Christmas tree, then set it with a tablecloth. At the center was a lit candle.

She laughed. "Fancy! Are you joining me?"

"Of course I am." He pulled out the chair for her and helped slide it back, then retrieved two fully laden plates from the kitchen. "Behold!"

Arranged on the plate was an entire Christmas dinner. "Wow! For me?" He'd set it all up going around the plate without mixing anything up: sliced ham, mashed potatoes with gravy, something that might have been broccoli casserole, and a roll.

He poured them each a glass of sparkling cider, then sat before his own plate. "Merry Christmas."

"Merry Christmas to you, too!" On the road, she'd figured she'd reheat the first frozen meal she touched and then fall into bed to forget the past three days, but the dinner in front of her looked delicious. "Did you spend the whole day cooking?"

"My mother sent this over, so you'll have to thank her. I couldn't help but notice your Christmas was a lot less Christmassy than ours, and I wanted you to have a holiday you'd enjoy before going back to the grind."

She looked aside. "That's sweet. You didn't have to."

Jonathan leaned forward. "You see—I knew I didn't have to. I did it because I wanted you to have a good memory of our Christmas together."

Our Christmas together. Singular. Which she hadn't even spent with him.

It didn't matter that the ham was a bit over-heated and the mashed potatoes were cold in the center. Nor did it matter that Brooke wasn't sure why you'd do something like this to perfectly good broccoli. Jonathan had wanted her to have a good holiday dinner, and that made everything perfect. She ate it all, complimented it all, thanked Jonathan for it all because he cared about her holiday, cared that she have a good time—cared enough to anticipate what she'd need and want.

He even got up to make her seconds, but she joined him in the kitchen for that because she knew how to reheat stuff. Then, while they were washing dishes, the doorbell rang, and the rest of his family arrived.

Brooke checked Jonathan for a cue. He was pleased, so she smiled.

Jonathan said, "You remember my sister, Gemma, right?"

Brooke had met Gemma a handful of times. Still, Gemma was over the moon, and hugged her tight. "Oh my gosh, it's been years! You look great for having driven five hours! I thought it was wild when Mom and Dad said Jonathan was marrying you."

His parents hugged her, too, and they asked about her trip. Brooke said, "Thank you for giving Jonathan a whole extra meal for me tonight," and his mother demurred that oh, of course, it was nothing.

Mr. Levesque announced, "I hope you like pie!" as he set

an apple pie on the counter. Jonathan moved their little table away from the lit-up tree, and they ate pie on the couches alongside.

Brooke sat back to listen to their rapid-fire conversation because they all seemed so excited. She felt full of food and lazy and just a little too exhausted for this, but that was fine because Jonathan was happier than she'd seen since he'd left seminary.

Gemma said, "Jonathan was telling us your plans for the main house and the carriage house, and I think it's amazing. Let me know how people apply for the residency program, because I know a bunch of artists who'd love a week to work on their stuff."

Brooke tilted her head. "Don't you feel it's unfair that Aunt Millie deeded the house to only Jonathan?"

"She explicitly didn't deed it only to him. She deeded it to Jonathan and whomever he married. And considering she did it as an act of spite?" Gemma rolled her eyes "She had the right to do whatever she wanted with her property, but come on. I want no part of it. As for the cash, she gave me and Jonathan the same."

Brooke set her empty plate on the table, and Jonathan got up. Brooke started to get up so he wouldn't collect the plates, but he said, "No, sit," and went to the tree to return with a stack of wrapped gifts.

Brooke tensed. "Wait, what?"

"Santa left your gifts here! Merry Christmas!"

"You're such a pain. Hang on." She scrambled to her feet. "Your gifts are upstairs."

She raced up the steps and dove under her bed for her own wrapped presents. Why was he doing this in front of his parents? He and she could have exchanged gifts with just the two of them in the library tomorrow night.

Downstairs, she handed two gifts to Jonathan, and one to his parents. Thank goodness Lilah had said his parents ought to get something, as a politeness thing. Even so, she burned with inadequacy to see her stack of presents was bigger than his. Worse still, she didn't have anything for

Gemma.

Also, while she'd been upstairs, Jonathan had cleared the plates. They were going to hate her.

It turned out Jonathan's family practice was to open all gifts at the same time, unlike at home when everyone had to go around the room opening in series so her brother ended up doing three in a row at the end. The first gift on Brooke's lap was from Jonathan, but as she slid her finger under the wrapping paper, she trained her eyes on him. She wanted to see his reaction to hers. Last week, she'd thought her gift was perfect, and now, she wasn't sure.

He opened his gift. "Fingerless gloves!" Relief flooded her at his expression. He'd commented on her fingerless gloves so many times that she'd had to make his own pair. His were made with worsted weight in a solid blue, just right for reading on a chilly night.

As he pulled them on, Mr. Levesque said, "Why do you wear those all the time?"

Gemma flopped back on the couch. "Dad!"

Mr. Levesque said, "I'm curious. Every time I've seen her, she's been wearing wrist warmers."

Brooke said, "They keep your fingers warm because they insulate your pulse point. But you still have your fingers free to knit or use your phone."

She wouldn't give the real answer, which was, "When I wear these, I feel calm. It's like having someone holding your hand all the time, except in this world, the only person who'll do that for you is yourself. Therefore, I knit my own hand-holder."

Jonathan flexed his fingers. "These are perfect, thanks."

Mrs. Levesque said, "And thank you so much for the dish towels. They're lovely."

They were. Brooke had knitted a pair in a basket weave style that included loops so Mrs. Levesque could hang them from the kitchen knobs.

Brooke said to Gemma, "I'm sorry I didn't make you anything. I didn't know you were coming."

Gemma waved her off. "I'm the rude one who's totally

crashing your party. Open your gift. I'm dying to see what Jonathan got his bride."

Was that a pot-shot? Brooke finished unwrapping the gift she was sure was another coffee table book...except it wasn't.

She stared at what was in her hands, trying to parse it the same way she'd tried and failed to parse a bacon-wrapped turkey. A piano songbook...?

Not just any songbook. This was music from the Paxley movies.

Brooke choked out, "Thank you."

She opened it on her lap, paging through, registering the notes and the chords and the words. Her favorite songs were here, pieces her piano instructor hadn't taught because Grandma wanted Brooke to play worthwhile songs. They were here. Now. All of them.

She looked up at Jonathan, still struggling to find her voice. "This is wonderful."

He didn't need to give her anything else, but there were still more gifts. Mrs. Levesque handed her the second, which was from her and Mr. Levesque. It was softer and squishier, and Brooke opened it to find a pair of pajamas that matched the ones in Jonathan's photo.

Gemma said, "I didn't know you'd gotten her one!"

"I thought she should be part of the tradition," Mom said. "I hope I guessed your size right."

Christmas pajamas. They'd included her.

Jonathan opened his second gift now, and Brooke wanted to wrestle it out of his hands because this was the better of his two gifts, and it was terrible by comparison. But then it was open, and he was holding a pair of handknit socks in a striped superwash merino. He beamed and said they were wonderful. But they weren't. They were just socks, and already in Brooke's lap were two amazing gifts.

Jonathan said, "You must have been sneaking around to knit these!"

His parents must think she was terrible. "You aren't

around in the mornings, and I do work at a yarn store."

Jonathan tilted his head. "Yeah, but socks take you twenty hours to knit, and given the size of my feet, probably closer to thirty. How did you even know my size?"

She smirked. "You wear shoes. And you do your laundry in the basement. It didn't take Sherlock Holmes."

Mrs. Levesque prompted Brooke, "Go on," so she opened the other gift from Jonathan's parents, this one hard-sided. She had no guesses. It didn't feel like a book.

Instead, she found herself looking at a collector's edition three-disc set of her favorite Paxley movie, with the special artwork and the additional commentary tracks.

Her brain didn't need to parse this. "Thank you!" She bounced in her seat. "This edition restores the song they removed from the first home video version, and it's also got a version of the song they added for Broadway!" She flipped it to the back. "Oh, and it's got the last interview one of the actors gave before he died. And there's a mini animation!"

Mr. Levesque stage-whispered, "I think she likes it."

She nodded. "I love it!"

Then she reached for the last one, from Jonathan, and it felt like straight knitting needles.

Brooke fought her immediate irritation. Knitting needles were, at the very least, an acknowledgment of who she was. Her mother hadn't ever gifted her anything having to do with knitting, not even when Brooke texted her a list. Still, Jonathan had lived with Brooke long enough to know she didn't knit with straight needles.

She opened the paper, and yes, knitting needles, but not a brand she recognized.

And then she realized—wooden. These were Jonathan-brand needles.

She ran her fingers over them, so smooth and amazing. The points were fine enough to knit lace, but not tapered too sharply. The caps at the end were spirals. She'd have to size them later, but they felt like fives or sixes, and they were about ten inches long. Perfect for something like a scarf or a dish towel.

He'd polished and sealed the wood to a high gloss. Brooke had no idea what words to use for what he'd done, but the needles were gentle as glass, and everything about them was perfect.

He'd spent his time planning for her, thinking about her, figuring out what she'd need, and then doing it.

"Are they okay?" Jonathan sounded unnerved.

Why was he doing this? They were friends, and they'd never exchanged gifts. They weren't really married, but here he'd learned to make something for her that he'd never made before. He'd taken all that time.

Her eyes burned, and her voice was soft. "They're wonderful. Thank you."

He relaxed into his seat. "I wasn't sure about the tips and whether they needed to be more tapered."

"The tips are fine." She had to say something. Whenever he'd told her about his work, there was special note about which kind of wood. "What kind of wood did you use?"

Turned out he'd gotten black cherry for these needles, and he told her how he'd researched different end caps and that he'd needed to use a special kind of varnish.

She hadn't stopped running her fingers over them. If she'd had yarn near right now, she'd have cast something on, just to feel these needles slipping through the loops.

Mr. Levesque slapped his hands against his thighs. "Well, we'll leave you two alone. I'm sure you're exhausted from all that driving."

Brooke settled her gifts safely at the coffee table, then saw his parents and Gemma to the door. As they were leaving, Brooke hugged Jonathan's mother. "Thank you, Mrs. Levesque."

She hugged Brooke back. "You can call me Mary. We don't need to be so formal."

Brooke hugged Jonathan's father, who said, "Same here. Dave."

Gemma said, "Call me Lady Levesque, Marchioness of

Burlington."

Brooke bowed to her. "Thank you for deigning to allow me in your presence, my lady."

Mr. Levesque (Dave) roared with laughter, and Jonathan exclaimed, "Seriously, Gemma?" Then he turned to his parents. "If it's okay, I'll still call you Mom and Dad."

He saw them off while Brooke stood a pace behind. Was this how family was supposed to feel?

Then they were gone, and Jonathan turned to her as if he had a bad case of nerves.

"Did you really like the knitting needles?" When she nodded, he hugged her again. "I'm sorry to spring the whole visit on you, but my parents wanted to give you their gifts. They promised not to stay too long so you wouldn't feel overwhelmed."

Brooke trembled. How had she gotten this lucky, to be surrounded by people who acknowledged her quirks and then not only didn't shame them, but worked around them?

She went into the kitchen to finish the dishes, but Jonathan said, "I'll do that."

"That's not fair. You set all this up for me." She started the water and squeezed out the dish soap. "You made everything so nice for my return. You didn't have to."

The words kept jumbling in her head. *I never expected that. My own parents didn't do that. What are you setting me up for?*

A Paxley piano book, one of her favorite movies, and pajamas like they got the rest of the family even though it wasn't Christmas Eve and she wasn't going to be a part of their family, and then handmade knitting needles.

The dishes went through the soap and through the rinse. Jonathan dried them, so after all that, she wasn't saving him any effort.

She kept trying to focus. "Your parents are very kind to me, considering."

Jonathan said, "Considering what?"

"They didn't want me to marry you in the first place."

"Mom has nothing against you. She thought it was a hare-brained scheme and was angry at Aunt Millie."

Brooke said, "They're both being nice."

The dishes and silverware were all in the rack now, and Jonathan was just finishing them up. "Do you want to watch your movie?"

Jonathan usually went to bed within an hour. She shouldn't keep him awake all night. "We can save that. It's late."

He said, "How about that interview you mentioned? How long could it be?"

He looked happy. She hadn't seen him relaxed like this in such a long time. "Sure. Let's get that set up."

He popped the disc into the TV while she thumbed through the booklet, and she held the mini animation cel to the light. The colors were brilliant, the character ebullient—and for the first time, Brooke knew exactly how that felt.

An hour later, Jonathan returned to the guest cottage, and Brooke got ready for bed. She wore her Christmas pajamas.

CHAPTER THIRTEEN

Brooke looked in control and well-balanced during the New Year's Eve party. "We've got a system now," she promised Jonathan, although he noticed that every so often she found a way to break free and give herself space.

Tonight was another full house. While they didn't have Colin or Austin (who had a full house of their own at the restaurant) they did have Lilah and Natalie, plus Emerson and Adrian and more than a dozen BCG members. This wasn't a BCG event. Lilah had said, almost as an afterthought, "If we had a New Year's Eve party, would anyone want to come?" and suddenly they had a roster of people bringing food and good wishes. Jonathan had invited Mom and Dad, and Gemma, and Father Tim, the last of whom surprised Jonathan by showing up despite having two Masses to say on New Year's morning.

They had music in the living room and a fire in the fireplace. Out in the firepit, Jonathan was burning some high-end cabinets that were flawed (that felt familiar) while inside, Brooke was burning her pine-scented candle in the stated hope of using it far enough that she could throw out the rest. Food kept appearing on the sideboard.

Once again, they'd borrowed chairs and tables. Oh, and at some time pre-arranged between Brooke and God Himself, she'd pushed play on *It's a Wonderful Life*. With subtitles, since the volume was off. No one was watching.

The menu was directed by Lilah: mountains of nibbles. Pans of hors d'oeuvres cycled in and out of the ovens. "It's easiest this way. Tiny plates, no silverware, and people gorging themselves without seeming to."

Jonathan had protested, but Brooke only said, "Lilah's going to do what Lilah wants to do." Instead of fighting a force of nature, therefore, Jonathan braced himself with an extra cup of coffee on the journey to midnight.

Adrian approached in the living room. "Your Christmas tree amazes me. If only you'd told me you had no ornaments, I could have provided some instead of arriving with a bag of chips."

"It didn't seem like something we needed." Next year, he and Brooke wouldn't be a couple any longer, so why buy ornaments together?

Jonathan himself had no Christmas decorations. He'd never needed any.

Adrian said, "Next year, make everyone bring one ornament."

"Hand-made?" Jonathan prompted.

Adrian nodded solemnly. "Make it a contest, only in the fine print, you keep all the entries."

Jonathan rubbed his chin. "Celebrating the birth of Christ with an act of theft. I'm feeling a little torn."

Mom came up to him. "More than thirty people. Not bad."

He nodded. "I think it's going well."

Mom said, "I figured Brooke would put on a Paxley movie. Speaking of which, when's her birthday? I can get her another, since she was so pleased with the first."

"May 19th," Jonathan said automatically. "Plenty of time."

Mom said, "Let me know which one you don't pick up for Valentine's Day, that way we can get her all set."

Getting Brooke "all set" made it sound like he'd move out and leave her with nothing but fantasy heroes and singing wildlife. Before he could protest, a timer went off. Jonathan stepped into the kitchen to take care of it. Was he supposed to buy her a Valentine's Day gift? What did men buy their wives for Valentine's Day?

Brooke was wearing oven mitts and pulling a tray of crab rangoon from the oven. "Need anything?" Jonathan asked.

Brooke scooped the crab rangoon onto a plate. "If you want to walk these around and tempt people, that would be a help."

The waiting pan had scallops wrapped in bacon, each speared by a toothpick. Would Colin be delighted by the bacon or horrified by the presentation?

Lilah said, "If you're looking for lots of 'somethings' to do, more knitting needles would be just the thing."

Brooke spun toward her. "Absolutely not! Those take a while to hand-craft, and if he makes any more, he's making them for me."

Warm inside, Jonathan said, "I need to know what sizes."

"All the sizes. She's a knitter." Lilah shook her head. "And then you need to start a complete set of double-pointed needles, just to be sure."

Brooke got a haunted look, but she shook it off. "I'm not asking for a thousand hours of his time." She handed a second plate to Lilah. "Get these in front of people."

When Jonathan hesitated, Lilah nudged him into action. Why had Brooke looked so haunted when Lilah mentioned double-pointed needles? Had she made the connection with a double-edged sword?

In the living room, Jonathan said, "I didn't think she'd used those needles yet."

"She made a washcloth at yesterday's Sit and Stitch. Said the needles were like a dream, but now she wants to make something real. As if a washcloth isn't real." Lilah tapped Adrian on the shoulder, and he and Emerson stopped talking long enough to take one crab rangoon apiece. "You know, I'd thought she was kidding about re-creating her entire apartment in the upstairs, but she totally did. Which is wild. I told her she could have the whole house, but instead she's cooped up in one little corner."

Jonathan caught Father Tim's eye from across the room. "And you had just as much luck with that as I did."

"I don't get it. It was nice of you to put locks on the door, and I love that she finally got out her artwork. It always miffed me that her grandmother said she couldn't."

Now Jonathan was miffed, too. "Why not?"

Lilah shrugged. "Wanted Brooke to be dignified like she was, I guess."

At the faux dining room table, Father Tim had set up a word-association card game. Jonathan waited until the end of the round, then offered everyone an appetizer.

Father Tim said, "You're trying to prevent your father's inevitable defeat by making everyone get grease on my cards."

Jonathan said, "If I wanted to prevent my father's inevitable defeat, I'd set off the fire alarm and run into the room spraying a fire extinguisher."

Dad laughed hard. Brooke approached from behind with a stack of napkins. "Here. And as a note for the future, it's also possible to say, 'Please stop playing cards at my party.'"

Jonathan paused. "Would that work?"

Brooke set the napkins on the table. "It might."

"But if it didn't, I'd have blown my cover for when I pulled out the fire extinguisher. Too risky." Jonathan held out the plate to her. "Eat one. You're being far too sensible for a New Year's Eve party."

Brooke took a crab rangoon. "Father Tim, even if Jonathan's being rude, it's my party, too, and I say you're allowed to play all the cards you want."

Jonathan set the plate on the sideboard, then rejoined Brooke in the kitchen. He said, "You could hand them all a humiliating defeat at that game. That's the best way to get them to stop playing cards at your party."

"*Our* party." She raised her eyebrows. "But I don't want to be at that table because then I'd be able to overhear your mother and Adrian talking politics."

Jonathan said, "If they're talking politics, that's an excellent time to make the punch."

Brooke brightened. "Shall I line up everyone so you can punch them?"

"Hah." He went under the counter for what should have been a salad bowl (and would be again) and then into the fridge for three bottles of juice and soda.

Brooke leaned her elbows on the counter and rested her face in her hands while the juice glugged out of the first bottle. "Are you sure this is going to work?"

"We did this in seminary for our Easter party, so yes. But wait." He handed her a bottle of lemon-lime soda. "Pour this in, and I'll be back with the best part."

Brooke said, "There's no party like a seminary party."

"You have no idea." He returned from the porch with a frozen bundt cake pan. Brooke's eyes widened, but he said, "No, no, trust me."

He flipped over the pan, then tapped until a thunk resounded against the counter. When he lifted the cake pan, before them was a bundt-cake-shaped block of ice.

Brooke applauded. "Whatever you've done, that certainly is a thing you did."

"Very funny." He set the ice ring to float in the bowl. "See? Punch is okay, but this makes it exciting. Plus, it made you look horrified, and that's half the price of admission right there."

She took a step backward. "I'm afraid to ask about the other half of the price of admission."

He smirked at her. "Maybe it's scallops wrapped in bacon."

Her nose wrinkled. "And maybe I'm going to regret asking."

He went into the freezer and came out with a container of lemon sherbet. "Actually, this is the other half."

She found ice cream scoops in the drawers, and they scooped the entire container into the punch bowl. Brooke said. "I take it back. This is suitably festive."

Jonathan raised his eyebrows. "As a sign of your humble realization, please clear a path for me to the buffet table so this will be ready to go for midnight."

Brooke said, "As you wish, most endlessly fascinating spouse of mine."

Jonathan lifted the bowl. "Is my title getting longer?"

"An endless title befits an endlessly fascinating spouse." She headed into the living room. "Make way! Behold, the mighty midnight punch bowl!"

An endless title, but not an endless marriage.

She was beautiful, and he concentrated on the bowl rather than on watching her move. Tonight she wore her hair long and loose, and she was dressed for comfort in leggings, a handknit tunic-style sweater, and clogs over her wool socks. He was wearing the socks she'd made him for Christmas, and they were wicked warm.

Everyone complimented the ice wreath punch. The whole house smelled of fried goodies, baked treats, cinnamon, and pine. Brooke settled on a corner of the couch with his needles and a skein of pearly yarn, plus some bright orange that didn't match. Jonathan talked to Mom, chatted with Emerson, then wandered back to the couch where Brooke was knitting. Another BCG member was on the opposite end doing something with leather straps.

Jonathan slipped into the empty seat in the middle. His thigh was right up against Brooke's, but Brooke didn't shift away. It was exciting and frightening at the same time. "Do the needles work?"

She held up her project, which was all of one inch long and had a singular row of garish orange at the base. The working yarn had flecks of blue and purple. The net effect gave it a softness, but he couldn't tell what the design was going to be.

"May I touch the yarn?"

She plucked the yarn ball out of her lap and handed it to him. She'd wound it into a cylinder-shape with the yarn coming out of the center.

This didn't help as much as he thought it would, so he went for the failsafe conversation-starter. "What are you making?"

"An infinity scarf." She turned the needles around, switched the yarn from the back to the front, and then did the entire row with one type of motion. "I'm using a lace pattern I originally designed for socks, but that's worked in the round, so I modified to work it flat. It shouldn't be too much of a problem, only on one row where I need to reverse a few of the stitches for shaping purposes."

She was in the expertise zone. Good. "What's the orange for?"

"Scrap yarn for a provisional cast-on. At the end, I'll pull it out so there's an entire row of live stitches, and then I can graft the ends so it's a long loop. I'm making it wide enough that I should be able to wrap it double without it hanging too much." She looked up, eyes wide. "Sorry. Were you following any of that?"

"Enough to know you're doing something complicated and you love what you're doing, plus you think it's going to work." What else did she, Lilah, and Natalie always ask each other? "What kind of yarn is it?"

She broke into a smile, and Jonathan went warm all the way to his handknit-socked toes. "This is a silk-cashmere blend I picked up at a yarn expo five years ago, but it never wanted to be knit up into anything. I knew eventually it would tell me what it wanted to become. When I was looking for something to make on your needles, I knew this was it."

Jonathan cupped the yarn in his hands. "And you don't have a pattern in front of you, so I assume you not only memorized it, but you're converting a memorized pattern in your head."

She sighed. "Would you need instructions if you went out to make a yarn bowl right now, just because you were making it a different size? Well, neither do I. Some things, once you know them, you know them."

"Fair enough." She'd started paying attention to her knitting again, but by now Jonathan knew she could let her needles fly without removing her attention from the rest of the room. If anything, her attention heightened when she was working. "What time should we switch the TV over to the ball dropping?"

"I timed the movie so it would end right before the ball drops, so long as no one paused the playback. Which I don't think they did."

She flipped the scarf back again, and Jonathan thought he might be detecting the beginning of a design. He didn't want to leave, though. She was seated and knitting, and right beside her, he felt comfortable. A warm house and pleasant guests and the roar of friendly noise all seemed oddly peaceful.

He stayed. He watched the subtitles on the movie, and he kept an eye on the time, and he held her yarn cake, and every so often she tugged another few inches from the center.

When the closing credits came on, Jonathan reluctantly pried himself out of the couch and set the TV to pick up the celebration at Times Square. Brooke turned off the music so he could raise the volume on the television. They called the guests in from the firepit, and soon the living room was crowded.

Brooke headed to the buffet table. "Everyone needs a glass of punch to toast the New Year!" and well before the time was up, she'd gotten all the cups filled while Jonathan stood behind her handing them out. Then it was 11:59, and everyone was watching the TV with small, whispered conversations. Jonathan stood behind Brooke with one hand on her shoulder as the seconds ticked upward. And upward.

Meanwhile the ball began to drop. Upward went the seconds. Downward went the ball.

12:00:00. The ball landed home, and the fireworks

started. The Times Square crowd cheered, and when the crowd in the living room also cheered, Jonathan's hand tightened on Brooke's shoulder.

"A toast to the new year!" Father Tim called out, and everyone raised their glasses. Brooke sipped some of her punch, and then she sagged back against Jonathan's chest while everyone around her was noisy and moving.

She'd been pacing herself until midnight, hadn't she? The ball had dropped, and now she was out of energy.

Jonathan wrapped his free arm around her, holding her to him as if he could be her bulwark against the noise that had been encroaching all night. She rested her hand on his arm, and the world was just right.

A new year. Anything could happen in a new year.

Brooke slipped out of his arms and headed toward the balcony. Jonathan wove his way through the revelers to follow her outside.

It was cold as blazes. She wouldn't stay here long. "Too many people?"

In the half light from the house her eyes were dark and lovely. "I needed a moment to think."

"It was wicked warm in there. I don't want you to get chilled." He stepped forward, but she looked fragile, and before he had a grip on himself, he wrapped her in his arms. "Take care of yourself."

She rested her head against his shoulder. "Thank you. You've made it a good year."

His heartbeat skittered. When she looked up at him, he bent his head and kissed her.

The warmth of her lips against his exploded through his soul with yearning, and then with guilt. He wasn't— He shouldn't be— He'd planned— Except here she was, and he closed his eyes because in the moment, it felt wonderful to have her here. Wretchedly wonderful, and perfectly off-kilter.

She looked bewildered. Their breath mingled between them.

That shouldn't have happened. He shouldn't have done

that. She must be furious, and maybe God was furious—but a man could kiss his wife. Even if they weren't married. A man could kiss his girlfriend. It wasn't wrong. But it was all wrong. This shouldn't have been his.

She giggled and touched his jawline. Fireworks burst through him to rival Times square. "You haven't even been drinking."

She wasn't furious, but Jonathan trembled anyway. "I'm sorry."

Brooke took his hands in hers. "Happy New Year to you, too," and rose on her toes to kiss him on the cheek.

Jonathan couldn't move. She hugged him, then walked back into the house. Jonathan followed.

He couldn't feel the cold any longer, nor the heat. He felt dizzy and guilty and ashamed and delighted, and none of it made sense. Meanwhile Brooke slipped off into the kitchen, but Father Tim cut off Jonathan before he could follow. "Thank you so much for inviting me. I'd stay longer, but I need to get out so I can say Mass tomorrow."

It ached. That should have been Jonathan's life, leaving Christmas Eve parties or New Year's Eve parties to say Masses the next morning. He shouldn't be kissing a woman. Except he was weak. He was in the wrong places, doing the wrong things.

Lilah and Natalie started cleaning up. Head swimming, Jonathan said, "You don't have to," but that triggered a cascade reaction of many guests putting their trash in the bags. Brooke skirted the edges of the room carrying leftovers into the kitchen, which she then boxed up and pressed people to take home. Finally, Jonathan brought back the nearly empty punch bowl, but then she avoided the kitchen.

Therefore, he avoided her, too. If she didn't want to talk to him, he'd respect it. He barely wanted to talk to himself right now.

Eventually he did go back to say goodbye as the final guests got their coats. Mom and Dad kept telling him what a lovely party it had been, and Aunt Millie would have been proud. Maybe she would have been. Maybe her ghost had seen that slip-up on the balcony and sneered. Lilah and Natalie were last to leave, hugging Brooke and then hugging Jonathan as well even though he felt filthy. "Happy New Year!" Lilah chirped, with Natalie echoing it a second behind. And then they were out the door, and Brooke stayed to watch them get into their cars.

Standing behind her, Jonathan said, "I owe you an apology. Everything got away from me."

"Really? I think the party went fine. You mom wasn't even teaching me how to be a good hostess this time, although I guess we weren't together often." She shook her head. "I'm going to make sure the food's put away, and I know I'll regret this, but I'll clean everything else in the morning."

Jonathan trailed her into the kitchen, nauseated. Brooke took a peek in the dishwasher, then turned it on. "I've got this. You look exhausted, so if you want to go home and go to bed, that's fine."

She wasn't angry. Had his kiss not even registered with her?

He'd never kissed a woman before. He'd never dated because he was never getting married. He'd taken Brooke to the prom, but all he'd done was hug her at the end of the night. Well, they'd slow-danced some, but he'd never kissed her because kissing meant love, and Jonathan was destined for celibacy.

His first kiss, and she'd blown it off.

She paused. "Are you okay?"

"Yeah." Should he confess what had actually happened? Or should he let it go and just try to keep better control from now on? She wasn't angry—now. But what if he told her? What if…?

What if she thought it was okay and just kept kissing him? What if he gave in to this flood of emotions that kept battering at the dam of his self-restraint?

What if Father Tim was right that this was going to be a lot tougher than he'd anticipated?

What if she found the whole idea offensive and only wanted the house?

Jonathan had started the new year by making a tremendous, unfixable mistake.

She squeezed his hand. "Earth to Jonathan. You need to get some sleep."

"Yeah." His voice was unsteady. "Thank you for tonight. For everything."

CHAPTER FOURTEEN

New Year's morning. *The first day with a whole year in front of us.*

She shook herself.

Well, in front of me. By the end of the year, Jonathan wouldn't be in it anymore.

She stretched out, warm in her Christmas pajamas. It was nice of his parents to treat her like a daughter. Her and Jonathan, "brother and sister."

Why did that leave her feeling disappointed?

She pulled on a robe because the house was chilly, then checked her phone in case Jonathan had texted. He hadn't. Poor guy. He'd been exhausted last night and looked one step away from escape when she'd dispatched him back to the guest cottage.

Downstairs, looking at the mess, Brooke remembered telling herself she'd definitely regret not staying awake to clean. Yeah, about that. But she'd been just as tired as Jonathan. Neither of their judgments had been all that good, like when he kissed her on the balcony.

They'd just watched the end of an emotional movie, and then everyone was cheering for the New Year. Brooke had been alone on the balcony, and he'd gotten carried away.

She remembered his face, but that wasn't excitement, was it? More like— Embarrassment? Shock?

She'd kissed him on the cheek afterward to reset him. Yes, he'd gotten a bit mixed up about how they'd deal with one another, but she didn't mind.

She wouldn't have minded if he'd done it again, either. He was sweet. He looked out for her and cared for her, and that was what mattered.

She pulled out her phone and texted, "I'm making coffee for when you wake up."

Coffee didn't feel like quite enough for New Year's morning. She could make something, but she had no idea what he normally did for breakfast. Omelets? Pancakes?

Everyone loved pancakes, so she mixed up the batter and readied the coffee maker, then sat at the table to knit more on her infinity scarf.

Jonathan's facial expression had been shock. Except why would he have been shocked that he kissed her? Her kissing him, sure, he'd have been offended. But he'd kissed her, which implied he knew what he was doing.

Unless he didn't.

Wait— Was that Jonathan's first kiss?

Brooke reached the end of the row with three extra stitches. She stared at the mess in her hands, but worse was the mess in her head. She could work backward to unknit whatever mistake she'd made in this row. She couldn't unknit whatever had happened last night.

She didn't think Jonathan had any prior girlfriends. Not that she was his girlfriend, but, whatever—she didn't know of anyone he'd dated. That was Jonathan's "thing," along with the priesthood dream. "The purpose of dating is to get married," he'd declared during high school, "so why would I date anyone? It wouldn't be fair to them."

That had to have been his first kiss.

What was going on here? He'd have wanted his first kiss to be meaningful if he'd given it any thought at all, and Jonathan gave everything a lot of thought. It was one of the things she liked about him.

What did it mean to him? And what did that meaningfulness mean to her?

An engine sounded in the driveway. Jonathan's car. Oh, right, Catholics went to Mass on January first. Father Tim had said something about that last night.

Brooke fought the urge to run. People made no sense. Jonathan had said— He'd said this wasn't a real marriage, just a way to spend a year while he unloaded a house and figured out who he was supposed to be.

He stepped out of his car, and Brooke smiled because he looked windblown and just a little tired, but also relaxed. What if he'd decided he was supposed to be her husband?

But then what did that make her, and what did she feel? She'd never considered going further with him because it wasn't an option, the same way she didn't spend time considering whether she should become an astronaut.

The front door opened, and she heard the zip of his jacket in the mudroom.

Jonathan was sweet in so many ways. Loyal and dedicated and thoughtful. She'd always thought, "That's why he'll be a great priest," but as she'd said to him before, those qualities also made him a great man. He was a confused man, though, and last night he'd kissed someone for the first time. This morning he'd find that same woman standing in the kitchen in his family's Christmas pajamas, offering him breakfast. That was only going to make him more confused.

He joined her. "I'm sorry I didn't see your text. I had the phone silenced."

"No problem. Coffee now?" Her hand trembled as she pushed the button to start the machine. "Is it okay to begin the year with pancakes?"

"Sounds like a great start." As she turned on the burner under the griddle, he went to the cabinet to get two mismatched plates. "I can straighten the living room if you have something you want to do today."

I want answers. That was always the issue, wasn't it?

People said one thing and acted another way—let alone the unspoken subtext—and when you questioned them, their answers were never the right kinds of answers.

Brooke said, "I'd planned on a day of knitting and reading." She got the butter and syrup, and she deliberately brushed by him as he was setting out the plates. He pulled back.

Noted. I'm okay to kiss, but not okay to touch. This would be easier if she had a checklist to determine what he wanted.

Also, what did *she* want?

Jonathan said, "If we're just going to have a relaxing day, we can watch your movie."

"Only if you won't be bored to tears. I know that's not your speed."

He chuckled. "I'll watch it with you."

That sounded a lot like how Brooke was when she first started dating someone. *A Renn Faire isn't quite my speed, but I'll go with you.*

Brooke cooked the pancakes while the coffee maker worked and Jonathan got the half and half from the fridge. Jonathan said Father Tim looked exhausted at morning Mass, but he'd asked Jonathan to tell Brooke again what a good time he'd had. Also, he'd joked with Jonathan about making sure the fire extinguishers were easily accessible, and Brooke smiled. Jonathan was in a good mood, with less tension in his voice. She brought the pancakes to the table, and he paused before eating.

She said, "You can do that out loud, you know."

He looked up. "What?"

"Saying grace. You don't have to hide it from me."

He offered her a smile. "Okay. Thanks."

This was how they were starting their new year together. And finally Brooke knew what she wanted: she wanted to talk to Lilah.

Talking to Lilah was problematic.

Brooke's first clue was Natalie's ten a.m. text, "Alert: Lilah is in fine form."

Brooke's second clue was how spaced-out Lilah seemed, staring off into the distance with a vague grin whenever she wasn't directly involved in anything, not giving good advice when she was involved, and always watching the clock. Sit and Stitch was in tumult, and Lilah had the attention span of a magpie in a glitter factory.

Brooke decoded it and pulled Natalie aside. "Quit being frustrated with her. I'll bet you one mini-skein she's engaged."

Natalie's eyes widened. "Seriously?"

Brooke plucked a mini-skein of yarn off its hook and handed it to Natalie.

During a lull in Sit and Stitch, as Natalie was packing up to leave, Lilah said, "Natalie, don't go yet. Excuse me, everyone?"

Looking rueful, Natalie pulled the mini-skein out of her pocket and handed it back to Brooke.

Lilah pulled off her fingerless gloves to reveal a gleaming solitaire. "On New Year's Day, Emerson proposed!"

When everyone applauded, Brooke called out, "Congratulations! And in honor of Lilah's engagement, everyone gets ten percent off everything."

Lilah hugged Natalie, and then Brooke, and then all the Sit and Stitchers asked to see Lilah's ring. It was a lab-grown orange sapphire set in white gold, and it matched her orange manicure.

After the congratulations, though, Natalie left, and Brooke took care of the shop while Lilah answered a thousand questions about her engagement, if they'd set a date, where they'd get married, and on and on. Lilah had no answers. Maybe they would rent a boat and throw a stick into the sea.

One of the crocheters said to Brooke, "You're so quiet, dear. Did you have a nice holiday?"

Brooke nodded. "It was fine."

Lilah said, "Show them Jonathan's needles!"

Brooke froze in place, but Lilah just gushed on. "They're so amazing and thoughtful!"

As a testimony to how in her own headspace she was, Lilah had missed all seven ways Brooke was signaling her no—don't—abort—rescind—quit—stop it—shut up. Lilah said, "Emerson gave me a ring, but Jonathan made Brooke a pair of custom knitting needles."

"Jonathan Levesque?" gasped one of the ladies. "Did he come home from seminary for Christmas?"

Brooke shot Lilah a glare, and finally Lilah got the message. She went pale.

"I see him all the time at Saint Lucy's." A woman in a red sweater looked up. "He's not in seminary any longer."

The first woman said, "Why not? That boy's always wanted to be a priest."

Brooke said, "He's been in Brighthead for months, working for a cabinetmaker."

The woman set down her crochet project. "Why did he leave? What happened?"

Everything Jonathan had said about "discerning out" had been so raw. So private. Brooke had no answer.

Lilah said, "He changed his mind," which in no way described the situation and at the same time made it sound worse, as if Jonathan were fickle. But, "It's complicated" would make it sound even worse than that— as if Jonathan had been thrown out, which was exactly the first thing he didn't want people to think, even if he thought it about himself.

Another woman said, "He left the seminary, and now he's hand-making you knitting needles as a Christmas present?"

Brooke strode to the display stand and brought back one of Jonathan's yarn bowls. "He sells these, too, if you're looking for his handmade pieces. They're beautiful and functional, and he even signed the bottom."

She set it on the table, fixing Lilah with a glare that made Lilah wilt in her own skin.

The red-sweatered women said, "Brooke's always with him. That's why he's making her gifts, and that's why he isn't a priest."

"He left seminary in May. I didn't speak to him until July." The looks around the table were a mixture of surprise and anger and something else Brooke couldn't identify. The crocheter looked horrified. The red-sweatered customer looked...well, grim. At least one woman took a look at Brooke's waistline.

Yes, obviously the demure and obscure Brooke Evart was going to baby-trap a seminarian. Via the postal service.

The crocheter sounded uncertain. "Weren't you dating that nice artist, the one with the show over at Fruits de Mer?"

Brooke flashed Lilah an icy look. "You're thinking of Emerson, who just proposed to Lilah." They could suggest Brooke was dating Colin, too, and she could nail the hat trick. "Did you see Emerson's exhibit over in the corner of the gift area, where you can buy one of his paintings and a matching skein of yarn that Lilah hand-dyed to match it? Of course they're a natural pairing. We shouldn't be taking away from Lilah's moment."

The red-sweatered woman said, "Don't take Jonathan away from the priesthood."

Brooke raised her hands. "I can't compete with God."

The crocheter muttered, "I should hope not."

With her hair standing on end, Brooke said to one of the newer Sit and Stitch members, "Have you ever used a yarn bowl?" and then set the woman's yarn cake in the bowl and threaded it through the curly cutout.

Since when was Brooke the kind of person to go to war with God? Brooke was the last person to issue ultimatums. If anything, she took far too much guff from people before finally deciding she'd had enough. But when she did, she was out the door.

Take Hal, her last long-term boyfriend. All his arrogance and put-downs were "just how he was" until the day Brooke had said to herself, "If that's how he is, then why do I want him?" At which point, she'd returned anything he'd ever given her and blocked him on everything. Had he tried to get back together with her? Yes. Had she listened? No, and that was doubly easy because the ways he tried to get back with her were all third-hand because (get this) she'd closed off every direct avenue of communication in advance. When he'd sent his mother's friend to the yarn store to tell Brooke that she'd never find such a great guy ever again, Brooke had replied, "Surely a guy as great as Hal knows how to get lost."

But even Hal hadn't gotten an ultimatum because Brooke knew: given the choice of Brooke or something else, people always chose the other thing.

Also, once she'd gotten to the point of deciding she could live without someone, why would Brooke let them make the decision about whether Brooke should stay?

The ladies around the table were silent. Lilah said, "Does anyone know what's going into the old shoe repair place on Edgemont Street?"

One woman said, "I think it's another convenience store."

Brooke didn't need to say, "Oh, good, another overpriced convenience store," because one of the ladies said, "Just what we needed, another overpriced convenience store," and gave her the chance to slip away. Conversation never ticked back up, though. Everyone was too horrified by the contrast of Lilah as a blushing bride and Brooke as the Whore of Babylon. Well, the Whore of Brighthead. While Brooke wrote in a ledger, the customers put away their projects and drifted away one at a time.

Weirdly, they weren't too uncomfortable to take advantage of the Lilah-got-engaged sale. And the newcomer did buy Jonathan's yarn bowl. Brooke also put the mini-skein back on the display. Bet or not, that was inventory.

After the last customer was out, Lilah turned to Brooke with her eyes huge, biting her lip.

Brooke said, "Yeah, I get it."

"I'm so sorry." You couldn't head off Lilah once she'd decided to say something. "It didn't even occur to me that they'd ask why Jonathan was giving you handmade gifts. I should have said he was test-running needles to see whether they would be worth selling."

"I'm not asking anyone to lie for me." Still, Lilah could have kept her mouth shut and not needed to lie. "I wouldn't want you to say that anyhow because that cheapens the gift. You'd already made a direct connection between Emerson giving you a ring and Jonathan making me needles. What other conclusions were they supposed to draw?"

Lilah looked miserable, so now was the time to get an opinion. "If you don't mind putting off wedding-planning for a few minutes, I need some help."

"Sure." Lilah followed Brooke to the register. "What's going on?"

"Do you have any idea what Jonathan is thinking about me?"

Lilah's eyes crinkled. "It's bad when the customers think he's pursuing you, but you think it's okay if I decide he is?"

Brooke's shoulders tensed. "I can't figure him out. He was emphatic about what he wanted and what he didn't want, but now that we're play-acting at all of *this*," and Brooke swept out a hand as though to encompass the half of Brighthead that surrounded Aunt Millie's house, "he's diving headfirst into the façade. I want to know what you think he's feeling. I have no idea."

Lilah said, "Honestly? You guys are tight. I'd just ask."

Brooke froze.

Hey, Jonathan? Why'd you kiss me on New Year's Eve? Like, was that a kiss-kiss, or was that for fun because you read in a book that non-priests kiss when the ball drops?

Yeah, but no.

Lilah recoiled. "Why don't you want to ask?"

Brooke shifted her weight. "That would be so uncomfortable."

"More uncomfortable than living with a man when you have no idea how he feels about you?" Lilah shrugged. "But you *are* living together, so if he wants to take it to the next level, won't he make a move on you?"

Uneasy, Brooke said, "How would he do that?"

"You know him best. How would Jonathan do something like that?"

Brooke chose to deflect. "I don't know him in this kind of situation. He's never dated anyone, unless you count him dating God Almighty when he decided to dedicate his life to the priesthood."

Lilah nodded. "Yeah, and he immediately went all in on that. He watched videos by priests and read books about vocations and told us all about the lives of the saints. He talked about it all the time."

Brooke said, "He went to the teen group at Saint Lucy's, and he offered me rides." She'd gone with him. Teen group got Brooke out of the house.

Lilah said, "Ergo, when he falls for someone or something, he immerses himself. He thinks about it constantly, and then invariably, he talks about it."

Brooke said, "I wouldn't know if he's talking about me when I'm not there, and I'm not that interesting."

Lilah waved her objection aside. "He started doing all sorts of church stuff once he decided to go for the priesthood, so he'd try to be near you. Does he do that?"

Brooke swallowed hard. "We live on the same property. It's all muddled up. We've been spending a lot of time together, but here's the thing—did he decide to become a priest because he'd *already* been spending a lot of time doing church stuff? Did he fall in love with the priesthood because of proximity?"

Lilah said, "Maybe it grew up together, so he found something he liked, therefore he went more often, and that reinforced what he liked, and then he spent even more time…"

Brooke closed her eyes hard. "Which would make it impossible to tell."

Lilah said, "You're going to need to wait for something obvious, like if he kisses you."

Brooke sputtered a laugh. "Even that might not be obvious."

"If he gets down on one knee with a ring and says, 'Brooke, let's take a drive to St. Lucy's and get God's approval for this gig,' you'll have to believe that." Lilah paused. "You're upset, though, and that's not fair to you. Open up the conversation."

"I don't want to lose him. He's been an awesome friend for so many years, and if I push for more than that after he said no—? What if he gets offended?"

Lilah hesitated. "Are you falling in love with Jonathan?"

Brooke opened her hands. "How should I know? That's why I need your opinion. What do I feel?"

Lilah bit her lip. "Okay, let me think about this one."

Awesome. If Lilah couldn't figure it out, it must be a disaster.

A customer entered the shop, so Lilah took care of her, and Brooke did the paperwork for Jonathan's yarn bowl. The BCG artists were in effect a lot of small-scale vendors. While it was an act of community service to give them exposure, it created more paperwork than Lilah had predicted.

The local busybodies were angry at Brooke about Jonathan. Once it became known that Brooke was living with him without a church wedding…? That animosity was going to explode.

It wasn't any of their business, but it was as obvious as the lighthouse in the bay that she'd stolen a priest.

Another customer entered before Lilah finished with the first, so Brooke filed away their discussion in the "unhelpful" category and returned to work. Lilah should be leaving soon. At this point in the year, Brooke never biked to work any longer (the frigid darkness was more than off-putting) but Jonathan would be in the kitchen when she stepped inside. He'd have some dinner waiting, although most likely it would be (should be) leftovers from the freezer.

Last night, they'd stuffed themselves with the last of the party nibbles while sitting on the couch, watching her movie and playing an entire disk full of extra features.

Had she stolen a priest? Or was she swooping in after the fact, a relationship vulture picking over the carcass of his vocation?

The shop was hopping tonight. A lot of people must be following through on their New Year's resolutions to knit an entire project. Brooke eventually sent Lilah home. They weren't going to get more time to talk, and Brooke could handle the customers on her own.

She just wished she had an answer.

After she locked up at eight, she found a bunch of texts from Lilah.

"I can't figure out how you actually feel, but I think I know what you should be feeling."

That was a start.

"You should be feeling comfortable with him, but I would guess you're also uneasy because you don't want to lose that comfort."

This made sense.

"He's a fixture in your life. But he's also treating you well. I can't say why he's doing that, whether because he's an awesome guy or because he loves you."

No new information there.

"But either way—awesome guy or in-love guy—I can see why you might want to go further with him. You said you don't want to lose him, but neither of those scenarios means you would."

Brooke replied, "How do you mean?" and then stood with her phone in her hand, waiting on a reply.

Lilah sent, "If you try to take things up a notch and he loves you, he'll respond. And if you try to take things up a notch and he's just awesome, he'll let you down gently. Neither one means a rupture of the relationship."

Brooke typed, "But I don't know if I want to take it up a notch."

Lilah texted, "I can't help you there."

That meant no one could.

CHAPTER FIFTEEN

Father Tim had said the marriage would be tougher than Jonathan anticipated, and now it was going to get even tougher than that.

Jonathan had joined Brooke, Natalie, and Lilah at Bright Stitches for a pre-opening meeting, which was also his very-early-lunch-hour meeting. The tough part wasn't going to be working the rest of the day without lunch. That couldn't be helped. The tough part was the obvious conclusion he couldn't avoid everyone else concluding.

Natalie said, "The Resident Artist should stay in the guest house."

Lilah shook her head. "It's not fair to Jonathan to take his home away. The artist has less privacy in the main house, but there's also better facilities, and it feels more welcoming to have them included in the family life."

Again that word, "family."

Brooke said, "I want them to feel included, too, but during Casey's presentation, she said the only thing she found awkward about her AIR was the privacy issue."

Plus, strangers in the house terrified Brooke. Strangers in the guest cottage would not. Lilah and Natalie knew about that. Whether they knew he'd camped out in her room, Jonathan wasn't sure. The solution was obvious. It just was going to take an hour to reach it.

If Jonathan had become a priest, there would have been plenty of meetings like these, only they'd have been called "parish council meetings," and they'd have extended into the night. If there was any bright side in not having a vocation, it was not having to attend parish council meetings for the rest of his life.

Leadership meetings of the BCG, though? That was another thing.

Natalie said, "I thought from the minute Jonathan suggested this that a separate, private building for the Artist in Residence was the perfect solution. I get that Jonathan and Brooke aren't really married, however you're defining it—that's cool, and I'm not arguing with the Catholic church even though I think it's dumb—but you still 'aren't really married' if you're both in the same house. The only difference we're talking about is where Jonathan sleeps."

Brooke said, "That's not the only difference at all. With the granny flat, Jonathan has privacy. He can go off and do his own thing if I'm being irritating."

Natalie said, "The main house is three thousand square feet. He's going to be able to go off and do his own thing unless you follow him everywhere, and that's not a level of irritation I've ever seen from you."

Brooke sighed. "He needs his own space."

"There are three entire bedrooms on the second floor where he can have his own space, and none of them shares a bathroom with your room."

Jonathan said, "It's more like, the boundaries become different when we're living in the same house all the time."

Brooke added, "He's got the granny flat set up just the way he likes it."

Natalie started to speak, but Lilah said, "Neither one of them wants to do it. We've got a workable solution now: Brooke double-locks her door, and the artist stays in the primary suite. Casey was one person."

"Yes, but she had a point. Having to share the space diminished her ability to work odd hours, and she didn't feel comfortable spreading out."

Brooke said, "You could have fooled me. We had beads all over the living room and dining room. Last week, I found a bead in the couch."

Jonathan laughed. "You didn't tell me about that."

"I pulled up a couch cushion looking for a DPN, and there was a seed bead hanging out."

Jonathan said, "Was the DPN having some kind of illicit tryst with it?"

"No, the DPN had managed to make its way all the way down into the couch's inner workings, and I thought I'd require a carpenter to set it free. But I got it anyway."

Jonathan said, "I'll build a little pedestal for the bead: the last souvenir of our first AIR."

Brooke shot back, "You only think it's the last survivor. Two years from now, I'll be sweeping and a bead's going to come skittering out from the baseboards."

Lilah had a dreamy look in her eyes. "Maybe you two should get a room."

Jonathan's stomach tightened, and Brooke snapped, "The whole discussion is getting him a room."

Jonathan said, "The unfortunate part, though, is I think they're right about the guest cottage."

Natalie said, "How hard would it be to clear out most of your stuff? You didn't move in with a lot."

"One of the seminary things was minimalism, so if the bishop moved your assignment, you could throw everything in the back of your car and be gone in two hours. Not that you'd ever get that quick of an assignment change, but you could." Now he could accumulate whatever he wanted. "I can spend a week with my parents whenever we have an artist."

Brooke tensed. Lilah drawled, "No... That's not going to work for her. Nor for me. I don't want Brooke alone when we've got strangers on the property, even with locks on everything."

Natalie said, "You and I could take turns staying with her."

Brooke snapped, "I'm not a child."

Natalie's mouth twitched. "You're a woman, and there's no woman on earth who'd feel comfortable with a stranger sleeping on the same property and having access to her house."

Brooke said, "Next year, Jonathan's going to move out, so I should get used to it now."

Natalie said, "Next year, Jonathan's going to move out, and the guest cottage becomes the Artist in Residence housing for real. Just move it up eleven months."

Lilah said, "There's the electronic locks and the security system."

"None of which mean a thing once the artist is inside the house." Natalie looked at Brooke. "If positions are reversed, this is exactly what you'd say to me, and you'd be right."

Brooke said, "You have a tenant on the floor beneath you. The tenant could kick in your door at any time. How is that different?"

Natalie said, "It's different because we've established I'm not worried about it. You are."

"Wait. Stop." Jonathan sighed. "I don't want you guys fighting. We all want Brooke safe—not just to be safe, but to feel safe." With Natalie's eyes burning a hole in his heart, Jonathan said, "Whenever artists visit, I'll use the primary suite."

Jonathan walked back into the main house, bracing himself before entering the kitchen where Brooke was reheating dinner. "Honey, I'm home."

"You've been home for a while." Brooke dumped a bowl of broccoli into the boiling water. "Thank you for doing that for me."

She might not thank him for very long, of course. "Remember when you said you were a difficult roommate? What if it's I who am the difficult roommate?"

Brooke raised her eyebrows. "We'll have to be difficult together."

He and Brooke ate together and cleaned up together, as always. Then they went to the primary suite with its fairytale castle over the bed, as well as all Jonathan's belongings in bags and boxes because this afternoon, he'd moved in.

Right now, Jonathan was terribly, terribly conscious of Brooke under the same roof.

She unpacked his clothes and set them into Aunt Millie's dressers. He unpacked his toiletries into the bathroom. Shoes, under the bed. It took next to no time, and any things that needed to go somewhere specific (his clock, his Liturgy of the Hours books,) Brooke put into a place where they were almost right. He could fine-tune it later.

She stood at the entrance and looked around. "We should get you a better comforter. Ice green isn't your color."

"What is my color?"

"Anything other than ice green." She rubbed her chin. "Surely we can find something that suits you."

"I don't plan to do anything other than sleep in this bedroom." That sounded a bit awkward, though, because abruptly Jonathan thought about the things a *really-married* couple would do in this bedroom, so he clarified, "I'm not going to notice the color in the dark while I'm unconscious."

"I would be conscious of it." Brooke, at least, hadn't immediately jumped to the wrong conclusion. "Not that it would keep me awake, but I'd find it annoying."

He sat on the bed. "It's not a bad room. I still think you should have taken this."

"And I still like my micro-apartment." She sat on the edge of the bed beside him, which made his hair stand on end. "That TV is so odd."

"Not odd. It's mounted on an arm so Aunt Millie could watch while in bed. At the end, she wasn't getting around much."

Brooke frowned. "I hadn't thought about that. It just seemed weird to have a TV on a metal arm."

"The mural," he said, and she gasped as she put it together—Aunt Millie hadn't wanted to fix the TV directly to the wall, but the front wall, which had no mural, had the windows, and it would have been impossible to watch TV with the light behind it. Ergo, the mobile arm.

Brooke sat on the bed. "Do you want to hang up your artwork?"

Jonathan had taken down his artwork from the guest cottage walls for the week. While he wasn't worried about the resident artist defacing any of it, it was all Catholic, so he figured it was more considerate to box it up. A crucifix, a few prints, and a half dozen icons would go back on the walls easily enough. "I might put up the crucifix."

Brooke looked aside and said nothing else.

Did she feel guilty about having him in the house? "What's wrong?"

"I don't want you to get mad, but can I ask you a question?"

Jonathan's mind raced through fifteen things he might be about to get angry over, but his mouth only said, "Sure."

"You kissed me on New Year's Eve. Why?"

He sat frozen, heart racing. *Deflect. Deflect.* "You thought I'd get angry at you for asking about that?"

She wrapped her hands around one another and jammed them between her knees, shoulders hunched. "It's not the kind of thing we talk about."

"What do we talk about?"

"Everything. We start a conversation about hiring a guy to snow plow the driveway and that morphs into a discussion about the American tax structure, why the continental United States doesn't have a fifth time zone, a quote from Søren Kierkegaard about time, and then oh, can you pick up milk on your way home?"

Jonathan shook his head. "It's like you know me."

"I'm part of these conversations, too, so yeah. We did that at one of the BCG meetings, remember, and poor Adrian was just staring like he wanted to ask for someone for a ride to Vermont where they're sane."

Jonathan tilted his head. "Are they sane in Vermont?"

"He's got a better chance of finding it there than at a BCG meeting." Her eyes narrowed. "But we don't talk about this kind of stuff. Relationship stuff. Because we don't have a relationship."

"I wouldn't say that." Jonathan's stomach was so tight it hurt. "We do well as friends, and I guess as semi-roommates, and this week we'll be real roommates."

Except for the pesky fact that he loved her, and the feeling wasn't easing off. The more they stayed with one another casually, the more it burned. He'd sit with her in the library to read, and he'd find himself watching her knit while she didn't realize. Her hands, her motions, the dark sweep of her eyes as she looked from the pattern to the project and back again. It was the casual familiarity that was doing him in, day by day, because the more he saw the real Brooke, the more he fell in love with her. She wasn't polishing herself up for him, and it wasn't an act.

She said, "I've had roommates before. I never kissed them."

Jonathan inclined his head. "Fair point."

"You said brother and sister when we got married, but I also never kissed my brother on the lips. So," she looked up, "I've been trying to figure out what it means. And I know you. Your gestures always mean something."

Jonathan flinched. "Always?"

She couldn't keep looking right at him, and he ached because again—the normalcy. The rhythm of the everyday. And at the same time, how wrong it felt to be in this position in the first place. None of this was what he intended it to be. He was going to end up hurting her. Brooke had been so afraid of losing him, but what if he ended up losing her, instead?

He said, "I'm sorry for not asking permission. I should have made sure you'd be all right with it. My judgment was shot because it was late and we were tired, and you were outside on the porch—"

...And she was so beautiful, and she was near, and he'd wanted to protect her, and they were alone for a sweet minute in the chilly midnight air...

She said, "But what did it mean?"

His lips were burning for her right now. "Are you angry at me?"

"I'm *about* to get angry at you because you keep dodging the question." Her voice was still low and even. "Why did you kiss me?"

Cheeks burning, he swallowed hard. "I really, really wanted to kiss my wife."

She looked right at him. Then, before he realized what she was doing, she put her hand behind his neck and her other hand on his shoulder. She leaned up close to him, face to face, while his heart pounded. "What if I wanted to kiss my husband?"

He drew her close, and she kissed him.

His eyes closed, and the warmth of her washed through him. Her touch, her body pressed against his, her presence. For a moment, she was everything.

She withdrew from him, looking down and aside.

They were alone in this huge house—alone on this huge bed—and Jonathan in his entire life had never felt more in danger. He was here to keep her safe, but instead, his behavior was jeopardizing them both. Even at that, though, he didn't want to stop whatever was happening.

He also couldn't be brave enough to continue. This shouldn't be happening at all.

Brooke took his hand, and he wrapped his fingers around hers. *I'm sorry. I'm derailing everything for both of us. We had an agreement, and I'm mucking it up.*

He couldn't even force out a joke to break the mood, something like, "Your brother never kissed you like that," because he craved the mood. He was in the front car of a roller coaster, at the top of the first hill where the back car is still locked into the gears but the front cars are hanging loose, filled with potential for the last of the restraints to let go. Momentarily the whole thing would rocket down the rails in exactly the way it was supposed to go. And, God forgive him, Jonathan was enjoying it.

But, oh, the guilt.

Instead he hugged her, pressing his face into her hair and closing his eyes. She was beautiful and delicate and brilliant, and he had all the grace of a rattling wooden amusement park car.

Brooke murmured, "I don't know what I want."

Jonathan's voice wavered. "Is it okay if I don't know what I want, either?"

She tensed. "Shouldn't somebody know?"

Jonathan's hands tightened. "In that case, I nominate you."

"Nomination declined." She pulled back from him. "You started it by kissing me. In fact, you started it by suggesting we get married. I demand you know what we want."

He laughed in surprise, and then she covered her face in her hands and laughed, too.

He said, "I thought I knew what I wanted, and then not only the rug but the whole floor got pulled out from under me. So as it turns out, I'm not good at knowing these things."

"We need a competent adult around to advise us. I already asked Lilah, and Lilah had no idea, either."

Jonathan swallowed. "Did she think you should have kicked me out for kissing you? Or is that why she told us to get a room?"

"I didn't even tell her you kissed me. She wanted me to talk to you because 'we need to communicate,' but it turns out, communicating isn't helping, either."

She stood up off the bed, and Jonathan fought the urge to pull her back, pull her toward him and kiss her again until she overwhelmed his physical senses and his common sense and finally his moral convictions. He had no idea how far he could push himself before he snapped. He had no experience, and here he was, plunging in the deep end.

He couldn't let her walk away, though. Not like this. "Then let's communicate."

She turned to him. "Is our original agreement still in force?"

Jonathan nodded. "Yes. In one year, you get the house."

She said, "Do you want to change any of the terms?"

How was she so focused? Jonathan had no resources right now to be logical, and here she was, talking about amending contractual terms. "You mean about living like brother and sister?"

She said, "Yes. To be clear, are you considering convalidating the marriage and then being married for real?"

Mouth dry, he shook his head. Convalidating the marriage so they were married in the Church sounded nice, but that made everything wrong from the start. Their marriage would have started wrong. It would be ending wrong. And as much as Jonathan loved Brooke, he didn't belong here. "I want to keep the terms as they are."

She let off a long breath. "Thank you. I guess we can communicate." She looked around. "It is a nice room, other than that weird door over the bed. Let me know if it opens and something comes out to talk to you."

It would probably tell Jonathan he was an idiot for getting entangled in this. But it didn't even need to because Father Tim had said from the start this would be difficult. Father Tim hadn't even realized Brooke would kiss Jonathan, or that Jonathan would have been ten days in love with her when she did.

CHAPTER SIXTEEN

The second Artist in Residence was a guy who stood six feet seven inches tall and created log statues with chainsaws. He had a square jaw, muscles for miles, a tattoo winding up the entirety of his left arm, and a set of black beads around his neck. He also, Lilah confided to Brooke after their tour of Brighthead, picked his own flowers to make potpourri and ran a feral cat rescue with his mother back in Massachusetts.

Brooke got one look at him and made an extra side tray of mac and cheese for his welcome dinner, since clearly this man burned calories faster than his dual rear-wheel Ford 350 burned gasoline. Yes, he'd brought his own tree trunks for carving.

"Thank you for your hospitality," he said after dinner. "I hope you don't mind if I get right to work."

Jonathan said, "Would you object if I watched? I can do a lot of things with a chainsaw, but I never saw anyone make art with one."

Off they went to the carriage house. Brooke inserted her ear plugs and stacked the dishes in the dishwasher before burying herself in the library to knit.

Jonathan returned after half an hour, chilled but exuberant. "It's amazing stuff. He started with a pine tree trunk, and even before I left, you could see the head of a dog forming."

Brooke popped out one of the ear plugs in time to hear most of the sentence. Jonathan finished up with, "The guy threw his jacket to the side and he's working with the carriage house wide open."

"He's his own heat source?" she ventured. "How does someone even get into doing chainsaw art?"

Jonathan said, "Maybe he'll tell us when he talks at the BCG meeting this weekend."

Brooke spent the night in her room, awakening every ninety minutes to the serenade of chainsaws. And to think, that guest at the November BCG meeting wondered if the neighbors would be disturbed by cars in the circular driveway.

At a quarter to six in the morning, Brooke awoke to hear —weirdly—no chainsaws. This was an excellent start to the day, and one she could heartily endorse.

Jonathan had likely slept better than she had. His room faced away from the carriage house, whereas Brooke's faced it dead-on. The granny flat would have been ground zero for sound, though. If Jonathan hadn't moved out for the residency, he'd have fled into the main house to sleep anyhow. And think about the artist, who'd have come into the main house at so-dark-thirty and then been awakened first by Jonathan at six o'clock and then by Brooke a little afterward.

Restless from the barrage of noise—even through her ear plugs—Brooke got out of bed and pulled on a handknit cardigan over her pajama shirt, and slippers over her wool socks, and fingerless gloves over her hands. Thus fortified, she headed downstairs.

Jonathan had unwittingly provided her a lot of information since New Year's. Yes, he'd informed her that he'd wanted to kiss her, and that he didn't want to be anything other than friends, (how was that supposed to work?) but from a practical perspective, he'd told her how he liked his coffee. She was awake, so she started it. Then she mixed up pancake batter, too, because she wasn't about to go back to sleep.

Were friends supposed to kiss one another? Brooke had never done that, but could she think of any friends who had? She'd never kissed Lilah. She barely kissed her own parents. Her brother got one hug at the beginning of a visit and a second one at the end. Jonathan's family was more affectionate, but Mrs. Levesque—Mary—had never kissed Brooke.

Given that, and given Jonathan's embarrassment, well, Brooke had to assume he'd suffered an unprecedented lapse in judgment. He'd been exhausted and excited, and when they were alone, he'd given in to an impulse he hadn't thought through. Now he wanted to forget it.

Unfortunately, Brooke had rather enjoyed that kiss. Prepared for it the second time, she'd closed her eyes and let his scent and his touch surround her, and for a moment, she'd felt something very close to yearning.

Not physical yearning. It had been a yearning entirely inside her heart, something she hadn't felt for years. She'd wanted him to love her. She'd wanted him to stay.

Except then he'd reiterated with conviction that he didn't want to. When the time was up, he still wanted to divorce.

It wasn't an unfamiliar feeling, but still, it hurt.

Jonathan arrived in the doorway, looking startled. "Why are you up?"

Brooke forced a smile which quickly turned into the real thing as she saw Jonathan's sleepy eyes and confused expression. "Mr. Chainsaw's dulcet tones aren't exactly good for sleeping. So, extra coffee?"

"I didn't hear him from my room." He looked over her shoulder at the griddle. "Might one or two of those pancakes be for me?"

She plated a stack for him while he got the butter and syrup, and then she poured coffee. The electric kettle bubbled, and she filled his thermos with boiling water, then got the last of the pancakes and joined him at the table.

He said, "Since he's here for a full week, and you intend not to sleep that whole week—does that mean I get coffee every day?"

"Don't push it." Brooke narrowed her eyes. "We've got a whole carriage house full of chain saws right now."

"Only two chain saws, two different sizes. Oh, but his compound miter saw has features I didn't know were possible." Then Jonathan must have seen the look on her face, because he raised a hand. "I'm not going to start doing chainsaw art! But I'm allowed to be impressed."

Right before Jonathan left, Brooke dumped the boiling water out of his thermos, filled it with the rest of the coffee, and sent him out the door.

Their agreement was still in force, but even so, Jonathan was funny and sweet and thoughtful. She should spend as much time with him as possible. And, if she got the chance, maybe he'd consent to kiss her again.

It wasn't even noon before Brooke had a very stern, unfriendly looking visitor at the shop. "I'm here for Lilah Marcille and Brooke Evart."

Oh, please. Was this a noise ordinance violation? "Welcome to Bright Stitches. How may I help you?"

"I'm Raymond Burgett, attorney for the Brighthead Garden Club. This is a cease and desist letter regarding you cutting down the apple orchard at the back of the Levesque property."

Brooke assessed his expression, decided this was the "serious face" from her map of faces, and then laughed loud and hard. As Lilah snatched the letter from his hand,

Brooke said, "You are such an idiot."

Now instead of serious, the lawyer looked affronted. "That's an historic apple orchard of note."

"That's an orchard on private property, and if we felt like cutting down every single tree and using the timber to put up a sign next to the mailbox saying, 'The Garden Club can pound sand,' we could do that. But just so you know, we haven't cut down a single branch." She pointed to the door. "We have all our leaves, and now you, too, can leave."

He huffed. "You were recorded cutting down trees last night, and there's a pile of logs beside the outbuilding."

"I'm sure there is, and we're going to cut down an equal number of trees tonight and every other night this week. Feel free to see yourself out the door."

Lilah said, "Also, before you try to sue us for cutting down trees, make sure any of the trees are actually down."

Brooke said, "If you're not familiar with tree law, cut-down trees will be horizontal, not vertical."

The lawyer said, "Chainsaws were heard all night long."

Brooke said, "Good day, Mr. Burgett. Any further conversation will take place through Theodore Hodges, my attorney."

She and Lilah folded their arms and watched in silence until he left.

The minute he was out the door, Brooke had her phone in her hands while Lilah was reading the letter. "I'm going to text Jonathan and make sure our guest wasn't taking down trees."

Lilah muttered, "It never occurred to me to include in the AIR contract that guests couldn't deforest the property, but for clarity's sake, I'll add that statement."

Immediately after, Jonathan texted back, "Meet me there," and Brooke left Lilah at the shop.

Jonathan met Brooke on the driveway, scanning her face for any kind of distress. "Did that lawyer harass you? Because I'm getting perfectly sick of these people."

Brooke's eyes were brilliant with anger, but her voice was controlled. "It was harassment of the legal sort. We only need to make sure the trees are safe."

They walked past the granny flat and the carriage house, both of which were dark. If Brooke wasn't exaggerating about their guest's all-night chainsaw party, it was no wonder he was still asleep. From there it was a quick walk to the apple orchard, and all looked fine.

"I knew he didn't cut anything," Brooke muttered. "The man arrived with a pickup full of logs." She folded her arms and tossed her head. "Oh, but you'll be pleased to learn this is *an historical apple orchard of note*, such that the Garden Club thinks we have blood on our hands for hewing them down."

Jonathan pulled out his phone. "What are the odds that the concerned Garden Club members are also members of the Historical Society?"

"The direct inverse of the odds that I'm going to bake an apple pie for the Historical Society's next meeting."

"Think of the special ingredients you could add to such a pie."

"That's exactly why no pie would be made. With my luck, their historic nondairy creamer would have spoiled, but they'd blame me for giving them all food poisoning."

Brooke stopped talking while Jonathan announced the date and time and that he was taking a video of the orchard for Raymond Burgett. She hated her own voice on recordings, so she'd be silent until he put away the phone. Back in high school, she'd had to leave the room when the

190

forensics teacher insisted on playing back their speeches for analysis. It didn't matter to her that Jonathan loved her voice. It wasn't the way she thought it ought to sound, and it made her anxious.

On the other hand, as someone who did love her voice, Jonathan was just as glad not to send any of her voice to the attorney who was about to get a whole lot of video dumped in his inbox.

Jonathan walked through the orchard, with Brooke keeping her steps quiet behind his. The air was frigid and dry, perfect for snow. The sky hung low and grey, and their breath frothed up around them.

This was a fool's errand, created for them by fools. And yet, walking with Brooke in the orchard was amazing in its own way. He led with the camera, picking his way with care, and together they traversed all three rows of apple trees.

At the end of the trip, he shut off the video, then turned to her. Her cheeks were pink with chill, her hair wind-swept, her scarf warm and tucked up around her chin.

She was gorgeous. If kissing her on New Year's Eve was amazing, kissing her now would be mind-blowing, with the orchard and the tantalizing foretaste of snow and all the pressure of the world around them. He and she in an oasis of dormant apple trees, away from artists and lawyers and crumbled dreams. They were here, one and one, with the afternoon settling around them in anticipation of an early nightfall.

Brooke kept gazing around. "I hadn't been back here much."

"We should pick apples next fall. Mom let the Garden Club pick apples this year, like Aunt Millie did, but since they're going to pitch a legal fit with no cause, I'll ask Hodges to send them a notice of criminal trespass so they can't set foot on the property next fall."

Jonathan put his phone back in his pocket and fumbled to pull his gloves back on.

Brooke held up her hands with the fingerless gloves.

"You should have worn yours."

"I keep forgetting them, and I didn't predict I'd be out here taking video." His fingers stung beneath the gloves, and he rubbed his hands together.

"You poor thing." She wrapped her hands around his, then tugged them toward her face. She breathed into her cupped palms.

Jonathan felt floaty. "You'd use your own breath to warm me up?"

He could stand forever in the chill and just have her near him, symbolically breathing her life onto him to restore warmth to the parts that felt numb and shut off.

"I just did, silly." She rubbed the fingers of one hand, then rubbed the other hand as well. "You need both hands to do your work."

They were right in front of each other again, and he only wanted her closer. Him and her, with the apple trees as their only witnesses. He felt guilty and confused. When she smiled at him, though, he felt peaceful because this was just right.

She put his hands together between her palms and held them tight. "Let me know when you're all warmed up."

"What if I never warm up?"

She frowned. "That's concerning, and I think we'd have to call an ambulance. Or a coroner."

What if he was meant to be with her?

The thought fell like a bomb into his brain. What if marrying Brooke had been his vocation all along?

He rejected it the instant he thought it. Maybe he didn't have a vocation to the priesthood, but that didn't mean he had to leap right into the first scenario that presented itself. Brooke was convenient. She was here, and she was an awesome listener, and she was beautiful. She knew all sorts of facts about the world, and she shared them with him because they were fun. Anyone would fall for her. That didn't mean everyone had a vocation to marry her. She deserved better than to have a man cling to her like a life raft because she was "convenient."

Jonathan pulled back his hands. "I'm warmed up now, thanks."

She tucked her own hands back in her coat pockets. "Then I need to get back to the shop. Lilah pulled an extra hour so I could verify that the trees weren't down. Can you send that video to her?"

"Yeah, but not from my phone. I'll get it on my computer and upload it from there."

Brooke put her hand through his arm as they walked back toward the driveway. "Send the video to the lawyer as well, just so he gets off our case."

"Speaking of criminal trespass, I'll also tell their lawyer on behalf of the trust that he isn't allowed on the property." He frowned. "I'm surprised he didn't serve my mother, since she's the executor."

Brooke shrugged. "It's not your mother they want to harass."

It was just harassment at this point, wasn't it? How unfair. And over nothing at all.

As they walked, Jonathan again felt that tug toward Brooke. She put her hand into his pocket alongside his own, and he held her hand in the pocket.

This was not going to end well. He'd already kissed her twice. If he didn't watch out, he was going to end up staying with her and then messing everything up even worse.

He'd been so sure about the priesthood. Since that had been wrong, how could he be sure about anything? It must be even harder to be sure of a vocation to marriage because not only did you have to discern whether you were called to marriage, but then you had to discern whom you were called to get married to.

Although the way people figured that out was to date. You'd date the person, and in doing so, you'd figure out whether you were compatible, whether your values matched, and whether your goals matched. You communicated to determine whether your neuroses interlocked well with theirs, or whether your mutual flaws all locked up with one another and stalled out the machinery.

At Brooke's car, again Jonathan felt that urge to kiss her before she left. Instead he said, "I'll text you after I've got the video somewhere you can access it."

He watched her drive off, then punched in the security code so he could flee inside.

The video moved from the phone to the computer in a minute and from there onto his cloud drive. It was easy to get the link to Lilah and to Brooke, and then Lilah thanked him and sent him an email address for the lawyer. Again, easy. Attached please find a video of the undisturbed apple orchard on the property at 28 Sky Ridge Drive on January 7th at two o'clock. You and all members of the Historical Society and the Garden Club are disinvited from setting foot on the property under penalty of criminal trespass. Have a nice day.

There. Now for the real issue. How does a man court his wife?

The internet wasn't going to cough up an answer, was it? The people who would ask that were probably trying to revive the wreckage of a marriage on the brink of dissolution, not discern a relationship's beginnings.

And then, it occurred to him. It occurred to him just how brilliant Brooke was.

He had her key. She'd told him he could go into her micro-apartment at any time. He called out from work for the rest of the day, then unlocked her door and looked on her bookshelf. Right there was the modern guide to arranged marriages.

How do you date your wife? You ask the thousands of people who've done it before you, and you learn what worked for them.

CHAPTER SEVENTEEN

Brooke changed her alarm to six o'clock in the morning. She moved her bagel cutter, her bagels, and her toaster oven downstairs, and while Jonathan had whatever breakfast he wanted (unfathomably, he changed it up every day), she would toast her bagel, drink her coffee, and see him off for his workday.

Jonathan didn't ask her why, which was good because she couldn't have answered with anything more than, "I like having breakfast together."

"I hope you'll kiss me again," would have sounded too forward. He hadn't made another move toward her, and he hadn't raised the subject again.

On Friday, Brooke closed Bright Stitches early enough to unfold thirty-two chairs in the basement so their guest could regale the BCG about chainsaw art. Lilah ordered pizzas and sodas, and that was Friday evening. The artist walked into the house hefting a log shaped like an elongated duck, and this leered over his shoulder from the corner while he proceeded to talk about how he'd gotten into creating art with chainsaws. "It turns out," he purred, "that when an instructor informs the class that not every tool is a good tool for creating art, some of the students will interpret that as a challenge."

Jonathan raised his hand. "Has the instructor since changed his mind?"

He chuckled. "After my tree-penguin won an award at the state fair, I delivered it to his house and installed it on his front lawn as a memento. He's never thanked me."

Brooke kept her face blank, hoping he wouldn't similarly express gratitude to the BCG.

Jonathan leaned closer to Brooke. "I hope he donates us the llama statue. I'll set it right at the edge of Sky Ridge Drive so the Historical Society can take us to court over that, too."

She ducked her head so Dear Mister Chainsaw wouldn't see her fighting laughter. He seemed like a gentle soul, but he also knew several tricks with sharp equipment.

On Saturday, after the fourth day of all-night chainsaws, Brooke and Jonathan folded up thirty-two chairs before she went to work. She spent a rather slow day helping customers and hoping that a benign chainsaw-malfunction would result in tonight's artwork being entirely theoretical.

Jonathan entered the shop half an hour before close, and Brooke battened down her smile before she tipped off the three ladies in the shop that this wasn't a business visit. "Did you spend all Saturday making more bowls?"

"You mean, bowling you over?" Jonathan smiled at Brooke, and it wasn't her imagination: one of the ladies shot her a glare. "As you can see, I've arrived empty-handed."

Pretending she didn't see the glare, Brooke said, "At least you won't have to leave empty-handed. Let me cut you a check for the bowls that sold since mid-December."

"Oh, good. The electric company has plans for that money."

Brooke snickered as she unlocked the drawer where they kept the checkbook. "It'll take a minute, so if you want to have a seat, I'm sure Mrs. Miller would love to teach you to crochet."

Mrs. Miller looked like she'd rather stick that hook right into Brooke's throat. Jonathan said, "Good plan. Maybe I'll understand whatever it is you're doing with those sticks."

He was here, and he was being friendly—and Brooke's hair was standing on end. Mrs. Miller said, "Jonathan, did you have a good Christmas with your family?"

Jonathan said, "I did, thanks! My sister got in on Christmas Eve so we could see the lights and go to Midnight Mass. We had Christmas dinner with my aunt and uncle and my cousins. How was yours?"

Brooke started writing the check for Jonathan's consignments. Mrs. Miller was a parishioner at Saint Lucy's. Was Mrs. Miller likewise a member of the Garden Club or the Historical Society? If both, then she could win the jackpot of reasons to hate Brooke.

Mrs. Miller said, "My son and daughter-in-law visited with their children. I'm sure your mother was delighted to have you back for the holiday."

Brooke's antennae were all the way up. Jonathan said, "Do you have pictures of your grandchildren?"

File that away as a conversational tactic: people liked talking about their families, but they loved showing them off even more. Mrs. Miller did get out her phone to show photos while Brooke set the check in a safe place on the counter, then rang out the third customer.

It was too early to close the shop. Brooke had her car. Why was Jonathan here?

Mrs. Miller finally said, "When are you going back to seminary?"

There it was—the trawl for fodder for the gossip machine.

Jonathan shook his head. "I'm not going back."

The other lady, who'd been quiet up until now, exclaimed, "Why not?'

Mrs. Miller looked at Brooke in a way that said she knew the reason Jonathan had left the seminary, and she found it entirely unpleasant.

Anything Brooke said would boil the hot water she was

already in, so she sorted today's mail. Bills, bills, advertisements, and fortunately no subpoenas. Also no apple fritter recipes from the Garden Club as an apology for piling onto the Historical Society's harassment campaign.

Jonathan sighed. "It was a difficult decision. My advisor and I went over a lot of things, but in the end, we decided I should go home. I'm at work with Wilson's again, doing cabinetry, and at least I got to spend the holidays with my parents."

The other lady said, "But I see you at church all the time."

Jonathan said, "I didn't lose faith. It just wasn't right."

Mrs. Miller pointedly turned her back toward Brooke, which was a relief rather than the offense she likely intended. "Have you spoken to Father Tim? I'm sure he went through all the same questions."

"We've talked a lot, trust me. I'm not sure what's going to happen next."

The second lady wrung her hands. "You should keep praying and try again."

Jonathan said, "You know the monastery Saint Lucy's uses for the annual retreat? I'm considering checking out their community."

Mrs. Miller said, "Maybe you're not supposed to be a diocesan priest. Maybe your vocation is to an order like the Dominicans or the Franciscans."

Jonathan straightened. "Maybe. We assumed a no on one was a no on all the orders."

Mrs. Miller added, "Whatever it is that's preventing you from being a priest, don't let anything or *anyone* stand in your way. "

Zing! That was Mrs. Miller taking a shot at Brooke over her shoulder, blindfolded, without even using a mirror. Except Jonathan said, "No one's preventing me. We're all doing our best."

Would these "customers" please leave already before their hatred swirled up into a roaring fusion reaction that swallowed the entire state of Maine? Because that, too, would put a quick end to Jonathan's trajectory toward the priesthood.

Mrs. Miller spoke like a woman who knew everything. It was helpful to have people like that around, especially when they were so willing to share their overabundance of knowledge. "You should get back into some ministries in the church, just so you can remind yourself why you started."

Jonathan said, "Father Tim has asked me to take over the bereavement group, and I'm thinking about it."

Brooke's head shot up. "You are?"

Both women looked at her, but Jonathan seemed sheepish. "I started reconsidering after Mass tonight. That's all."

Mrs. Miller said, "Why shouldn't he lead the group if Father Tim asked him to?"

Brooke pumped her head. "Of course he should if he wants to. Jonathan was emphatic when he said he wouldn't, so I was confused."

Mrs. Miller said, "And where did *you* spend Christmas?"

She must suspect Brooke had been lying in wait outside the doors at Midnight Mass, shivering in a tiny red dress and sparkly six-inch heels. "I did morning shift at the shop on Christmas Eve, and then drove to Boston to see my parents and my brother, same as I do every year." So sorry to deny Mrs. Miller her juicy gossip. "Whenever you're ready, I can check you out." She glanced at the clock, hoping that was subtle. Brooke was no good at subtle.

First the other lady brought up her yarn, and eventually Mrs. Miller did, too, though appearing unwilling to leave Jonathan undefended in Brooke's den of iniquity.

That brought Brooke close enough to end of day that she flipped the sign to "closed" and locked the door. "Oh, your check." She fetched it from the counter. "Why are you here? Truly bored after the Saturday vigil?"

Maybe Father Tim's homily had been about taking pity on people, so Jonathan thought, "I should run that group after all. And maybe spend time with my wife."

Jonathan flushed. "The chainsaws are already in full force, and the kitchen faces the carriage house, so I was wondering..." He looked aside. "Thanks for the check. I was thinking, since it's going to be so noisy, maybe, you know—"

What was happening here? He was clearly about to ask if they could grab dinner somewhere quiet, so why be this nervous?

He glanced at the check. "There's enough here for me to take you out to dinner, and there's that vegetarian place that opened in the plaza with the grocery store, so, if you wouldn't mind—"

Good grief, was Jonathan asking her on a date?

"—since, you know, we don't have plans, we could go for dinner."

She nodded. "Sure, that would be great. Let me get my coat. Should I ride in your car?"

Come to think of it, this might be Jonathan's very first date. Unless he counted taking her to the prom as a date. But that had been more like a favor.

If this was a date, did he plan to kiss her again at the end of it? He had no choice but to walk her to her door, since they were staying in the same house, but maybe he'd walk her right up to the micro-apartment and kiss her there.

In which case, yes, she did indeed hope this was a date.

Jonathan drove. He asked if the music was okay, and he told her she could adjust the heat. Was he being nicer than usual? Had he dressed up a bit?

In the restaurant, he was halfway through the menu before looking up with his eyes huge. "Is there food you feel comfortable eating here?"

Brooke patted his hand. "I'm picky, but I promise you, I can survive anywhere. I ate college dorm food for four years."

Jonathan sighed. "I should have had you look over the menu first."

She closed the menu. "I've decided to have the falafel, so you've already worried far too long."

They also decided on a cashew, cheese, and fruit plate for an appetizer, and Jonathan opted for a portabella burger.

"Why the veggie place?" Brooke asked. "Planning for Fridays in Lent?"

He shrugged. "I wanted to try someplace new, and Father Tim recommended here."

The tables were tiny, and everywhere the walls were draped with bead curtains. Brooke couldn't quite name the vibe, whether they were striving for peace or Nirvana or a new age of enlightenment for the whole planet. Their faint background music was full of chimes, and they featured an entire cider menu: apple cider, pear cider, cherry cider, and a few others. "What do you think cherry cider is?"

Jonathan said, "Let's find out," and when the server delivered the appetizer, he asked if they could have a sample of it. Brooke fought the urge to crawl under the table and hide, but the server agreed to this.

Also, the "cashew, cheese, and fruit plate" was *cashew cheese,* and fruit with crackers. So the cheese was made with cashew milk? Sure, it tasted great, but you could do that?

The server returned with a shot glass full of cherry cider. "Do you want to try it first?" Jonathan asked.

Brooke's bravery fled right out the window. You could ask for samples at a restaurant? Why had she never known this? Her grandmother would have beaten her with a stick if she'd even dared to ask, but here was the server, thrilled that these first-timers were trying something new. "Why don't you try it?" Brooke ventured, so Jonathan sipped, then passed her the glass.

Now she was twice as unsteady because you weren't supposed to share glasses, either. Except a kiss would be his lips on hers, so his lips on a glass followed by hers on a glass wasn't that much weirder, was it? She braced herself and tried the cider.

She hesitated. "A bit bitter, but pretty good."

As though all this were perfectly normal, Jonathan said, "We'd like two cherry ciders, please," and the server left as Brooke wondered how to steady the boat under her. It was all getting to be too many unusual things all at once. To tally: the ladies of Brighthead hating her for stealing a priest, followed by Jonathan asking her on a date, followed by a completely new restaurant where all the food was unfamiliar to her, followed by expanded rules for dining out. And a new drink to go with the new food. She needed a touchstone. Instead, she clenched one hand under the table and began running her fingers over the back of it with the other.

She took a deep breath. "What changed your mind about the support group?"

Jonathan shrugged. "I haven't been volunteering with the church since I returned, and that was always a staple. Teen group, doing the readings at Mass, clean ups and fund-raisers, all that. I thought it would hurt if I volunteered because it would remind me of all the things I wasn't going to be doing, but Father Tim needs someone, so I may say yes."

Brooke said, "You still don't know anything about bereavement."

Jonathan sighed. "Father Tim promised it isn't about giving advice. I have to prepare the coffee, make everyone go around the room and say their names, and then let them talk."

The server delivered the cherry cider and let them know their meals would be ready soon. The place was relatively crowded, and Brooke rubbed her fingers through each other harder, then jiggled her leg.

Breathe. Jonathan was here, and he knew what he was doing.

He said, "Also, I was thinking... I don't know if you'll object to this, and it's totally fine if you do, but it did work well this week to have the resident artist in his own place. I know neither of us wanted it that way at the start—"

He was about to ask to live in the main house, and Brooke's brain leaped ahead by several bounds to figure out why the very request was unnerving him. Although she wasn't one to talk, since this restaurant was unnerving her.

"—but if you think it would be okay, I was thinking maybe it works better if I'm not moving back and forth between the buildings every time we host a resident artist, so maybe I should keep staying in Aunt Millie's room."

She'd keep waking up early and making coffee with him. She'd get her bagel toasted while he said morning prayer, and then she'd sit with him while he had his cereal or a bagel of his own. He'd come back downstairs, dressed in jeans and work boots and a flannel shirt. She'd see him off every morning. It was a little more time they'd have together.

He looked up, anticipating her refusal. Brooke said, "I'm fine with it if it's easier for you."

Their meals arrived. Her portion of falafel seemed like what Jonathan would have cooked for the entire seminary class. She'd never finish this. Jonathan's portabella burger looked good, and he cut off a piece for her to try. She gave him some of her falafel and tzatziki sauce. "This is a nice place. Thank you for suggesting it."

"Thank you for coming with me." He looked more relaxed now than when they'd started, which was just as well because his tension had been amplifying Brooke's.

They'd be living together. The arranged marriage book talked about the adjustments you needed for that, but a lot of them weren't necessary. They had separate beds, separate bathrooms, and didn't even wash their laundry together. Except now, they could do more things side-by-side. She'd wake up in the morning knowing he was here. Not just nearby, but actually here.

She looked aside. He was doing a lot for her. She ought to do something for him, too. "I know you're not pushing for this, but do you think it would be okay if I started going to church again with you?"

He stopped mid-bite, then swallowed fast. "Sure. I mean,

you probably should talk to Father Tim, but otherwise, yeah. Um... If I go to the seven o'clock Mass, is that too early for you?"

She'd begun waking up at six every day. "I can do that." The church ladies were going to have a righteous fit when they saw the pair of them sitting in the same pew. But church together was something they used to do in high school, so it was something they could do again now.

Jonathan looked unnerved and pleased at the same time. "Since you asked me what changed my mind, what changed yours?"

"We used to go back in high school." She put more falafel on his plate. "I'm not going to finish all this myself, so we might as well work on it together."

A perfect gentleman, Jonathan drove Brooke back home, which was probably less romantic because it was also his. Still, he opened the car door for her, and he opened the house for her, and he ushered her inside.

The chainsaws were roaring. It still wasn't clear whether Jonathan had used that as an excuse for a date he wanted anyhow or whether he'd genuinely needed an escape. But then he took her coat to hang up. "Do you want to watch a movie?"

Dinner and a movie sounded very much like a date. Really, Brooke just ought to ask him what was going on, since men entering monasteries next year shouldn't be dating the wives they intended to divorce in ten months.

On the grounds that you don't ask questions you don't want the answers to, she only said, "Which one?"

The chainsaws reverberated through the living room enough that they had to crank the TV volume. "This isn't working," Brooke said. "I'm sorry."

They paused the video and tried to figure out a better solution. Move the TV and all the equipment into the library? This was Brooke's TV, so there wasn't another in the micro apartment. Which left the one in Jonathan's bedroom.

He looked super uncomfortable. Brooke said, "It's a big bed. We can both sit on it at the same time."

That didn't make him less uncomfortable, but upstairs, Brooke rearranged things so he was on one side, and she was on the other, with the bolster pillows lined up between. It was just like sitting on opposite sides of the couch. She set her knitting on her lap, a clear sign of "do not touch me." Moreover, this was an action movie with some comedy. If Jonathan was concerned about her being overcome with passion, he could rest easy.

The movie opened with a bang, but after the first act, Brooke got bored. She was full of food and short on sleep (those extra morning hours had to come from somewhere) and eventually she was too tired to keep knitting. She settled further down the bed and watched with her head on the pillow.

This was a good date. Jonathan may have felt like he had no idea what he was doing, and maybe he'd cobbled together the entire plan at 7:35 before springing it on her at 7:45, but it was still a good date. He'd taken her someplace nice, and now they were watching a movie, and it was all very good.

Brooke startled awake when the knitting needle moved out of her fingers. Jonathan jerked away, exclaiming, "I'm sorry!"

She sat up in his bed, head muzzy. The TV was off. She had her yarn ball clutched in one hand.

Jonathan had changed into pajamas. "You fell asleep, so I was going to take the couch, but I thought sleeping with a knitting needle would get you stabbed."

He looked unnerved. Gingerly, she sat up. "I'm sorry. I missed most of the movie."

"You didn't miss much. It wasn't that great." He set her

knitting on the dresser. "You can go back to sleep."

She got up. "You can have your bed. I'll go to my room."

And then, like a gentleman, he walked her home. At the micro-apartment door, she faced him. "Thank you for everything."

He gave a nervous smile. "Thank you, too."

"But there's one thing more to make it a perfect date."

His eyes widened, but she'd been looking forward to this all night. She was not going to let him drop her off without a farewell kiss.

She put a hand behind his neck, stretched toward him, and guided his mouth to hers.

He drew out the kiss for longer this time, as if he'd learned from the first two. His lips were soft, his touch gentle. Then she stepped away, unlocked her door, and stepped inside. "Good night, fascinating spouse."

He looked pleased and baffled. "Goodnight yourself, esteemed wife."

She stepped inside and locked both locks.

CHAPTER EIGHTEEN

The BCG's third Artist in Residence was a quilter who regarded the guest cottage and declared that yes, she could use this space, and could Jonathan please carry her sewing machine and serger from the car? And would he mind shutting the door on his way out?

No, Jonathan would not mind. He was just as glad to be parted from that artist.

They rolled through the rest of January and February,. Jonathan awoke every morning to find Brooke getting the kitchen ready for breakfast. They started the day together, then split off to do their own things for work, and at night he'd get home and maybe get dinner started, maybe reheat something. (Her idea of prepping meals and reheating them was clever.) After dinner, they'd spend time together in the library or watching TV.

She said his wood-turning skills were fascinating, but hers? Watching her going to town on graph paper or making arcane crochet maps out of arrows and Ts and loops was breathtaking. She'd hover over the table, sketching and planning, then doing mock-up stitches. There was math and there were mean words directed at the yarn and there were "stitch dictionaries," and then she'd laugh and be pleased. For a few minutes.

She'd finished the infinity scarf with his black cherry needles, which after so much knitting had conformed to the shape of her hands. He hadn't realized that would happen, but they'd yielded ever so slightly.

Brooke said, "Lilah says yarn absorbs your emotion, but I think the needles absorb it more."

Jonathan prompted, "Did they absorb my emotions when I made them?"

She wrinkled her nose. "Maybe. Maybe every time I knit with them, I read your mind just a little."

Maybe a little. Maybe when she'd kissed him, it was because the needles told her how he felt.

Brooke's newest design was a crocheted shawl for Lilah's wedding. "We got inspired after Shelly Novick knit her own wedding dress, and all three of us are participating." She looked pleased. "My design. Lilah's dyeing the yarn, because of what I said before about emotions soaking into yarn. And Natalie's going to crochet it."

Jonathan said, "And then when Natalie marries Colin, she'll wear it, too?"

Brooke nodded. "That's the idea."

Brooke was the only one without a use for that shawl. At least, not yet. Maybe someday. If it hurt her, she didn't mention it.

Brooke set up Jonathan's prayer corner in his bedroom. She nailed up a crucifix over the kneeler, then experimented with placements by laying pictures on the furniture. She giggled that nothing would irritate Aunt Millie more than all these Catholic pieces, but Jonathan had another thought. Namely, if he and Brooke were to start anything in here, at least he'd have a crowd of saintly onlookers to deter them.

The TV in his room was, it turned out, the much better TV. They watched from his bed, and (saints aside) that got less uncomfortable the more often they did it.

Valentine's Day posed a challenge, but Brooke suggested ordering in and streaming a concert from one of Jonathan's favorite bands. She refused flowers, so instead he bought her a book about archaeology. She got him a book of meditations on the history of wood in colonial America, which Jonathan hadn't even suspected would exist at all. They spent the end of Valentine's Day by the fire pit in the snow, each of them reading under a throw blanket with Brooke leaning against his chest and occasionally telling him about an interesting paragraph.

After their second date, Brooke began calling them adventures, which relaxed Jonathan because that gave them leeway to get things wrong. Adventures weren't always dinner. They went to an ice castle exhibit and free concerts at the public libraries. Brooke was clever at finding interesting things to do, and sometimes they went with Lilah and Emerson.

At the end of every adventure, Brooke would kiss him. Jonathan enjoyed the adventures, but he always looked forward to the kiss.

And then there was one adventure, one boring movie, that ended up with a lot of kissing and then a lot of confusion, and Jonathan tried to be more disciplined because he didn't want to hurt Brooke by pushing her too hard. Yes, she'd enthusiastically consented when hand-holding turned to cuddling, which turned into them lying side-by-side, but then he'd forced himself to turn away and get calm. No matter how much their not-a-marriage felt comfortable and sustainable, they weren't really married.

That had to be wrong. The right path for your life should involve sacrifice and hard work, but there wasn't hard work here. Instead there were vigorous conversations, the easy routine of breakfast and dinner, and Brooke coming over to him every so often with her phone screen lit up so she could read him an interesting fact about sourcing shoe leather or the line of succession during the Ming dynasty.

If dating her should discern his path, it wasn't helping.

Work continued on the carriage house whenever the BCG got any money. The floor, the tables, the lighting—those were easy, and they managed all that with donations from the members, both time and materials. No skylight, though.

Brooke started accompanying Jonathan to St. Lucy's on Sundays, and on Tuesdays, Jonathan took over leading the bereavement support group. Oh, the awkwardness—at first. The people were in need, though, and Jonathan warmed right up to meeting the need. They came five or six to each meeting, although not always the same members. Several were widows or widowers. A woman was there who'd lost her daughter, then two years later, lost her brother. One woman spent her entire first session unable to speak. The next week, she said her name, but nothing else. The third week, she told her story: at age forty-five, her husband had died, and she was too traumatized even to leave the house. This support group was the only place she'd been able to go alone since the funeral.

It was good to be here. There was work to be done.

In mid-March, Father Tim called Jonathan's cell and asked to speak to Brooke, and the next week, she subbed for the musician for the early Sunday Mass. Jonathan resumed doing the readings.

Was this right? Here he was, inculcating himself in parish life again, when he might uproot after the end of the year. He'd miss the community. Even worse, he'd miss Brooke. He'd miss their late-night conversations or her random factoids or the way she wore fingerless gloves pretty much all the time. He'd have to make his way through a life where he didn't walk into a room to find graph paper covering the table and Brooke muttering imprecations about invisible increases and how to purl five together through the back loop.

The church ladies wanted him to go back to seminary and "just finish up." They were sure he'd make a good priest if he pushed through whatever it was. They handed him brochures for religious orders. "Don't let anyone divert your vocation," they'd scold, as though Jonathan hadn't fought to force God not to divert his vocation.

Brooke stayed out of those conversations. When they divorced, it was going to be hard on her, too. As much as Jonathan was getting used to her, surely she was also used to him. She'd made him part of her routine. Come December, the house would be empty, and she'd be back to living in that one room.

Late in March, the parish held its annual retreat at a monastery an hour from Brighthead. "You should give them a dry run," Brooke said, habitually avoiding his eyes. "If they're your runner-up vocation, it makes sense to scope them out."

The thought was uncomfortable. It was too much like seminary—and what if the answer was still no? What if the monks hated being his second choice? "I've been on retreats before."

"As a pre-priest." She was far too sensible. "Not as a pre-brother."

Jonathan said, "You come, then, too."

Brooke gave a subtle roll of her eyes. "I've got no idea what God's calling you to."

He replied, "But I value your opinion."

They left on a Friday night, stayed in separate cells, then on Saturday and Sunday attended the talks and the public Liturgy of the Hours. Jonathan visited the monks' woodworking shop, then spent an hour talking to their vocations director and Father Tim together.

The vocations director said, "We find the beauty of life in the ordinary. Many times, the ordinary is what we've been put on Earth to do. There are sacrifices, but every life has its sacrifices. The question is whether these are your sacrifices to make."

There was peace here. It wouldn't be a bad place to spend the rest of his life, even if he couldn't be a priest.

On the drive home, he said, "What do you think?"

Brooke sounded subdued. "I think you'll be happy with

the routine and the work they're doing."

He said, "And did you have a good time?"

She chuckled. "It's weird traveling, you know? I've never gone anywhere, just here or Boston. Even for college, I stayed in Maine. It was fun visiting somewhere new."

By the time they'd gotten home, Jonathan had a plan.

He texted Lilah, who immediately looped in Natalie, but made a stipulation. "Tell her first. Brooke doesn't do well with surprises."

Jonathan agreed to tell Brooke before finalizing anything, and then he got on his computer.

CHAPTER NINETEEN

After a Mass where Brooke had played the piano and Jonathan had done the readings, she hung out in the church hall cleaning up from the coffee and donut social. It was easier doing this than getting the evil eye for leaving with Jonathan in front of the judgmental church ladies. She'd rather put trash into bins than deal with their assumptions.

She wasn't stealing a priest. For one thing, Jonathan didn't want to be stolen, remaining firm about staying the course on their agreement. For all that he was dating her, (and kissing her once a week,) he still planned to divorce her in November, spend Christmas with his parents, and enter a monastery in January.

Even to Brooke, the monastery sounded enticing. Every day, there'd be the same routine of awakening, rising, meeting with the community, dispersing to work, eating again, and going to bed. Every day, punctuated by church bells followed by ritual prayers you could look up and follow, all the variety coming in the form of the prayers but everything otherwise the same. It felt safe and predictable, and if Brooke had felt even the slightest call to a religious life, she'd already have been filling out applications for any community that would take her.

She couldn't compete with that. She wouldn't even try to compete for Jonathan against both God and the Church. But until that time, she could join him at Mass.

Jonathan returned from dumping the last of the coffee out of the urns. "We're all set in the kitchen."

Brooke finished pushing chairs back under tables. "We're set out here, too. Is it safe to go?"

Jonathan laughed as though she were joking. But of course it was safe for him. The church ladies loved him.

In the parking lot, they headed for her car. Jonathan said, "If you don't mind, I have an errand to run before we go home."

Had they run out of milk? Maybe his parents wanted him to pick up something. Jonathan directed her toward the Main Street municipal parking lot. There, she pulled out her knitting, but he said, "Come with me," so she shoved it back in the bag and followed him onto the sidewalk.

There were a couple of law offices on Main Street. Had the Historical Society again made its presence known? But no, instead he opened the door to an office she'd never paid attention to. *A travel agency?*

A woman met them before a wall of posters with beaches and mountains. "Jonathan Levesque? So glad to meet you!" She shook his hand, then turned to Brooke, who introduced herself with a flustered mumble. "Yes, Brooke Evart. I'm excited to meet you, too. Come on, let me show you what I've put together."

Brooke looked at Jonathan for her cue. He was beaming.

Oh, no, was he planning a pseudo-honeymoon? She didn't want to go anywhere. Did he want to drag her to the Vatican so they could push through the crowds to hear about saints and look at the relic of the wooden table where Saint Peter used to pray? Because no. Brooke didn't even have a passport.

She stalled out rather than move forward. "What are you

doing?"

Taking both her hands in his, Jonathan said, "I planned something for you, but I'm not confirming it until you give your approval."

She shook her head. He lowered his voice. "Please. Hear me out, and then think about it."

Her legs were rooted in place. It hurt to look into Jonathan's eyes, but she couldn't look away while the world turned into static. What had he done? What did he want her to do?

The travel agent handed something to Jonathan, who handed it to Brooke.

She found herself staring at a folder with a familiar logo splashed across the front, along with people in character costumes, and above that, "Welcome to your Paxley Vacation!"

She kept staring at it while the pieces clicked together in her mind, one after the next. Paxley vacation. Brochure. Travel agency. Jonathan.

No. No, he hadn't.

Jonathan rested a hand on her hair. "For your birthday, I want to take you to Paxley in Orlando."

He was smiling, his eyes tender, his smile tentative.

She looked back at the folder. It was packed with paperwork and brightly colored brochures. There was an itinerary and an explanation about a meal plan and a separate itinerary for flights. Right around her birthday.

This was real. He wanted to do this.

He put his arm around her. "Come sit down. Everything is reserved, but not paid for. Jen is going to talk us through the whole thing, and then you can tell us whether to put down the deposits."

Her knees were locked. When she spoke, her voice cracked. "We can't afford this."

Jonathan chuckled. "Aunt Millie left me a chunk of change. I can afford it."

Brooke's eyes watered. "That money was for you."

Jonathan said, "And I choose to use it to annoy her."

That was startling enough that Brooke laughed silently, her shoulders shaking.

"See, I knew I could make you laugh. Take a look. I think you're going to love what we planned."

Jen the travel agent introduced herself as a Paxley Trip Specialist, which Brooke had never known was a thing because she'd never considered a Paxley trip a possibility. Jen explained the way the admission tickets worked and how they'd divide their time between the different Paxley parks. Jonathan wanted them to stay on one of the resorts within Paxley itself, and he'd also opted for a meal plan. Jen had combined offers and discounts to get them reservations at character breakfasts, as well as VIP seating for one of the fireworks displays. They'd be able to have their souvenirs sent directly to their hotel room rather than lugging them around the park, and then the hotel could box them up to mail home. They'd wear bracelets that fast-tracked them onto some of the rides. The park would take photos for them and upload them all to their account. At the end of the day, they could go back to their resort hotel and crash-sleep until doing it all over again.

Brooke's hand tightened harder and harder on Jonathan's. Because—

Why are you doing this?

A gift this huge—a time commitment this long—and going with her to a place he'd never had the slightest desire to go—? All that was something you should do for someone you loved, not your contractual partner whom you kissed once a week.

Jonathan's small gestures always meant something because he put thought into everything. A gesture this huge—it meant everything. Was he offering her more than a trip to Paxley? Was he offering her his love?

Jen said, "On Monday, before five p.m., I'm going to need a final yes or no. Jonathan said you'd need time to think about it, but unfortunately I can't hold the reservations longer than that."

Jen had even selected a specific room. It was

overwhelming—so much information, so much surprise.

Jonathan put an arm around Brooke's shoulders. "If there's anything you want to do that we missed, or anything you don't want to do, we can change it."

One after next, the brochures showed families looking happy, characters in costume, rides and photo opportunities and fine dining and plush hotel rooms. It was everything she loved. And she could do it with Jonathan.

With someone she loved?

Yes, with someone she loved. Someone who loved her. Maybe he didn't know it, but he was doing something loving toward her.

Brooke's parents had sent a picture of them and Gavin at one of these events. Brooke had never mentally inserted herself into that picture. Postcards had arrived after her parents had returned from Florida, and she'd read them in her grandmother's kitchen, then magneted them to the refrigerator with the pictures facing the metal doors so she didn't have to see what couldn't be hers..

That could be her and Jonathan. She had only to say yes.

Yes to flying and standing in line and sleeping in a weird room and getting used to unfamiliar noises. Yes to all the things her grandmother thought were childish and her mother never acknowledged at all. Yes to the things Jonathan had never given a second thought to, until the moment he saw Brooke loved them, at which point he'd begun to love them, too.

He was offering love. She needed only to say yes to that, too. Say yes, accept it, and hope he realized that's what he was doing.

"Yes." Her hands tightened on the folder. It was selfish to say it, and she was going to do it anyhow: take his trip, take his heart, and offer her own. "Go ahead and book it."

CHAPTER TWENTY

If Jonathan had even the slightest thought that this wouldn't be worth it, he'd lost that thought when Brooke packed and re-packed her suitcase, telling him Paxley trivia the whole time.

It turned out she'd never flown, so through that whole process, he'd guided her and kept preparing her for what the next step would be.

For their first day at the park, Brooke created a mini-itinerary that should have them hitting all the most important points, and in the best possible order. "Some land wars weren't waged with this precision," Jonathan mused.

"We have only four days. We need to make them count." And then, with the specificity of a pattern designer, she proceeded to make them count. She knew which rides to go on, planned how long each would take so they'd be able to get to their meals, and also set aside time for her emotional shut-down breaks. The park had set up a scavenger hunt, looking for special hints and hidden surprises, and she worked that into the itinerary as well. They saw exhibits and shows, and they went on the rides, and they spent money on souvenirs.

Brooke was delight itself, at least until the moment she got tapped out and needed to sit somewhere to recover. Then after ten minutes, she'd be delighted again until the next time she tapped out.

Brooke wanted pictures with the characters. She wanted to know everything about the "behind the scenes" work. She took a thousand pictures and discarded half while standing in line for a ride, just to make room for the next thousand.

She took pictures of him, and he of her. He made sure to get plenty of selfies together, and they had the park take pictures of them side-by-side in front of all the landmarks. She sent pictures to Lilah and Natalie, and that was only the first day. They ate dinner at one of the better restaurants, then used the hotel pool until they were both so tired they could barely stagger back to the room and sleep.

Their room had two beds. It would have been cheaper to get a single king, but no. At home they watched TV together in Jonathan's bed, but so far he'd held out against sleeping in the same bed. He didn't trust himself. She was beautiful and warm and kissable, and she'd never consented to being a tool for his physical gratification. They weren't married. He was leaving Brighthead next year.

The next day, they hit a different area of the park, again with a battle plan and a strategy. Strangely, Brooke seemed to have factored in that they'd be tired and sore from the day before, so this involved more sitting and watching, and more frequent breaks. They ended the day earlier, ate and swam in the early afternoon, and then headed back to watch a parade and a light show.

Every penny had been worth it, and it hadn't even been his money to begin with.

The hotel rooms had channels that showed all the Paxley content, so Brooke stayed up watching it at night. When she talked, she smiled.

It was a grave injustice that her parents hadn't brought her as a kid, but their neglect had paved the way for Jonathan to bring her now, which meant he'd gotten to share her joy. In a way, maybe that made up for it.

Before they went to sleep, Jonathan reached for her hand across the space between the beds. He'd given her all his extra pillows, leaving her snug in a tall nest. "Are you having a good time?"

She half-lowered her eyes. "I am having the best time."

He shut the lights, warm inside.

Day three. He'd scheduled a lunch with several cartoon characters. After that, they went back to the higher-end souvenir shops, and Brooke went wild. He'd never seen her just spend like that. Normally she'd buy something only after deliberation and comparison-shopping. Most of her clothes were several years old. (He knew she'd worn some of those T-shirts during high school.) She had exactly as many pairs of shoes as she needed.

Here? She bought artwork, a mug, a stuffed animal, more stuffed animals, and a felt banner. He suggested jewelry, but she didn't want that. Neither did she want clothing. What she did want was art.

He didn't look at the total as the cashier tallied it up. "You're going to need a bigger wall."

Brooke had them scan her resort bracelet so it would all get charged to the room and appear on their table as if by sorcery. "Fortunately, it's a big house."

"You'll need to move out of that one room," Jonathan teased.

Looking him right in the eyes, she winked. "Maybe I will."

He went warm inside.

Now they held hands while walking or while waiting in line. She leaned against him when they watched a performance. The longer the day went, the more he found himself reaching for her, too. And kissing. She kissed him when they got off a scary ride. He kissed her when she was nervous to let a kangaroo eat out of her hand. On a bridge surrounded by fountains, they kissed each other.

This was their last full day here. Tomorrow, they'd have the morning, but they'd leave for the airport in the early afternoon. At sunset, with his arms around her, they watched the parade and the fireworks a second time. After the bursts had ended and the music faded, Brooke kissed him with an energy that ricocheted all the way through his body. Brooke seemed quietly exhausted as they rode the shuttle back to the resort.

They snuggled in her bed to watch one final film, and it was just right. Their last night here. She cuddled him with that pillow fort shielding them both from the world, watching with her head on his shoulder, holding his hand, breathing lightly. The film would have a happy ending. They all did. Jonathan wanted her to be happy like that, too. If only.

When the credits rolled, she didn't move away from him. He shifted, but then she leaned over him—and he flattened into the pillows because she was about to climb on top of him...only instead, she took the television remote off the nightstand to turn it off.

He didn't want to move as she put it back, again with her body brushing over his. Or rather, he did want to move —but move toward her rather than away. She pulled up the blanket and snuggled him with her arms around his waist and one leg over his.

She closed her eyes, and Jonathan was lost. He reached up just enough to turn off the light, then sunk back into the pile of pillows and blankets.

"Thank you so much." Her voice was a breath in his ear. "Thank you for bringing me here. It's been the best."

His heart pounded. "I'm so glad."

She nuzzled him, and his skin was like lightning. "Everything you've done for me... You're wonderful. I love you."

He closed his eyes. "I love you, too."

In the dark, she wrapped even tighter around him. "I love you so much. Don't go."

He didn't want to go. She was warm and relaxed. His body ached, and he closed his eyes. He could smell the hotel shampoo and the extra-clean bed sheets, and they were tangled up with one another.

Brooke nuzzled his jaw with her lips, then guided his face toward hers and kissed him. Kissed him gently. Then she pulled back a hair's breadth and whispered, "Good night."

Good night was—impossible. Impossible. He wanted her more than he'd wanted anything in his life, and she was right here. He couldn't focus on anything else.

In his arms, she was asleep in minutes. He lay with her head resting on his chest, just above a heart on fire.

For the past two nights, he'd lain in the opposite bed, hearing her breathe and feeling comforted by her presence. Now she was pressed against him, her breath light over his neck in a sweet rhythm, and he absolutely wanted her.

How could he possibly be loved by someone so beautiful and sweet and thoughtful? He shouldn't be in a plush bed with someone so tender-hearted. His plans had him in a narrow bed at a seminary, aiming for a life of celibacy and prayer. His alternative plans had him pointed in a similar direction. Instead, somehow he was here, cuddled with Brooke.

He put his hand in her hair. He tucked her closer to himself, then turned just a bit to nuzzle her temple.

This didn't feel wrong, except for the times it felt all wrong. But then the day caught up to him, too, and his thoughts kept falling apart in his mind. The soft bed, the warm blankets, the amazing woman at his side—and finally, sleep.

Then—bliss.

He awoke with a start, burning with disgust at himself and grief for what he'd just done to Brooke, having sex with her without being married, his mind wrestling with apologies and the shock of having just given Brooke his virginity—and then he realized no, wait, no, it was okay, he'd been dreaming. It was a dream. He was in her bed, yes, but she'd rolled away from him. They were both fully clothed. He'd had a dream.

Careful not to awaken Brooke, he made his way out of her bed and into the bathroom.

Regret ghosted around him under the buzz of fluorescent lights. His self-discipline wasn't going to keep holding. At some point, he was going to let himself off the chain for real while he was awake, and then he'd break her heart. Last night, he'd thrilled to think she was about to lie on top of him. When they went home, it would be more of the same: watching movies in his bed followed by breakfast together in the morning, and how long until they just skipped a step and stayed together during the time in between?

Had Father Tim said it would be more difficult than anticipated? He should have said impossible. Jonathan had been co-existing with his love for Brooke since Christmas, and here it was May, and she'd fallen in love with him, too.

He was breaking her heart. Dating her was supposed to be a test-run to discern a marriage vocation, but he'd been selfish. He hadn't considered that while he was test-running his vocation, she was test-running it, too. She'd given him space in her heart, and at every step of the way, she'd accepted him exactly as he was, limitations and all.

This wasn't fair, neither to him nor to her. Falling in love now made parting next November all that much harder. It would have been easy to dissolve a legal marriage and leave the friendship intact, then go before an annulment board with all the documentation to prove a "defect of form," and solidify the case by stating the marriage was never consummated. That annulment would be a rubber stamp.

Leaving her now, if she'd fallen in love with him? It would hurt them both. Her letters would be painful for her to write and for him to read.

It had been easy to consider a life of celibacy when he'd never dated and never fallen in love. That was part of his plan: keep to the narrow path to make the sacrifice straightforward. It made no sense to build a future with someone and then destroy it. He should have stuck to the plan.

Jonathan went back to bed. To his own bed. The cold sheets were lonely without a pillow fort and his sleeping wife, but it was where he belonged.

He couldn't get back to sleep. His mind whirled.

You should only sacrifice good things, and you can only be tempted by good things. That was a given, as far as Jonathan was concerned. When you donate to the food pantry, you pull the good stuff off your shelves. Ancient farmers who sacrificed crops would sacrifice "the first fruits." All good stuff. Sex and marriage were good things, so it made sense to sacrifice those to become a priest. Not everyone would agree, and that was fine, but that was Jonathan's understanding. Sex was tempting precisely because it was a good thing.

He was supposed to be discerning his vocation, not distracting himself with dates and kisses and cuddles. He shouldn't be playing with Brooke's emotions, and then playing with his own all week, and then on Sunday reading for the Mass and trying not to stumble over a prayer for increased vocations to the priesthood and religious life.

What if...? And what if, and what if, and what if?

He awakened again when he heard Brooke getting out of bed, but he kept his eyes closed and hoped she wouldn't join him. Hoped she would. Wished he could just have had what he wanted and not be responsible for deciding any longer.

CHAPTER TWENTY-ONE

The longer their final day went, the more Brooke felt uneasy, as if Jonathan were pulling away. Except, last night, he'd said he loved her.

Her heart felt as if it were completely outside her body, absorbing Jonathan and everything around him. He loved her. He was married to her, but also, he loved her? What did that mean for the future? Did that mean they weren't going to divorce after all? Or did that mean he didn't want to ruin her birthday by letting her down gently? If she hadn't reiterated how crazed she was feeling for him last night, would he have added, "But Brooke, I love everyone"?

She'd never felt like this before, being given so much space by a boyfriend to figure out her own feelings. Always there had been pressure: pressure to kiss him, pressure to declare her love, pressure to give whatever gratification he wanted. Jonathan had asked of her exactly nothing. Where she felt weak, he stepped in to strengthen her. When she saw him faltering, he let her bolster him without shame.

He'd accepted all the idiosyncrasies that everyone else belittled her for. If she'd freaked out because of a guest at her grandmother's house, her grandmother would have yelled at her. Her roommates would have told her to get over herself. Even Lilah sometimes got short with Brooke when Brooke didn't understand a subtle interaction Lilah expected should be obvious. Meanwhile, Jonathan had worked around Brooke's quirks and made sure she felt safe. Somehow, in the middle of all that safe feeling, Brooke had also felt seen. And then appreciated. And then loved. And then she'd fallen in love, too.

She hadn't intended to fall in love. She hadn't intended to tell him, but when he turned out the light and was still there with her in bed, the gush of emotion overwhelmed her judgment. She loved him—and not just because Jesus told people to love everyone. Brooke loved him special.

Then she'd awakened without him, and now he seemed reluctant to hold her hand. He hadn't kissed her good morning (not that he normally did) but did actual couples do that? Or was that just in the movies? Hal hadn't been affectionate that way. Emerson had never kissed her at all.

During a snack between rides, Brooke pulled out her itinerary. "Is there anything else you want to see?"

"I'm good. This is for you."

"But you're here too, and I care about you having a good time." She reached for his hand, and he tensed. "We have two more hours in the park, then our final lunch, then the airport shuttle."

Distracted, Jonathan watched people walking by. Brooke wanted to make a joke about hitting the gift shop one more time, but Jonathan wore a facial expression she couldn't identify. Not worried. Also not angry. Not tense. Why were faces so varied? Haunted? Yeah, she'd go with haunted.

If he didn't want to get close to her, and he looked haunted, then what did that add up to?

By noon, Brooke was anticipating a nap on the plane. They ate a nice meal at the resort hotel, then they were in the lobby with their luggage for the hassle of getting to the airport. That took longer than it should have. The airport was packed, and Brooke struggled to keep up with Jonathan.

Half this vacation had been waiting in line, but it had been fun standing in line with Jonathan, looking forward to good things. Here she was in a line that wouldn't budge, and Jonathan seeming like misery itself.

She said, "What's wrong?"

He should have said, "Nothing, why?" Or he should have said, "I'm nervous about making the flight," even though they still had an hour's time cushion. Instead, he said, "Before we get home, we need to talk."

Brooke frowned, about to say, "What about?" when her words caught in her throat and she couldn't speak.

He needed to talk to her about last night. About saying he loved her, when really, he didn't. He cared for her as a friend, but Jonathan, the most honest guy in the world, had lied last night. Caught up in the moment, he'd mistaken exhaustion for love, and now he needed to remind his misbehaving business partner that she'd never been his from the start—and he was even less going to be hers.

The line moved forward, and he pushed his bag ahead, but she stayed in place. He came back and got hers, too, and then took her hand to draw her forward. Everything was a roar of sound—the loudspeakers and people passing and machines beeping and transactions happening. Her body was in a different space-time continuum, and her mind was fixated on a thousand details that all added up to nothing because—sort them as she might—none were important.

Jonathan didn't say anything further. They needed to talk. He was going to wait for her to draw it out of him, except that was like sucking the poison from someone's snake bite and swallowing it yourself.

He'd just gifted her the trip of a lifetime. She'd gifted him her heart in what she'd hoped would be another gift of a lifetime, but he didn't want it.

Which, well, she should have expected. As usual, Brooke

had misread all the cues. She'd interpreted attention as love even though love had never been on the table.

Jonathan had a vocation to something, and he was still discerning it. Marrying Brooke was a temporary stop to unload a house that was itself an insult, and then they'd once again live separate lives. Jonathan had a vocation to be single, and if Brooke were honest with herself, it was probably the same for her. She was too picky and too quirky for a guy to want to build a future. Whatever guy wanted to marry her would have to hammer off all her rough edges and form-fit her into whatever mold she should have assumed from the start. Jonathan hadn't done that, and she'd mistaken his acceptance for love. He'd only accepted her as she was because he'd seen no long-term reason to change her.

Jonathan took her arm, and she realized once again the line had moved. He said, "You're quiet."

Was she? Her thoughts were a wall of noise, and she'd have done anything to silence them all and retrieve the perfect peace from when she'd fallen asleep in his arms.

She hadn't even gotten the chance to hope she could join him again tonight. She'd awakened with him in the other bed, meaning he'd extricated himself as soon as she'd let him, and now he needed to hammer up a taller wall.

He was supposed to be a priest. Or a brother. Priests and brothers didn't have wives. They didn't fall in love, not even if a woman fell in love with them.

They were close to the front now, and whenever the line moved, he shifted both their bags, and she followed. A curious distance separated Brooke from everyone, even as the presence of so many people crawled over her skin like spiders.

Noise hadn't felt like that at the amusement park. That had felt more like water currents swirling. To be fair, though, she also hated that sensation and wore a T-shirt to swim.

At the front, Jonathan produced their tickets and

handed over their bags while Brooke stared a thousand yards away. Sometimes the check-in attendant asked a question, and she answered without engaging. No one gave me anything to carry on the plane. Yes, I have my ID.

The attendant put their bags on a conveyer belt, and Brooke watched her belongings disappear behind a curtain. "You'd better go straight to security. Your flight leaves in an hour, and I hear the lines are long."

They got into yet another line, and Jonathan took her hand again. It was guiding her, not loving her. Her limb felt like someone else's hand, someone else's life, and she was trailing along behind it.

The group in front of them and the group behind were chattering about stupid things. Movies and people they knew and complaints about the price of airport food. Jonathan was looking at her, and Brooke stared in the general direction of his face. With her eyes unfocused, she could fixate on a spot between his eyebrows.

He must have thought that gave them privacy. More than they'd have on the plane. He said, "Last night, after you went to sleep—"

Please, don't.

"—I just...don't know what I'm doing. I'm an awful mess, but you know that."

Please stop.

He sighed. "I'm not being fair to you. I have no idea where I'm going to be next year. I mean, it's just— I didn't mean to jerk around your feelings."

Except he had.

He'd been dating her. They'd cuddled. They'd kissed. He'd been looking out for her. For crying out loud, he'd married her. Not in that order. But even so.

He said, "I need to back off. I don't want to ruin your life, and I don't want you to be stuck with me just because you're here and I'm here."

He was dumping her for her sake?

He said, "I'm sorry."

He needed something from her. Words. She said, "I

understand."

That was neutral. She wasn't good enough for him, and she could understand that. She'd told the church ladies she couldn't compete with God, and of course she shouldn't want to. She understood that, too. But God could have anyone, so why take Jonathan after Jonathan had fallen in love? That, Brooke couldn't understand. Was it some weird posturing on the part of the Almighty to say, "You, come to me. You, stay over there"? Was this Brooke's punishment for daring to fall in love with someone who happened to be the most thoughtful and accepting person she'd ever known, but also happened to be set aside for some other path?

Jonathan said, "Are you sure you understand? Because I don't."

A thought popped up: he was prompting her to banter. When they bantered, they connected, and they both felt better after connecting. He wanted her to shoot back with a rejoinder that would make him laugh, and then he'd make her laugh. Once they could laugh, they could get through anything because they'd be a team again. So far, the team of the two of them had gotten through a lot of things. Being a team had made Jonathan smile again, whereas when she'd first seen him after he returned from seminary, he hadn't been able to smile at all.

He prompted, "Of course, there's a lot I don't understand, so I can just add it to the list."

He couldn't banter with himself. If he wanted to live as a celibate, though, he'd have to get used to that. Or maybe the other monks could learn to banter with him. He'd drive off to live in community with their everyday structure, and somewhere in there, he'd find someone to trade jokes with. Maybe he'd joke around with Jesus.

It couldn't be Brooke. She didn't have it in her right now. "No, I do understand." The people trudged forward in an endless line that would never reach its destination. "We took things too far, and everything snapped back."

The security agent pulled Brooke's bag off the X-ray belt and rooted through it while Brooke put her shoes back on. Jonathan had been sent to another X-ray on a different line.

The agent pulled out Brooke's knitting, on Jonathan's handmade needles. "These are dangerous and can't go on the plane."

She looked up. "Knitting needles are permitted. I looked it up on the TSA website."

The agent said, "They're too long."

"They're ten-inch straight size six wooden needles," Brooke said, raising her voice, "and your agency website says they're permitted."

The agent said, "I need to ask you to throw these away or give them to someone who isn't going on the plane."

"I don't know anyone else in Florida." Brooke pulled out her phone to look up the TSA website. "It's on your own website that knitting needles are safe!"

Jonathan came up behind her. "What's wrong?"

"She's trying to confiscate my knitting needles!" Brooke's voice pitched up. "But they're safe. They let them through on the trip up, and the website says knitting needles are safe."

Another agent joined them. "Ma'am, if she says they're dangerous, we can't let them on the plane."

"But he made them!" Her phone wouldn't load the page —service in here was awful. "He made them for me, and they're not dangerous. Your own website says I can have them or I wouldn't have brought them in the first place."

The agent shifted his stance and squared his shoulders. Jonathan said, "You know she's right. Knitting needles are permitted."

The agent said, "These can stab someone. I say they're dangerous."

Brooke looked at Jonathan, then back at the agent. "Can you hold them off to the side and mail them home?" They shook their heads. "Can we put them in my checked luggage? Can the pilot keep them in the cockpit and then give them back at the end?"

No, no, and no.

Jonathan said, "Brooke, we need to get to the gate. They're wrong, but they're not going to budge. I'll make another set as soon as we get home. I promise."

Her eyes were blurring, and she could barely hear anything. "That's the nicest gift anyone ever gave me, and you're just going to take it?"

Jonathan said to the agent, "Take the needles. We need to get to our flight."

The agent pulled the needles out of the project and threw Jonathan's handmade cherry wood Christmas needles into the trash.

Jonathan propelled Brooke by the arm through the crowd, down a long corridor, and up to a gate with another crowd. Brooke stood with her arms wrapped around the backpack she hadn't even put back on her shoulders, and she shook. Hard.

This was punishment. She'd reached for too much. She was going to lose everything of Jonathan.

At the gate, Jonathan handed over their boarding passes, and the flight attendant let them on. That would have been the final kick in the teeth, if Jonathan had gotten onboard but they'd stopped her. Only then, maybe she'd have been allowed to leave the secure area, take her needles out of the trash, and mail them home. Or just go back through security when someone else was on duty, someone who followed the law rather than her whim.

At their seats, someone was already in one of them. Of course. "You're in my seat," Jonathan told the woman.

She pointed to the baby in a seat against the window. "They put my baby here and me all the way in the back.

The baby can't sit alone."

Of course not.

Jonathan hit the button for the flight attendant, then had Brooke sit in the empty space.

The flight attendant examined their boarding passes, then asked Jonathan if it would be okay if he took the seat at the back.

He said to Brooke, "I'm sorry."

Sorry again. Sorry for a lot of things. So was she.

CHAPTER TWENTY-TWO

Brooke slept late the next morning, and Jonathan readied himself for work without making noise. He didn't have to dump boiling water out of his thermos before adding the coffee because she was always the one who warmed the thermos for him, and he'd forgotten to do it. He'd just pour the coffee into a cold thermos. That's how it had been before. She'd begun warming it up for him to make it nice.

That night, she returned from work looking tired and chilled. "I've got dinner ready," he said. She thanked him for making it, and she helped him clean up afterward.

Conversation was minimal. He tried to get her to laugh about anything, but she stayed flat. "I'm tired."

He went into the library to do evening prayer, but she went upstairs. Ten minutes later, when she still hadn't joined him, he texted. "Are you coming back down?"

She replied in a minute. "I'm going to stay up here. I've got work to do."

Work usually meant designing or testing a pattern, but for weeks now, she'd been working on those in the library. He texted, "TV tonight?"

"I need to get this done."

He'd broken her heart. He'd broken both their hearts through his own arrogance, and it wasn't fair. He hadn't listened when Father Tim said this would be difficult because he'd never minded the idea that something would be difficult for himself. Making it difficult for Brooke, though? That was unbearable.

The next day was the same. She didn't look at him, didn't laugh with him. The light was gone from her eyes, and her smile was gone entirely. He asked her to play piano, but she declined, saying she'd practiced in the morning. She stayed a little while in the library, but then went into the kitchen to wind yarn, and she didn't come back.

Third day: she didn't come down for breakfast. It was over. They'd had a good vacation, gone too far emotionally, and now they couldn't return from the brink.

He got some black cherry wood to remake her knitting needles. He wrote a nasty letter to the TSA about violating their own policies, for all the good that would do. Which was none. Her package of souvenirs arrived from Orlando, so he carried them into the library, but when she got home from work, she said she didn't have the energy to sort through the box.

Everything was in ruins. Their friendship had mattered to Brooke more than the house, and now she was walking away from it.

While Jonathan was talking to his parents at the coffee and donut social, Father Tim approached. "Is Brooke all right?"

Jonathan hesitated.

Mom said, "Did she not sleep at all on the trip?"

"We both did a lot of walking." Brooke was cleaning one

of the tables even though technically the coffee hour was still going on. Alone. Two of the volunteer church ladies were chatting at the other side of the table, and a third joined them.

Dad said, "Go help her with that," so Jonathan escaped the conversation. He had no idea how he'd have explained, regardless. Father Tim might or might not have understood. His parents would likely remind him this idea was ridiculous from the start.

Or maybe not. Maybe this had been part of the plan all along: maybe he still had a vocation to the priesthood, but he was being tested for his loyalty. Oh, or even more— what if God was using this time to train Jonathan to be a better priest later? Because after this experience, Jonathan would have a better understanding of temptation. He would understand the mechanics of a marriage. All of that would be useful when counseling parishioners who needed help.

God might not have taken everything away, after all. Maybe God was only delaying, and if Jonathan kept discerning, eventually God would reveal that Jonathan had needed a sabbatical before getting ordained, and having done that, Jonathan was good to go.

Someone intercepted Jonathan, Allie from the bereavement group. "Look at me! I managed to show up!"

"Awesome!"

She laughed. "When you weren't here, they all ganged up on me about going to church. Last Sunday, I didn't get through more than ten minutes, but today, I stayed for the whole thing."

Jonathan folded his arms and made himself look sage. "The important question is, did you get a donut?"

Her eyes widened. "Well, but—" She waved at the table. "People."

Allie sounded a lot like Brooke. "You worked hard to come here for the first time after losing Jake. I'll put a donut in a bag for you to take home, and I think there's lids for the coffee. It's not social, but you deserve a reward for your effort."

Allie looked uncertain. He called, "Brooke?"

When he explained, Brooke smiled with her customer service face and reassured Allie she'd take care of it all.

That was how Brooke operated: quietly taking care of it all. Except he'd come to like it when she talked more.

Then from the edge of his hearing, Jonathan heard someone mutter, "Chalice chipper."

He pivoted, breath hard, and looked right at the cluster of church ladies. Two of them were looking right at Brooke.

Chalice chipper?

Jonathan said, "Excuse me a moment," and he strode over to the church ladies, all of whom smiled at him.

No, not going to have that. In a dark voice, he said, "Did I just hear you gossiping about Brooke?"

One of them had the decency to look unnerved. Jonathan went on, "Because if you're gossiping about her and me, I should hear exactly what you have to say."

The unnerved woman said, "She's a very nice girl."

Jonathan folded his arms. "She's a woman, not a girl, and did I just hear you call her a chalice chipper? Because if so, I need to set the record straight."

In his peripheral vision, he saw Brooke return with Allie's donut and coffee, so he faced the three church ladies head on.

A familiar-looking woman huffed. "Isn't she? You started hanging around with her, and now you're not going back to seminary."

Jonathan narrowed his eyes. "You think I compromised all my morals for her? Would you even want me to be a priest if I'd do that?"

The woman who looked familiar said, "She's trying to seduce you away from your vocation. She knows a good thing when she sees it, and she's attacking when you're vulnerable."

Jonathan tilted his head. "You think Brooke is more powerful than God?"

The unnerved woman gave a tittering laugh. "Jonathan, dear, of course not, but—"

He ticked his voice up a bit. "Because if there were someone I thought was more powerful than God—powerful enough to overwhelm someone's free will and destroy God's plan—then I sure as heck would be *extra nice* to that person, not gossiping about them just out of earshot."

Were these women the reason Brooke didn't want to leave right after Mass? Didn't want to be seen standing too near Jonathan for too long? Had she been getting community flack for months and kept it to herself, the way she had in middle school and high school?

She'd been standing in the gap for him for years. He'd been trying to protect her, but she'd been protecting him. Protecting his freedom to make decisions. Protecting him from feeling pressured.

Jonathan looked the first woman in the eyes. "I don't want to hear that slander again. I discerned out of seminary long before I resumed talking to Brooke. She's been my biggest supporter in discerning my vocation, and she's never wanted anything other than for me to find the right path for my life. If you're implying she'd lure me away from God, then you're insulting both her and me."

The unnerved one said, "We're not insulting you. Of course you approached this seriously. But you could still go back."

"Have you not been listening? I *can't* go back to seminary." His voice grew tense. "The whole point of discerning is to figure out what God wants. If God wanted me, God had me right there. I didn't flip a coin and leave because it landed on tails. I didn't get a letter from Brooke and think, 'I should marry her and get a job making custom cabinets.' None of this was a whim."

She said, "But honey, if you tried harder—"

"I can't fight God! You don't honor God by doing exactly the thing God said you're not supposed to be doing. Once God says no, what's the reason to insist? For status?

Because it made me feel good? Would *those* be the qualities you're looking for in a priest?"

The second woman pursed her lips. "Brooke is distracting you."

"I'm not in seminary. What would I even be getting distracted from?" Except hadn't he had that same argument with himself in Orlando? Hadn't he said falling for Brooke was keeping him from figuring out if he should marry her? Sometimes God sends enemies to say things your friends won't say.

Brooke and Allie were approaching. He'd better get a grip.

Jonathan squared his shoulders. "I don't care what you think about me, but leave her out of it. Do not make me say that again."

The second woman backed up a step just as Brooke drew up alongside.

Brooke said, "Anything wrong?" Then, to the rude woman, "Oh, hi, Mrs. Miller. How's the colorwork hat coming?"

Jonathan lowered his voice a notch. "We're just having a discussion about self-preservation and making good decisions."

Mrs. Miller added, "Or bad decisions."

Brooke made her voice brighter than it had been talking to Jonathan for the past few days. "Colorwork hats are never a bad decision, but if the floats are too tight, the trick for keeping them loose is to knit the hat inside-out." She turned back to Jonathan. "There's still a lot of coffee in the decaf urn, so it's too heavy for me to lift alone. I'll need help getting it to the sink to dump it out."

Mrs. Miller said, "He's so helpful, Brooke. Don't you think he would still make a great priest?"

Jonathan's vision whited out with rage.

At his side, Brooke said, "I've been saying that for years. He's thinking of joining a monastery in January, and they'll be lucky to have him."

Allie added, "It will be sad when he goes, but he's been

239

so good to look out for our group. Sometimes you need a protector, and God sends the right person."

Brooke still wore her customer service face. "I admit, I wasn't sure why Father Tim talked you into leading the group, but it sounds like it was just the right thing. You've been so helpful to everyone."

Mrs. Miller folded her arms. "Think of how many more people you could help if you went back to seminary."

That wasn't happening. But maybe it was time Jonathan figured out who it was he should be helping.

He drove home with Brooke quiet in the front seat. "Have the church ladies been harassing you?"

Brooke looked out the passenger window. "Not much."

Jonathan's hands clenched on the wheel. "You should have told me."

"Told you that people jumped to conclusions and gave me wicked side-eye? You've been there when it happens." Her mouth twitched. "They can think what they want. It's not as if—"

She drifted off, and Jonathan couldn't bear to ask her to finish that thought.

It's not as if what? Not as if this were her community? Not as if she'd ever stood a chance of parting him from his vocation? Those were true. She'd gone back to Saint Lucy's because of him. And she'd never stood in his way.

He said, "I tried to straighten them out today."

She huffed. "Good luck with that. They tagged you as a pre-priest, and they're going to track you that way for the rest of your life. You could be married and have ten kids, and they'd still be waiting for your wife to drop dead so you could take Holy Orders and score all seven sacraments."

"Ten kids?" Jonathan prompted.

Brooke said, "Nine girls and one little boy they'd spoil like crazy. They'd crown Jonathan Junior as the heir to your unused vocation and scare off any girls he was friends with—assuming nine older sisters didn't do it first."

Jonathan laughed. "What would their mother do?"

Brooke said, "I'm sure I have no idea," and stopped the banter cold.

Jonathan pulled onto Sky Ridge Drive. "Brooke, I feel terrible about this."

She kept looking aside. "I never thought you were in control of the gossip machine."

"I feel terrible about how our trip ended. I messed up everything, and I'm sorry."

"Are you?" She tilted her head. "'Sorry' implies you'd have done something differently, and I don't think you would have. Also, it's not entirely on you. It took both of us to mess things up in that spectacular a fashion."

Jonathan prompted, "At least we're good at something when we work together."

"I don't want to be good at that." She drummed the fingers of one hand against the opposite forearm. "It's more my fault than yours. You said in January that the agreement was still in force. You *said* it. I'm terrible at subtext, and when you started dating me and started kissing me, I thought that meant you changed your mind. I should have clarified, except I didn't want you to say no." As he pulled into the driveway, she huffed. "Whatever the church ladies were speculating about me, it's close enough. I'm certainly not better than they think I am, even if they think I'm horrible for all the wrong reasons."

Jonathan said, "You're being hard on yourself."

She said, "And you're a liar when you're trying to spare my feelings, so let it go."

She got out of the car, and Jonathan scrambled out his side. "I haven't lied to you."

"*I love you too, Brooke.*" She walked up the steps and

punched in the key code. "*I mean, I love everyone because Jesus said to love everyone, and I love my enemies, too, therefore I'm sure you're in there somewhere. Maybe you're one of those neighbors I'm supposed to love.*"

Jonathan caught up to her in the living room. "I was not lying to you. I fell in love with you back at Christmas, and I've been fighting myself ever since."

"Ooh," she breathed. "Love your enemies, then, even when that enemy is yourself. You should have fought a bit harder, because taking me on dates and kissing me? Not the way to fight your feelings."

Jonathan rolled his eyes. "I was trying to figure out my feelings. I've never done this before."

"We both got married on the same day," Brooke exclaimed. "I'm just as inexperienced as you are. Not to mention, I didn't have a formation director meeting me once a week to help me figure out my life pathway or whatever it is I'm supposed to have been doing all this time."

"Like that did a world of good." At least she was talking to him. She wasn't bantering, but bantering was just playful arguing, so if she argued—well, they were communicating.

Her eyes were brilliant. "I'm not trying to do good to either of us right now. I'm trying to survive. I have no idea how to salvage any of this, and I still don't want to lose you as a friend. Even if I do want to break an egg over your head." She swallowed. "Leave me alone. I don't think you love me, not the way you think you do. I believe you that you have no idea what you're feeling, but I can't help that. And yes, I believe you have no idea what you should be doing with your life, other than the fact that for some reason, doing it with me is not an option."

He stood breathless. Speechless.

"I'm trying to respect whatever it is God's telling you to do." She opened her hands. "What more do you want? The church ladies said I was a distraction and a chalice-chipper. Well, undistract yourself. Get a tube of chalice glue and patch it together. You told me to back off, and I backed off. Now you want me not to back off. I stink at reading minds."

Jonathan lowered his gaze. "I'm sorry."

"You don't even know what sorry is. It's something you say when you can't figure out why everyone isn't going along with what you want." She sighed. "Forget it. I'm going biking on the rail trail."

She disappeared upstairs, and Jonathan went into the kitchen for a glass of water.

So much for protecting Brooke from the town gossips. It had been going on for months—apparently in front of his face.

What good was it to fashion up his whole life to shepherd the nebulous parishioners of a theoretical parish, but then expose someone he loved to the judgment and anger of her community?

Brooke wasn't a distraction. She was a whole person. Jonathan had considered all the sacrifices he would have made to become a priest, but she was making sacrifices, too. She'd given up her home and hours of sleep. She'd given up her routines. She'd given up her reputation.

He could give some of that back to her. Maybe it was time to stop discerning and start doing.

When she returned in biking gear, Jonathan intercepted her. "I'm going to remake your knitting needles like I promised."

She avoided his eyes. "I'm sorry I yelled at you. You're doing your best."

A lot of good that was. "My best isn't enough, but at least I can replace your knitting needles. It was sweet that you said they were the best gift anyone had ever given you."

Brooke shrugged. "You were thoughtful. I thought that meant something."

It had meant something. It still meant something. Jonathan said, "Maybe I should get a bike, too. I could ride with you."

She said only, "It's not necessary," and wheeled her bike out the door.

Jonathan watched her pedal first down the driveway and then down Sky Ridge Drive.

It was time to stop discerning and make up his mind.

CHAPTER TWENTY-THREE

Sunday's fight still bothered Brooke on Monday morning, but she shoved it out of her head because what other choice did she have? She had to work. She had to prep the house for their upcoming Artist in Residence, even though (yes) they had a professional cleaner coming in to take care of the guest house. That didn't mean the main house could be a disaster.

Yet another reason to stick to the micro-apartment. She could strew her stuff wherever she wanted and then lock the door.

The Paxley souvenirs had survived their trip home in a box, and Brooke's next assignment would be finding enough wall space for everything she'd bought. The thought of opening that box nauseated her in ways she couldn't describe. Every night since coming home, she'd gone to bed with her pillow fortress and weighted blanket, and she'd remembered Jonathan in that cocoon with her. She would remember her exhaustion and the overwhelming need to tell him how much she loved him... and then she'd burn with shame that kept her awake.

He'd be right down the hallway, flinching with

secondhand embarrassment at how she'd spurted her feelings all over him. Maybe it was keeping him awake, too.

Natalie and Lilah's souvenirs needed dispersal, though. Brooke endured unpacking the box only so she could bring them to work. Lilah got a wind chime and a headband with trademarked character ears sticking up, which she promptly put on her head. Natalie got a hoodie, and then they both got suncatcher artwork.

Lilah set hers aside and folded her hands on the Sit and Stitch table. "And now, you get to tell us what went horribly wrong on the trip, because you're not yourself."

Brooke opened her mouth to object, and Natalie said, "And no, you're not tired."

Brooke closed her mouth, then started to speak again, and Natalie said, "You may be tired, but you're not *only* tired."

Brooke looked from one to the other, and then at the shop door. No customers.

Natalie said, "I'll lock the shop for half an hour if you need it, but really, just spill. What happened?"

Brooke started spinning the yarn buddy. The ball bearings growled, and whenever it slowed down, she'd twirl it again.

Lilah handed Brooke a crochet hook and a skein of cotton yarn. "What did Jonathan do to you?"

Brooke made a slip knot and started a foundation chain, counting even though she had no idea how far across she was going to make this thing. Whatever it was. Cotton and a crochet hook probably meant a dish scrubbie.

Natalie got up from the table, and a minute later Brooke was still processing the sounds as Natalie got back: she'd taped something to the door and locked it up. Closed for emergency meeting?

Somewhere at the top of her throat, Brooke finally unlocked her words. Yes, she and Jonathan had been getting closer. It hadn't been imagination. He claimed he'd loved her since Christmas, but when she said she loved him, too, he'd braked hard. He still had vocation stuff to work through. It was hard to love him and be with him everyday knowing he loved her but didn't want to be with her. He wanted things to go back to the way they were when he'd made her feel safe and appreciated, except he wanted her not to feel safe and appreciated.

Brooke didn't look up from her dishcloth, but she could tell Natalie had her elbows on the table, her fingers woven through one another, and her face in the little cup they made. Lilah hadn't moved or said a thing.

Natalie finally said, "If I ask, there's at least two guys working for Fruits de Mer who will beat him half to death."

Lilah said, "No violence. She loves him."

"That makes it worse."

"No violence."

Natalie sighed. "This is a mess. I was nervous about you two getting married because he didn't love you."

Lilah's voice raised. "And I was nervous because he did! Of course he loved her, it's just that he's like me, an idiot who got so mono-focused on one thing that he never bothered to actually ask himself whether it was going to work."

Natalie recoiled. "That's not fair."

Lilah got to her feet. "It's absolutely not fair—to Brooke! Ever since I've known Jonathan, he's been the one who locks into a plan, doesn't question it, and then runs it right to the end of the line. Then he doesn't take correction when things fail. It's no wonder he got three years into seminary before realizing the priesthood wasn't going to work. I'm frankly surprised he ever got to the point of admitting it. And then he did the same thing with marrying Brooke."

Brooke looked up. "How?"

"If he fell in love with you at Christmas, then what kind of pig-headedness was it to tell you in January that you two were going to stick to the just-friends plan?" Lilah opened her hands. "And then to double down on that pig-headedness by starting to date you?"

Natalie's eyes were huge. "I have never, not once in my

life, heard anyone describe Jonathan Levesque as pig-headed."

"Because he's so darned nice about it. Hey, I'll help you with that. Oh, I've got this selfless sacrifice up my sleeve. And here, I'll do all these awesome things for you. Meanwhile the signs are lit up like the town common Christmas tree that the wheels are about to fall off." Lilah paced away. "Now, add in that once he declared himself a future priest, an army formed around him to keep reinforcing that plan, so if he ever had any doubts, plenty of people would push him right back onto the rails."

Natalie muttered, "While talking garbage about Brooke at the same time."

Lilah's eyes narrowed. "Really? Because I might suddenly have a use for those guys from Fruits de Mer."

Brooke said, "Jonathan shut them down. And we all thought he would have been an awesome priest."

Lilah's eyes narrowed. "I bet if he looks back, there were warning signs that he didn't acknowledge. He never dated anyone because he intended never to get married, so the places he could have gotten those warning signs from, he never even went there. But dating you in order to figure out if the priesthood was for him? That's bizarre beyond belief."

Natalie said, "He's sending mixed signals."

"He's sending mixed signals *to himself.*" Lilah opened her hands. "How is Brooke supposed to figure out how to handle him if even he doesn't know?"

Natalie said, "I think he does want to be with Brooke."

Lilah snapped, "But he also wants to be a monk."

Brooke reached the end of the row and chained one to turn and start the next. "He doesn't want to be a monk. He wants God to change the verdict about the priesthood, and since he can't coerce God, he's going to try a religious order. A monastery is the consolation prize. I come in a distant third or fourth or tenth."

Natalie said, "None of that is fair to you. He brought you to Paxley on what looked like the perfect honeymoon, and then he broke your heart."

"That's what I don't understand. He sees me. He sees me with all my stupid flaws, and he's fine with me." Brooke turned, chained, and then worked a row back across the dishcloth. If Lilah was right that emotions infused yarn, this scrubbie was going to get dishes cleaner than a pressure washer loaded with bleach. "He looks out for me and learned to care about all the things I care about, but then he tells me to pretend he's my big brother. Therefore, I start to treat him like I'm his kid sister, but he doesn't like that, either."

"Would *you* like that?" Lilah folded her arms. "I'm deadly serious here. You've got that big house, but you've crammed yourself into a tiny corner because that's what always happens to you. People give you crumbs and demand you be thankful, so you tell yourself it's enough. Jonathan has a big heart, and you're willing to cram yourself into a tiny corner rather than move into the big uncomfortable space that would be all of him."

Brooke shook her head. "He won't let me."

Natalie said, "What Lilah's saying is, in the absence of being allowed to move into the entirety of his heart, are you content to keep yourself confined to the corner of it? Do you want to be living on crumbs of affection and whatever he happens to send your way when he forgets he's supposed to be *vocating* or whatever it is he's doing?"

Brooke set the quarter-done dishcloth and hook on the table, and she stared at her hands.

Natalie said, "I wouldn't be okay with that. If you love him, and he refuses to admit he loves you, then it's too painful to stay."

Lilah said, "I've got space. We'll set up a micro-apartment in my barn the same way you have it in the house. You can live there until you get another apartment. The contract only says you have to be married for a year. It doesn't say he has to drag your heart through the gutter."

A mixture of joy and dread broke over Brooke when she saw lights on in the kitchen. Jonathan was home.

She encountered Jonathan in the living room. "Hey." She tried keeping her voice steady as she dropped her bag on the couch and pulled out a brand-new dish scrubby.

Jonathan said, "Don't take off your jacket. Let's get dinner out."

Brooke went cold, but she pulled off her jacket anyhow. "I can cook. We've still got leftover chicken."

He said, "It'll keep."

"But that's what I was planning on having." She went into the kitchen and left the new dish scrubby alongside the sink. The freezer yielded the appropriate container. "I'm thinking lemon chicken and orzo soup."

Jonathan said, "I'm thinking I could take you out tonight."

"I'm also thinking we shouldn't be going out because you're supposed to enter a monastery in seven months, so a dinner date would be wildly inappropriate." She set a pot on the burner with a clang. "Would you mind grabbing the chicken broth from the pantry closet?"

He touched her shoulder, and she jerked away.

Jonathan said, "What's wrong?"

She let her eyes bore into his just in case it made him as uncomfortable as it made her. "What do you mean, *what's wrong?* You said you wanted distance. I'm respecting that. Do you think respecting you is wrong?"

Jonathan backed up a step, and then his shoulders dropped. "Fine. We'll eat in tonight."

Who even goes out for a date on Mondays? Half the restaurants in town closed on Monday because they'd just worked the whole weekend.

Maybe he was planning to do the drive-through burger window, and they could come home with paper packets of fries. It would be faster just to make the soup. Brooke wasn't heartless, though. She also popped a tube of biscuits and set those in the oven.

Jonathan picked up the dishcloth and didn't drop it screaming in pain, so Lilah's theory about yarn absorbing emotions must be incorrect. "This is new."

"Someone left me alone with cotton yarn and a crochet hook when we didn't have any customers." Brooke tried to relax her shoulders while Jonathan started setting the table. "Do we still have soup crackers?"

She should move her stuff back to the kitchenette in the micro-apartment. Then when Jonathan didn't want to cook, he could take himself out to dinner and linger over dessert with God, communing about the latest papal encyclical and how it related to the Council of Nicaea.

It didn't take long to defrost the cooked chicken and heat up soup. After she got that going, she whisked up eggs and lemon juice. Orzo, in. They needed a side vegetable. Carrot sticks seemed easy enough. After dinner, she'd go upstairs and work on a pattern. Maybe fingerless gloves laced with vines that went all the way to your elbows and made it look like your hands were tied. Meanwhile, Jonathan hovered, uncertain.

Natalie was right about Jonathan mixing signals. He had no idea what he wanted. A life full of confusion was not a life that had any room for Brooke.

The soup was good, at least. Grandma used to make this. Jonathan usually liked it, too, but tonight he was quiet. Or maybe it was Brooke who was quiet because the couple of times he did start a conversation, she answered briefly. That was her: vocation-killer and conversation-killer.

Finally she said, "How's that job going, the one with the knotty pine cabinets?"

"We still can't find pine that's knotty enough for our customer." Jonathan made a face Brooke would have to describe as "irritated." "The first pine had an insufficiency of knots, so we went back to the supplier and requested the knottiest of knotty pine. That pine, you'll be distressed to learn, was too knotty."

Brooke wouldn't recognize knotty pine if it fell on her in the woods, but she'd been hearing about this saga for a while. "Can the customer visit the distributor to pick out one with just the correct ratio of knots to pine?"

Jonathan pointed at her. "That's what I said. The customer didn't want to travel, though, so that's when I decided we live in an age of miracles. I took pictures of every plank of pine in the distribution center."

Brooke broke some crackers into her soup. "A forest of knots."

"They were all wrong. I've decided the customer doesn't actually want knotty pine. She wants to drive us knotty."

Brooke kept a straight face as she took an unfair pot-shot at Jonathan Levesque, the Master of the Mixed Signal. "It's hard when the customer thinks they know what they want, but even they don't know."

Jonathan missed it entirely. "It's worse when the thing the customer thinks they want doesn't even exist."

Fair point. Brooke said, "Do you now convince the customer that knotty pine was never right for her in the first place?"

"My boss has tried," Jonathan said, proving once and for all that Brooke was the worst person in the world when it came to delivering subtext. "She won't let it go. She's dreamed of knotty pine for years, so she keeps insisting it's out there, somewhere, the perfectly knotty pine."

Brooke took another spoonful of soup, then gave a bland, "Imagine that."

Jonathan had relaxed. He always relaxed when the conversation came quick and light. Sometimes he was even relaxed when the conversation was quick and heavy. She enjoyed it, too, and that was the problem. Every day, this would keep happening, and eventually Brooke would return to interpreting his affectionate comfort as love. Or interpreting his love as love, since he said he loved her.

After dinner, Jonathan got nervous again. Brooke would get the dishwasher started and then retreat upstairs to let him be nervous alone in the library. Except he stopped her before she could vanish. "I have something to show you."

His voice was higher-pitched than it should be. He had her sit on the library couch, and then he opened his backpack. Inside he had a new set of wooden knitting needles.

She frowned. "Why'd you do this?"

"I promised I would. They came better than the first set, although I still hope that TSA agent awakens every night from dreams of me standing over her, plunging the first pair of wooden knitting needles through her heart."

Brooke said, "That will just convince her she was right to take them, and other knitters will suffer."

Jonathan said, "It's also not Christian forgiveness on my part—but then I think, I'm not the one who's supposed to forgive her, since she didn't steal my knitting needles." He leaned forward, hopeful. "Do you like them?"

"Yes, they're wonderful." The warmth wouldn't come to her heart, but intellectually, they were as smooth and straight as before. It was always amazing to watch Jonathan rotating wood against sandpaper and then using his calipers to make sure everything was the right diameter. "Thank you."

He said, "They aren't conformed to your hands the way the other ones were, but maybe in time."

It wouldn't happen. He'd made the first ones in the grip of impulse and love, but these he'd re-made out of obligation. Brooke couldn't knit with that.

He said, "Okay, and this, I'm super proud of." He handed her a yarn buddy.

She laughed. "I didn't know you could do that!"

"I didn't know I could do it, either. In fact, I'm not sure I actually did, but I can pull everything apart and make it over again, unlike the yarn bowl. Which I still should fix up for you."

"It's fine the way it is." Blast it, he was getting under her skin again. She couldn't help it, especially when he looked so earnest.

He opened his backpack. "And this is the final thing I wanted you to see."

He pulled out a thick book, and Brooke gasped because it was a photo album. It said, "Our Paxley Trip" on the hard cover, and then inside, on the first page, was a photo of them together in front of the main entrance.

"Oh." Her voice broke.

He sat next to her on the couch, and she didn't even edge away because here was their whole vacation, all these amazing moments captured for them. Some of the photos were from the exhibits and the rides, and others were ones he'd taken of her, and a couple she'd taken of him, and several of them together, taken by the park photographers.

In the ones together, Jonathan so often had his arm around Brooke's shoulders. On the rides, she was frequently holding (or clutching) his hand. They'd been together those days, him and her, no focus other than enjoying their hours in paradise. Everything had been taken care of—food, a place to stay, transportation. There'd been no question of whether he was supposed to become a professed religious, no foreboding that someday God might drop orders in Jonathan's lap and force him to march off to a meaningful life elsewhere.

No, in this album was the joy and silliness of taking their picture with life-size characters who previously only inhabited a screen or Brooke's wall or Brooke's imagination. Just her and her dreams, even if they were ridiculous. He'd been willing to be part of the ridiculosity. For a little while.

Like the vacation, the photo album came to an end too soon. She turned the last page, and there wasn't a final photo, but instead, text: *"Will you marry me?"*

She stared at the page.

It wasn't that her brain couldn't parse it. This wasn't like gawking at a weirdly shaped ham and deciphering that it was actually a turkey wrapped in bacon.

This was more like...? Blast it, she needed that chart of emotions again. Outrage?

With her voice flat, she said, "Why?"

He repeated, "Why?"

She snapped the cover closed. "You don't want to marry me. You said explicitly that you wanted to back things off and figure out what God wanted you to do with yourself. Yet here you are giving me a gorgeous photo album that must have taken hours to create, and then at the end you ruined the whole thing by asking me to marry you when you don't want to get married."

This explained why he wanted to take her out to dinner. He'd have dropped this on her in the restaurant. Her refusal to go to dinner was at least saving him the humiliation of getting turned down in public. Imagine if he'd gotten on one knee?

Jonathan's eyes widened. "I do want to marry you. You've done a lot for me, and I owe it to you. I hurt your feelings when I didn't mean to, and you've been making so many sacrifices for me that you deserve to have me stay with you and make it right."

She shoved the album onto his lap. "That is the most offensive thing you've done to me in all the time I've known you. You have no interest in marrying me. If I were stupid enough to say yes, you'd go through with it. You'd put on a brave face, and I'd always know it wasn't what you wanted. No, I am not marrying you just to be second-best forever."

He recoiled. "What do you mean?"

"I mean, you're not over your ex." Brooke stood away from him because having him that close was making her skin crawl. "You're still obsessed with the priesthood you never got a chance to try. You're an ex-seminarian before you're a man or a carpenter or my husband. I can't marry an ex-seminarian."

Jonathan got to his feet, leaving the photos on the couch. "I *am* an ex-seminarian."

"You should be other things, too. You're still discerning your vocation, whatever that is."

Jonathan said, "I'll set it aside. I'll make you my vocation."

"Not good enough." She'd better not start crying now or he'd think she was upset, and really, she was just spent. Exhausted, not as in tired, but with the strength sucked out of her soul. She didn't have the means or the willingness to connect with him. "I don't want to be your project, or your obligation. I don't know why even God would want to be that. Either the priesthood or a marriage should be a joyful joining, but you're making your life all about clenching your teeth and making a sacrifice."

Jonathan tilted his head. "You think there won't be any joy?"

Her eyes narrowed. "I will never feel joy knowing I'm the second-best path you took because the one you really want —and still really want—is covered with Road Closed signs. I'd rather you be enthusiastically wrong about being a priest than regretfully faithful about marrying me."

Jonathan stepped toward her, but Brooke raised her hands. "You're not listening!" Her voice wavered again. "You're not available for a relationship, let alone a marriage. You're still entangled with your last relationship, and you can't even see it."

He squared his shoulders. "I owe it to you to marry you."

"I'm freeing you from any debt right now. I forgive whatever you think requires you to bind the rest of your life to mine." She tightened her fists to drive her fingernails into the palms of her hands. Stay on top of the emotion. "Marriage is more than duty and sacrifice. I'm not going to have you marry me as an act of service."

He said, "You wanted me to be with you. You asked me to stay."

"Not this way!" She clenched her hands harder. "I'm done being everyone's second choice—or third choice, or fourth choice. If I get married, I want it to be to someone who loves me." Jonathan opened his mouth, and she cut him off. "You don't love *me*. You're in love with the idea that you'll finally fulfill a tremendous obligation at great personal cost. Great Hero Jonathan, sacrificing himself. But what about me? Every day, I get to wake up next to someone who's my whole world, someone who's more important to me than life itself—and who, just like everyone else I love, feels like they're stuck with me."

Jonathan walked to the opposite side of the library. Bingo.

Brooke lowered her voice. "I can't sign up for that. I'm sorry I've ruined yet another of your vocation plans. Maybe I am a chalice chipper."

Facing away from her, he shook his head. "Don't say that. My vocation was in ashes before I got back to Brighthead."

She stared a hole in his back, but he didn't turn. "You don't believe it's ashes because you keep breathing on it to make some spark burst out of it like a phoenix. Maybe you can be a religious brother or maybe you can join the Dominicans or maybe you can fast on a pillar in the desert while people pilgrimage to you for sage advice. If I'm the one who hammers a spike through the soot where your vocation's heart used to be, you're going to resent me forever."

He folded his arms. "You're saying you have to be my last resort."

"If that's what you're taking away from this conversation, then I'm absolutely right to turn you down." She picked up the knitting needles, since he'd promised to replace those anyhow, and on consideration, she took the yarn buddy. She'd leave that album right there on the couch. "Thank you for replacing what the TSA stole from me. I'm sorry I can't be the one to replace everything that got taken from you."

CHAPTER TWENTY-FOUR

One of the light bulbs flared and burnt out when Jonathan turned on the lights in the church meeting room, and all he could think was, "Good." Let the other three do the work for the fourth. He should text the parish office, but whatever. Someone else would turn on the lights in this room tomorrow, see they were down one, and let maintenance know. Or maybe change it themselves. Who cared?

Jonathan dragged the chairs into the formation the bereavement group members liked (whatever) and then made sure the tissue boxes were in their strategic positions. Why was he doing this, again? Oh, right, because Father Tim didn't want to be doing it, so he'd looked for a convenient person to offload it on.

By the time eight o'clock rolled around, the bereavement group was ready to start. Jonathan opened with the prayer printed on the meeting notes, then explained their procedure to the new member. "Let's go around the room and quickly introduce ourselves," he said, knowing that as they made their rounds, the "quickly" part was going to vanish like yesterday's dreams. He went first, hoping to set the standard. "I'm Jonathan Levesque, and I'm your meeting facilitator. I'm only here to keep things on track and point out any resources that might be of help."

"You do a lot more than that," said Allie.

Jonathan forced a smile. "Allie, why don't you lead off with your introduction?"

Allie didn't deserve his anger. None of these people did. He'd better get his attitude under lock and key because this group was arguably the most fragile in the parish. How many people did Jonathan know who'd walked away from religion when some mean-spirited representative of God said something insensitive? Please, God, may he never be the cause of that.

Allie said, "I'm Allie, and I'm forty-five. My husband died eight months ago, and until I started coming to this group, I couldn't even leave my house. But when I did start coming, everyone here was helpful. I'm hoping that if I stay, I'll be able to help other people, too."

Jonathan said, "Just to jump in—we don't want to set the bar too high. When grief is new, it may seem impossible to help other people. So if you're thinking, 'I can't save anyone else while I'm drowning,' you're absolutely right."

Allie said, "We're here to lean on each other. But even so, it's so helpful when I look around and think to myself, if all these people can go through this and be so amazing and generous and strong, then maybe I can get through it and survive."

The next person started their intro, and Jonathan tried not to tune out. Survival sounded like a good goal. Although, why? He wasn't sure what he was surviving to do. God didn't want him as a priest, and Brooke didn't want him as her husband. And boy, had she not pulled punches when she said it.

Tonight's group consisted two widows and two widowers, one bereaved mother who'd been attending for the past two months, two who'd lost parents, and one who'd lost his twin. One of the widows had also recently lost her father and then a few months later her dog. And yet, every day, she got up and went to work.

After introductions, a man raised his hand. Jonathan said, "Frank, you have a question?"

Frank twisted his ball cap in his hands. "My wife died fifteen months ago. Last week, my daughter invited me for dinner, but she had a friend there. She calls that woman her work mom, and turns out, it was a setup."

Murmurs around the room, along with some people shaking their heads. Jonathan said, "Did you feel pressured?"

Frank huffed. "My daughter likes her well enough, so I guess that's a good recommendation. Work mom, and all. My daughter said, 'Martha, you and Dad can keep talking about this over dinner. How's next Friday night at the pizza place?' and Martha agreed, so now I have a date."

Jonathan's eyebrows went up. "I'm not sure whether to laugh at her audacity or feel bad that you got roped into this."

One of the women said, "Call the woman back and tell her no."

Frank frowned. "Do you think I should?"

Allie said, "I don't think it's a should or a shouldn't. Do you like this person enough to go to dinner with her?"

Frank twisted the hat again. "I wouldn't mind seeing her."

Jonathan said, "Then I think you should go," because of course Jonathan had vast experience both with dating and bereavement and was completely qualified to give this advice. Why had Father Tim tapped him for this, again? Although Father Tim likely didn't have much more experience than Jonathan did.

"It's hard, though, going for that first date," said another man. "It feels almost like cheating."

Frank gave a nervous laugh. "I don't want to forget Jodie. She was a huge part of my life."

Allie said, "People always say to me, 'What would Mike have wanted you to do?' and my response is, Mike wouldn't have wanted to die, so I don't think his opinion counts."

Once the group was talking freely, Jonathan's job was to let the support happen on its own. He'd only had to step in once when the support turned into a pile-on.

Frank said, "Would you go out on a date, though?"

"It's only been eight months. If I had to go on a first date again, I'd choose pizza because it's low-key. The thing is," Allie said, abruptly lowering her voice, "when Mike died, I didn't just lose Mike. I lost the whole life I thought we were going to have together."

"Yes!" exclaimed Elizabeth, one of the widows. "That's exactly it! It's not just losing the person—it's losing the whole dream."

Jonathan's heart shuddered. Like losing the dream of the priesthood.

Frank nodded vigorously. "My daughter thinks I'm being stubborn, but my dream was to live to my old age with Jodie. Another woman...? It feels wrong."

Allie's head pumped. "Because she's part of your identity, even if she's not there anymore."

Jonathan said, "How do you make peace with that?"

It slipped out. He shouldn't even be talking.

"You grieve it," Allie said. "That's what you said to me, that it's healthy to grieve. I had to grieve over the little things, not just the big ones. Things like when I needed an oil change, I brought the car myself. That was always Mike's thing, and it hurt. I'm capable of booking my own oil change, but it was a little wrong thing."

Frank nodded hard. "You're right. I'm saying goodbye to the life I thought I was supposed to have."

Across the room, Elizabeth said, "My sister-in-law started dating two weeks after her husband died, and I kept my mouth shut because it's not my life, but I thought, that can't be healthy."

Allie said, "The grief books say sometimes if you do that, it's because you're afraid you're going to be left with nothing."

Left with nothing.

Jonathan glanced at the door. What would happen if he just walked out? Maybe call the parish voicemail to report the dead lightbulb. Maybe leave.

"Like Jonathan said, grieving is about making peace with what we've lost so we can accept what we still have. And that stinks." Allie sighed. "It made me too afraid to leave the house. It's making you reluctant to meet with this woman."

Frank twisted that poor cap again. "This isn't the life I wanted to have. But my daughter says I can't hold onto the one I lost, either."

Jonathan battled nausea.

Elizabeth said, "I look at it this way, like my life was me driving down to Boston, only there's a car wreck. Now, I can call for a tow truck and get myself a new car. I can call roadside assistance and try to get it repaired. Or I can call for a ride back home and stay there. But I can't push the wrecked car back onto the highway and expect to arrive in Boston."

Jonathan said, "How do you pick which of those options is best?"

"We're in a church hall, so I'm supposed to say you pray over it." Elizabeth laughed. "But I think really, it's just, we muddle through. You figure out where you are and how much of a car you have left, and where you've come from, and where you've been. But at some point, you have to say goodbye to that car. You won't get anywhere if you keep dragging the wreckage. Sure, keep the license plates and the keys, but most of it—? You've got to say goodbye."

Jonathan stared at the carpet. *You've got to say goodbye.*

Frank looked uncertain. "So you're saying I should go on the date?"

Jonathan said, "I think what she's saying is that starting something new means you need to make peace with releasing what you thought you'd have."

Before the end of the bereavement support group, Father Tim stopped in, and Jonathan was just as glad to let him take over. Also, wise and perceptive Father Tim noticed the burnt-out bulb and made a note to replace it.

Allie and Frank both shook Jonathan's hand before they left. "Thank you so much," Allie gushed. "You always say just the right things."

Jonathan hadn't said anything.

Frank finally set that tortured ball cap back on his head. "I'll let you know next week how dinner goes."

Father Tim stuck around to put the chairs in their regular places, and Jonathan kept trying to get his balance back.

"They've become attached you," Father Tim said, then paused. "You're uneasy. What's going on?"

"I don't know what's going on any longer." Jonathan shoved a chair back into its spot, wishing he could do the same with his life. "I'm getting hit with things from every direction, and I'm not sure how to deal with them."

Father Tim sat on one of the chairs they hadn't yet put away. "Hit me with them, too."

"Did you give me this group because losing my vocation was the same as losing their spouses?" Jonathan swallowed. "That wasn't fair."

Father Tim raised his hands. "I needed someone to take the group."

Jonathan clenched his fists. "I know it's not on the same scale, but they talked about losing their whole future all at once, and losing all their community and all their plans. I don't know how to take that."

Father Tim nodded. "Go on."

Jonathan paced. "Tonight, they kept saying how

necessary it was to grieve. I don't think I ever grieved for losing my vocation."

Father Tim said, "You keep saying you lost your vocation. You didn't lose it. You were mistaken about what it was."

"I lost the future I planned. Last week, Brooke walloped me by saying I never let it go, and tonight, they were talking about having to let go." Jonathan shuddered. "But letting go leaves me with nothing, which is also what they said."

Father Tim hummed. "What else did Brooke say?"

Jonathan laughed, but sardonic. "She went for my heart with a keyhole saw. I don't know how to get out of this now. You were right that marrying Brooke was harder than I thought it would be, but it's also too easy. I mucked it up, and now I'm not sure what I'm even supposed to be doing."

Father Tim's brow furrowed. "In what ways is it too easy?"

At least he hadn't asked the ways in which Jonathan had made it far too difficult. "It's easy living with her. We fit around one another and accommodate one another's routines. She was worried that I'd get irritated with her quirks as a roommate, but we give each other space. I let Brooke do Brooke, and I do me, and that works fine. We've got common goals and shared standards, and we both decide the kitchen counter is getting cluttered at about the same time."

Father Tim laughed. "How is that a problem? Is it possible you really should marry her?"

Jonathan said, "That can't be my vocation because vocations require sacrifice. And anyhow, I asked her to marry me, and she refused."

Father Tim raised his hands. "Wait, hang on. First off, a person's vocation is not supposed to be difficult. It's going to have difficult aspects, and it may be rigorous, but you would be designed to follow that vocation."

"Right, but for the priesthood, chastity and obedience

are difficult."

Father Tim shook his head. "The overall vocation shouldn't feel like a fight. If it felt like a fight all along, then you shouldn't have gotten as far in seminary as you did. They should have caught that early on."

Jonathan folded his arms. "My parents always say that a good marriage also requires sacrifices."

Father Tim nodded. "But not sacrifice in the everyday. A sacrifice is when she wants to move near her aging parents and he wants to stay where he grew up. Or he wants to retire early, but her job is so stressful that he lets her retire instead and keeps working for another five years." When Jonathan frowned, Father Tim added, "The everyday shouldn't be a struggle. Ask your parents. When there's no particular struggle going on, your vocation should feel natural."

Jonathan said, "I thought Christians were all about making sacrifices for love of others."

"Not the grinding kind. You're making it sound like every day should be running uphill." Father Tim put his hands on his knees. "Now, what's this about asking Brooke to marry you?"

Jonathan sighed. "I offered to get the marriage convalidated. The church ladies have been calling her a chalice-chipper and spreading gossip. She's given up so much for me. I owe her, so it makes sense for me to settle down with her and give her what she wants."

Father Tim said, "And she refused?"

Jonathan nodded.

Father Tim prompted, "Her reason being that she doesn't love you?"

"Her reason being that she does love me, and she thinks I'm only offering to stay because I feel some kind of obligation toward her."

"That's how it sounds to me, too."

Jonathan walked all the way to the window and stared at the dark parking lot. "Brooke said I'm still entangled with my ex, by which she meant the priesthood, and that she thinks I'll resent her if I marry her because then I'll blame her for never achieving my actual goal."

Father Tim sighed. "She has a way with words."

"Oh, she had quite a few words to have her way with, too." Jonathan rested his head against the window. The chilled glass helped calm him. "She said she doesn't want to be second best forever. She said everyone else she loves acts as if they're stuck with her, and that I keep digging up the corpse of my vocation because I'm not convinced it's actually dead."

Father Tim paused a long time. One of the instructors at seminary said to do that if you weren't sure how to counsel someone, and you were hoping they'd keep talking so you could get a bead on what they actually needed to hear. Either that, or you could pray desperately for help in that silent moment.

Which Jonathan also should be doing, but right now, his heart felt gouged out with a spoon.

Father Tim opted for a change of subject. "If you tell me who was harassing Brooke, I'll step in and tell them to knock it off."

"I already did that, but I'll let you know if it happens again."

"Also, if she did want to convalidate the marriage, you two are about as prepared for marriage as any couple I've ever counseled. I'd dispense the marriage prep requirements and marry you on the spot. You both have a good grasp on what a Catholic marriage entails, which is why, I'm guessing, she knew to turn you down."

Jonathan's jaw tightened. "I suspect I should consider that a compliment, but pardon me if I don't take it that way."

A long silence. Finally Father Tim said, "What was the conclusion you reached tonight during the group?"

"That I haven't grieved over leaving the seminary. Brooke accused me of being a permanent ex-seminarian. But I'll always be an ex-seminarian by virtue of having left the seminary."

Father Tim said, "By that definition, I'm also an ex-seminarian."

Jonathan laughed despite himself.

Father Tim said, "Do you define yourself as a former high school student? How about a former soccer player? A former Scout?"

Jonathan sighed. "Point taken."

Again there was silence.

Everywhere Jonathan looked, there were dead ends. He should have been gearing up for an assignment that would be the rest of his life, and instead he couldn't even marry his own wife. Leaving seminary felt like failure, and in the year since, he'd only compounded it.

Father Tim said, "Do you feel stuck?"

Jonathan glared out the window. "I feel like an idiot."

"No." Father Tim's voice was lower-pitched. "Anger, even anger at yourself, is a defense. What are you truly feeling?"

Jonathan said, "Abandoned."

He didn't even think before it came out, but now the word was sitting there, naked in the light—the fear because all along he'd had something that kept him moving, made him special, set him apart—only he'd never had it at all. He'd built a life and a personality around one thing, and then when he'd flung himself out in the void knowing the safety net would be there, it wasn't.

Father Tim said. "And now, tell me the rest about discerning out."

Jonathan recoiled. "I told you everything."

Father Tim said, "No, you didn't. Because I think you fought it. I think you fought it for years."

Jonathan shook his head, heart pounding.

"The way you're talking now, I'm guessing you stuffed it down for as long as you could. You knew what to say to the vocations advisor and your formation director, and more to the point, you knew what not to say. If you didn't tell them about that nagging feeling—"

"Please."

Jonathan couldn't manage more than the one word.

When Allie first showed up at bereavement support, hadn't she been the same way? Unable to introduce herself, unable to speak? He didn't even know who she'd lost for the first couple of weeks. Because if she didn't say it out loud, maybe it hadn't happened. Maybe if she didn't admit her husband was dead, she'd have him back.

It could have been over for Jonathan years ago. Except he knew he'd make a good priest, and if he just hung in there, eventually he'd find the key and the gates would swing open. God would relent. The rest of the path would spread itself up before him. The peace would come. It had to come if he just kept denying the uneasiness.

He bit his lip hard, and he couldn't face Father Tim.

Father Tim's chair creaked, but he didn't cross the room. Jonathan wouldn't have been able to stand his touch if he had.

Jonathan hadn't given up. His heart had been saying what Brooke had in January: "Should we change the plan?" Jonathan had replied to himself, over and over and over, "No, we're going to stick to what I decided."

Jonathan was shaking. He leaned hard against the wall to quell it, but his hands still trembled.

It was time to let go. Time to face everything that had happened and agree: it was time to let go. If he was in an untenable spot right now, it was a spot into which he'd methodically entrenched himself.

Brooke had been right to refuse him. She was being nothing but generous when she said proposing was the most offensive thing he'd done in all the time they'd known one another.

He'd held on so tightly that everything good had broken apart in his hands. No priesthood. No Brooke. It was all his fault, and all because he hadn't wanted to face the losses in front of him. He'd slithered out of the pain he should have been feeling, and now, if the pain was too great to bear, it was only that great because every day he'd piled more denial onto the basic pain, delaying and delaying and delaying the inevitable payday when he'd have to acknowledge it all.

I wish I'd never even heard of the priesthood. He squeezed his eyes closed. *I wish I'd never had a vocation. I wish I'd never heard of God or been Catholic.*

How could he deal with this? What had he done to himself, and what had he done to Brooke?

Father Tim spoke quietly. "What do you need?"

Jonathan trembled. "I don't know. What do I do?"

Father Tim stood. "My answer is always to pray about it. As for the rest, I think that's up to you."

Jonathan said, "Am I supposed to get married?"

"That's not for me to answer, but you heard what Elizabeth said about not jumping ship too quickly. Don't do anything right away."

Brooke had said Jonathan wasn't available for a relationship. He stared out at the parking lot, and his throat tightened. He could barely breathe.

"The church is unlocked." Father Tim unwound a key from his key ring. "Stay as late as you want, but lock up before you leave. Push the key back through the rectory mail slot."

Then they closed up the meeting room and turned off its three remaining lights.

At ten-thirty, a text came in from Brooke. "You didn't come home? Is everything okay?"

Jonathan took that as a sign to go back. He texted, "I'm on my way now."

With the church dark and the key back through the mail slot, he got into the only truck left in the lot.

The bereavement pamphlet said Elisabeth Kubler-Ross's five stages of grief were denial, anger, bargaining, depression, and acceptance. That sounded like a travel itinerary, and the first time Jonathan had recited them to the group members, the more experienced ones had guffawed and told him no, you could experience all five during the same morning and then after lunch discover two new stages. The point was not to get stuck in any of them, and Jonathan had spent the last year cementing himself in bargaining.

Tonight, he'd experienced everything except acceptance, and what did that even feel like anymore?

At home, Brooke came halfway down the stairs. "Is everything okay? Did someone need special counseling?"

Jonathan looked up from the bottom step. "Yes." His voice was unnaturally hushed. "A lot of that."

Brooke's face softened. "I'm sorry. You look worn out. But I'm glad you were there for that."

Shaking his head, Jonathan stared at the step he was on.

Brooke came further down. "Do you need to sit up for a while? Or do you just need space?"

Her face looked strained. She'd been worried about him, and as always, he'd been wrapped up in everything going on inside himself. Jonathan said, "One of the men tonight —he wanted to date again. It's been fifteen months. He's afraid to move on because that means accepting the loss."

Brooke's face fell. "That must be so hard." She came the rest of the way down the stairs. "Do you want to talk?"

He did still want to talk about it, was the problem. Except not with Brooke. And not with anyone else. And not with God or with himself. He just wanted it all out of his head, all the confusion and the realization that none of his plans were going to happen, and his identity was built on a conceit that never was. "There's so much."

She was close enough to take his hand. A month ago, she would have. "It's kind of late, but do you want to watch something?"

He'd treated her shamefully, but she still cared about his well-being.

"I'm going to bed." He met her eyes, but she glanced away. "Thanks, though. I'm sorry you waited up for me."

She went down the hall and locked her door. Probably double-locked it. He wasn't about to check.

No means no. He couldn't ask her to renew the relationship. Not until he got his head and heart sorted out, and even then, he should respect her no. He should treat her right. He should give her clarity. He should give her everything he should have been giving all along.

In his own room, he readied himself for bed and looked at Aunt Millie's castle headboard with its large door at the center, a door that was never going to open because there had never been anything behind it in the first place.

About to turn out the light, he stopped himself mid-reach. Then he opened the bedside drawer and grabbed the fingerless gloves Brooke had made for Christmas. He pulled those on, and wearing them, that was how he went to sleep.

CHAPTER TWENTY-FIVE

By summer's end, Brooke was scared by how quiet Jonathan had become. It wasn't him punishing her for turning down his proposal. He was quiet with everyone. If anything, when he did talk to her, he was softer in tone, more considerate in feeling. He gave her all the space she wanted without pressing her.

Jonathan had resumed making bowls. Brooke would come home from work to find the lights on in the carriage house, and then she'd bring dinner out to him. He'd take a break to eat, sitting on a stool on one side of the lathe and her on a stool on the other side.

So many bowls, all at once. Endless stacks. Jonathan chain-sawed apart a sixty-foot pine that had fallen last summer, and every day, he turned it into two more bowls.

Last year, he'd called them therapy bowls. Whatever had happened at that meeting, it had punched him in the gut, and ever since, he hadn't been able to draw his next breath.

Brooke wasn't stupid. It couldn't have been just about a widower wanting to date again. But what?

Without answering her unasked questions, he kept

spending his time scary-quiet. At coffee and donuts, sometimes he'd sit with his parents and Father Tim, and even then, he wasn't talking much. He never again brought up loving her. They didn't cuddle on his bed to watch TV. They ate together and cleaned up together, but a wistfulness ghosted around Jonathan that Brooke couldn't identify. The only thing he seemed to look forward to was the bereavement support group.

In early July, he drove home with a tremendous box in the back of his pickup. He and a work friend spent the entire weekend on the carriage house roof, and at the end, Brooke had her skylight. She stood in the center, neck craned back, smiling at the natural light. She'd been right. Letting in the light meant they could see all the colors better. Jonathan said he was happy that she was happy, but he didn't seem happy. He never seemed happy.

His face was mostly what Lilah's facial chart would have called "neutral," but that was so very much not like Jonathan's usual self. Brooke kept thinking he seemed devastated. And not by her. He filled the summer with therapy bowls and silence, accompanied by the occasional thousand-yard stare.

Whenever any of the church ladies came close to Brooke, he fixed them with a glare. This, granted, wasn't doing anything for her reputation, but at this point, Brooke no longer cared. If they gossiped about her, at least they did it out of earshot.

As if to make up for it, the bereavement support members became friendly with her. They asked her to sit with them at coffee and donuts. They all wanted to talk up Jonathan, and she would agree with them. He's very nice. He's sweet.

Until one day, mid-August, when all the church ladies gave Brooke the undisguised evil eye—and none would talk to her. As in, she asked if there was more creamer in the kitchen, and they walked away.

It was off-putting and odd, but having dealt with large-scale silence on a longer term in the past (*hello, middle school!*) Brooke put it out of her head. The thing you could count on with the silent treatment was if you didn't notice it, eventually someone would break silence to make sure you did.

Silence got broken before the end of coffee and donuts, but not by the church ladies. Rather, it was Allie from the bereavement group. "I heard today that you and Jonathan got married!"

Brooke went cold, but Allie was beaming. "Oh, don't worry, sweetie. I don't think you stole him from the priesthood—and whatever arrangement you have, I'm sure you both know what you're doing." She leaned closer to Brooke. "But I'm telling you now: the Historical Society is going to challenge the house and your marriage at the next Town Meeting."

Brooke blinked. "Excuse me? What on earth would that even mean?"

"They don't want your artist group to get the house, and they think the town can stop it from happening. I know this is nonsense," Allie added, "but you ought to be there."

Brooke sighed. "Do they have a warrant article for us, or are they planning just to spring it on everyone? No, never mind, I'll get Lilah on it. She's on the Economic Development Board."

Brooke pulled out her phone and sent out the alert, then froze in place and looked around the room.

How many people knew they'd gotten married? There was Jonathan, Father Tim, and Jonathan's parents. None of them were gossips. As of a couple weeks ago, the church ladies thought Brooke was only attempting to seduce Jonathan, so it couldn't have been general knowledge. Moreover, how would any of them have known about Aunt Millie's will and the trust and the house?

She looked again at Jonathan. His face was that same neutral-to-wistful expression she'd come to expect. She met his eyes and braced herself not to look away, until after a moment, he said something to his parents, then crossed the room to her. "Are you all right?"

She set her jaw. "Our enemies the historians know about Aunt Millie's trust and how we're handling the house. They've identified me as a priest-thieving slut, so I'll have to go to the town meeting."

Jonathan's eyes narrowed. "What are they going to do? Our own lawyer couldn't break it."

"If only we'd known they could challenge the will, we could have gone to them last October and saved you a lot of trouble."

Jonathan grabbed her hand. "You're no trouble."

Knowing she'd caused no end of trouble, Brooke slipped her hand from his. "The point is, I can't conceive of what they're planning. But whatever it is, I need to be there."

Jonathan didn't reach for her again. "Together. Whatever they had planned, they need to hit us together."

Town Meeting was always on a weeknight, for reasons no one in Brighthead knew but were enshrined in the town charter. Brooke would close the shop early. Let anyone who wanted late-night yarn get mad at the historians.

Jonathan texted her right before six. "If you close now, we can get dinner first."

Brooke texted, "If I eat the pasta I packed in the fridge, I can still get dinner first."

He texted, "I'll be there in ten minutes. We'll split the pasta."

She replied, "Or you could bring a sandwich...?"

His reply to that was to show up without a sandwich. "Pizza. You said that was the only acceptable dinner for moving, and things may start moving tonight."

In a booth near the back, Brooke cut the crust off her pizza first. "We're going to have a nice contingent of people around us, at least."

"I saw that on the message board." Jonathan looked up. "I've been trying to figure out how to tell you this for a while, so do you mind if I just say something uncomfortable?" Without giving her a chance to say she minded or didn't, Jonathan clenched his hands. "I'm sorry for the way I treated you. You deserved better than that, and I was out of line."

She rummaged in her head for whatever he thought had offended her. "Treated me, how?"

Jonathan sighed. "You said everyone you love acts like they're stuck with you. Your parents—they definitely act that way. Your grandmother did, too, and that was wrong. But then I came along, and I also didn't accept you the way I should have."

Brooke puzzled at him. "On the contrary, you accepted all the weird things I do. Of all the people I've ever known, you're the only one who hasn't tried to change me."

Jonathan bit his lip. "I turned you into the stand-in for my vocation, and that was objectifying you. I mean, you do weird and wonderful things, but they are kind of wonderful because they're a part of you. That's the irony. In school, I benefitted from the ways I was quirky, while you suffered for being quirky."

Like now, when Brooke was eating her pizza with a knife and fork. It felt neater that way, but her school friends had roasted her for it. Jonathan never did. When he'd brought the pizza back to the table, he'd brought silverware unprompted. She said, "Go on...?"

Jonathan sighed. "All along, having a vocation was what made me special. It was the thing that let me say I wasn't like other people. Everyone else had to figure out what they'd grow up to become, but I was this luminous being with a life plan charted out for me."

Brooke chuckled. "And you were what, thirteen? That's how most thirteen-year-olds think."

"Most thirteen-year-olds opt out of being the Chosen One sometime before college. Me, I just kept getting petted for it. Oh, is Jonathan still on track to become a priest? Is he volunteering with the cleanup committee? Even the other kids in school were like, 'Hey, Father Jonathan.' I built my identity around that."

Brooke looked at her hands. "But you would have been an awesome priest."

His eyes flared. "I would have been a terrible priest! Can you imagine my arrogance if I'd actually gotten ordained? Father Jonathan, the Chosen One?" Jonathan shuddered. "No, thank you. That's not giving glory to God. That would have been giving glory to me."

Brooke looked up. "So now that you've realized that, having become humble—"

"No, it's over." Jonathan sighed. "I never thought I'd say this, but it's better this way."

Brooke's eyes widened. Was that acceptance? Had he spent the past two months grinding down his own resistance and finally accepting what he'd been giving lip service to for the past year and a half?

All summer, he'd been grieving?

Because if he'd been grieving—if he'd been accepting that there was no vocation and no pedestal and no one heroic life pathway he had to make great sacrifices to follow—what did that mean for her and for him?

Did he still love her? Were all these apologies and explanations a run-up to him inviting her back into his heart?

Jonathan was still off in his own conversation. "I couldn't face giving up on my vocation, not when even I didn't know myself as anything other than Father Jonathan. Coming home was horrible. I created so much pressure to force it to happen in some form or another. And then—"

Brooke ventured, "And then you married me because somehow that made you more a priest?"

"I keep thinking back over my thought process, and I'm not sure if it was a way to stick it to God, or if it was a way for me to leap into the darkness and grab the next thing that came along. Neither of those is fair to you."

Brooke said, "You were getting rid of a house. And you were furious at Aunt Millie."

"I'm working on the anger. She was misguided, but it's more charitable to pretend she was leaving me a safety net in case I left the priesthood on my own, not trying to bribe me away from it."

"Fair enough." Brooke ate the crust without cutting it up. Crusts were different. "It's ironic that people accused me of competing with God for you, when it was you doing all the fighting."

Jonathan sighed. "Here's what I didn't expect, and I didn't realize it until now. I came to you trying to hold onto my past. By contrast, you accepted me as I was, in the present. You were right that I spent a year trying to resurrect my vocation in a different form, whereas you encouraged me to accept myself. Not my job, not my function. Just me. And I appreciate that."

Maybe he did still love her. Brooke took his hand across the table. "Thank you." Then, trying to make herself brave, she said, "You know how at the beginning, I was so scared we'd finish up the year and wouldn't be able to keep being friends...?"

Jonathan flipped his hand over beneath hers and clasped back, but for a brief flash his face was...was it devastated? Immediately, he returned to looking brave. "If we can stay friends, even after everything, that's what I want. In fact, it's very important to me that we do."

Brooke fought disappointment. He still wanted to divorce. Giving up on his vocation meant he was also giving up on the vocation substitutes—the primary one of which was her.

It made sense. If he'd been reaching out to her because of the fear he'd be left with nothing, then once he was no longer afraid, he no longer needed her.

It would hurt to keep interacting with him afterward, but she didn't want to let him go. Brooke said, "Our friendship is important to me, too."

Jonathan looked relieved. "Then it's settled. We're still

going to be friends, but I think we'll succeed only because you've helped me become friends with myself."

Lilah cast on a sock from the toe while they waited to begin the Town Meeting, and she started working her way up the foot. At her side, Natalie was crocheting a scarf, and sitting behind them, beside Jonathan, Brooke was working on a mosaic colorwork shawl in black and pink. The final product would be crescent-shaped, the top half pink with a black design, and the bottom half black with a pink design.

The key to winning a Town Meeting, with its idiosyncratic New England voting style, was getting all your friends to show up in blocs. The BCG had turned out in force. Additionally, Jonathan's parents were seated in the same row as Brooke and Jonathan. A contingent of bereavement support group members were in place, and also Father Tim. At least Father Tim's presence made sense because Saint Lucy's was an important presence in the town. Jonathan had joked that one of the skills necessary to become a priest was the ability to sit through boring meetings, and here was Father Tim, proving it.

Jonathan touched the edge of the shawl where it hung over Brooke's knee. "I can't do wood turning during the meeting."

"Not without violating Robert's Rules of Order." Brooke chuckled. "This is my second time making one of these. The first shawl, I hated everything about it. The colorwork looked nothing like the design photos. Lilah told me it was okay, but I couldn't stand it. It wasn't the way the designer wanted it to look."

Jonathan shook his head. "And yet you're making it again."

She arched her brows. "Let me finish. After I cast it off, I hurled the thing into the washing machine and then the dryer to make sure it thought good and hard about what it had done." She snickered. "And wonder of wonders, it ended up looking—well, hang on." She pulled up her phone and poked around until she found the photo, then handed it to Jonathan.

He exclaimed, "But that's beautiful!"

"Right? In the wash, the yarn bloomed—meaning the yarn fluffed out and made a halo, and that filled out the colorwork so it looked exactly like the designer's plan." She laughed. "It's a joke in the yarn world that 'oh, that will block right out,' and this time, it did."

Jonathan tilted his head. "I've never seen you wear it."

She shook her head. "The only way I could force myself to finish it was to tell myself no one other than me knew what it was supposed to look like, so I could donate it. I felt obligated to follow through. That's why I'm making another one."

Jonathan gave a rueful chuckle. "Do you think I got thrown in God's washing machine?"

"And then you bloomed?" She rested a hand on his knee. "Maybe it made you more beautiful than you would have become otherwise."

He said, "An arrogant green and blue shawl with an unbloomed mosaic pattern?"

She smiled at him. "As opposed to a humble blue and green shawl with exactly the pattern the designer intended."

Grandma used to drag Brooke to Town Meeting. Grandma said it would make Brooke civically conscious, but really, Grandma wanted to hear all the arguments. Brooke had made it a life goal never to attend again, and yet, here she was.

For the first hour, the town of Brighthead debated (argued) about building a new firehouse, expanding the library, adding a sidewalk on Route 188 near the apartment complexes, and fund-raising for the rail trail. Lilah had economic board business to discuss a couple of times, which was nice. The rest was dead boring. Brooke finished the first colorwork section and moved on to the border before the colors would flip-flop.

"The next item on the agenda is the Brighthead Crafters Guild, and their allegedly illegal use of the house at 28 Sky Ridge Drive."

Lilah stood. "As the president and founder of the Brighthead Crafters Guild, I'd love to learn what town ordinances our group is violating."

The chair waved her down. "The issue at hand is whether you're using a residential property for commercial use, and also, how you've obtained the property."

Lilah said, "There's nothing commercial going on. The owners of the property trust have graciously allowed us permission to use the property for our meetings. Private residences can still be used for meetings, correct? Or are we introducing a town ordinance against book clubs and new mom support groups?"

The alderman said, "Michelle Hargrove? This was your motion."

Of course it was. Michelle stood and folded her arms. "You're operating an artist-in-residency program out of that property."

Lilah said, "To be clear, you want the Town of Brighthead to regulate whether homeowners can have overnight guests?"

Brooke snickered, but Michelle was unamused. "Renting out the property makes it commercial space."

Natalie stood. "Resident artists pay no fees to stay at the house, so again, not commercial. They're guests. Please call off your witch hunt. All you're going to discover is that we understand the state statutes as well as you do."

Lilah said, "In fact, better."

Michelle said, "You frequently have cars parked all over property and large numbers of guests."

Lilah said, "To be clear, your motion is to prohibit parking on driveways, as well as backyard weddings and at-home graduation parties?"

Michelle said, "This isn't a wedding. You're an organization hosting a meeting."

Natalie stood. "You want to prohibit church groups from having Bible studies?"

Michelle said, "You are trying to find loopholes!"

Lilah shook her head. "We are interpreting the rules as given. You're the one ransacking the law for a loophole to destroy the Brighthead Crafters Guild. You know we haven't done a single thing that's illegal or in violation of town ordinances. If we had, you'd have filed a court order or called the cops rather than coming to the town meeting."

Michelle folded her arms. "You don't even own the property."

Lilah turned to Mary Levesque. "Mrs. Levesque, as the executor of the estate of Millie Levesque, and the manager of the trust that currently owns the property, do you grant permission to the Brighthead Crafters Guild to continue using the property as the caretakers see fit?"

Mary said, "All permissions granted."

Michelle stepped forward to the alderman. "They didn't even obtain the property under moral means. The property was left in trust to Jonathan Levesque on the condition that he got married. Brooke Evart married him with the sole purpose of obtaining the property."

Brooke got to her feet. "Mrs. Hargrove, may I ask if our marriage is in violation of town ordinances? Because unless you intend to introduce a motion stating that couples in the state of Maine can only marry with your personal approval, it doesn't matter why Jonathan and I chose to get married."

Michelle strode toward Brooke. "Your own mother says you aren't really married."

Ah, so Mom was the source of the gossip. Of course she was.

Brooke pulled a paper out of her knitting bag. "This is a copy of my marriage certificate, signed and notarized. The State of Maine says we're really married.

Michelle smirked. "But Jonathan Levesque is the super-Catholic boy wonder, and according to the Catholic church, you're not married."

Brooke met her halfway up the aisle. "The terms of Aunt Mille's will don't stipulate he has to enter a sacramental Catholic marriage. Given that Millie Levesque's intent was explicitly anti-Catholic, she wouldn't have cared. Neither will a judge."

Michelle raised her eyebrows. "Do you know what they call women who sell their bodies for money?"

Brooke put on her customer service smile. "I don't know what *they* call such women—but *you* call her Brooke Evart."

About to reply, Michelle looked up and to the side, and that's when Brooke realized Jonathan had joined her.

"How dare you?" Jonathan's voice was steely. "You've gone beyond town politics and into personal detraction. My aunt's will is between her and her heirs. My marriage to Brooke is between her and me. You're the one who's demanding that the town interfere in the normal usage of a personal property, and for what? Because the BCG initially wanted to purchase an abandoned church? Instead, you're dragging down the institution of the Town Meeting as your personal slander and gossip-festival."

Michelle folded her arms. "You married her to give her a house? What are you getting from the deal?"

Brooke murmured, "I asked him the same thing."

Jonathan squared his shoulders. "I've gotten to live with the most amazing woman I've ever met. I got the chance to discover a depth of friendship and acceptance I'd never comprehended in my entire life. I got the opportunity to give someone joy and open my family and my home to someone who's more special to me than life itself. I've spent time with the best woman in the world. What more could I want?"

Michelle folded her arms and glared at Brooke. "To marry her for real."

Jonathan said, "In a heartbeat."

Brooke said, "I'm in." Then she spun toward him. "Wait, really?"

He started. "We were just talking about staying friends. You mean, I didn't ruin everything?"

She grasped his hands. "Was that a real proposal, via Michelle Hargrove?"

Jonathan exclaimed, "Yes!" He got down on one knee and took her hand. "Brooke Evart, my guiding star and the reason I was born, will you do me the honor of becoming my wife?"

Brooke pulled him up to his feet, and he was laughing. "Yes! Yes, of course!"

Across the room, Father Tim stood. "Would it please the Board of Alderman to have me convalidate their marriage right now, or shall I wait until after we adjourn?"

Brooke put her arms around Jonathan's neck and pressed her face into his shoulder. He nuzzled her hair, and she tightened her grip.

Michelle exclaimed, "This is an act! You're trying to distract us from what's actually going on here!"

A voice rang out from the back of the room. "Michelle Hargrove, young lady, you sit yourself right down."

There was Lavender Paul, marching up the center aisle. She thundered, "You've monopolized this meeting for too long with your vendetta against a bunch of perfectly nice women."

Michelle said, "You can see—"

"All of us can see exactly what you're doing, miss!" Lavender Paul pushed Brooke out of the way. She was wearing the pink and orange shawl Natalie had crocheted for Brooke during last year's all-night crochet session. "These ladies have been nothing but good for Brighthead. They run a store and pay property taxes, and they bring smart and clever people to this town. They have artists come in who make beautiful art, but you won't have it because they're not *your* people." She pushed even closer in front of Michelle. "Now you're dragging out our town meeting with your nonsense, and this isn't even close to the way a meeting should be run. You had the nerve to bring up Brooke's mother, but I went to school with *your* mother, and your mother would be ashamed of you!"

As Michelle backed away, Lavender Paul turned to the rest of the meeting-goers. "Two years ago, you tried this on me, too, tried to railroad me into not putting art in my yard. I've been putting more and more art in my yard and on my house ever since, and you can't touch it. Think about what happens when you get the backs up on a whole flock of creative artists who have the power to change what everyone thinks about Brighthead. If you're gossiping that my fifth of an acre is an eyesore, what happens when you've got painters and sculptors and musicians using the whole world as a canvas to label us as a haven of narrow-minded people just like Michelle?"

Brooke backed up and bumped into Jonathan, who put his hands on her shoulders.

Lavender turned to Jonathan. "For heaven's sake, man— kiss her and then have Father Tim set a date, otherwise this meeting's going on past midnight."

Jonathan faced Brooke. "I don't want to get on the bad side of Ms. Lavender Paul."

Brooke snickered. "Me neither."

Jonathan bent to kiss her right in front of the whole Town Meeting, and Brooke's heart went out of her body to engulf his.

This was real. She could get married to her best friend— for real.

CHAPTER TWENTY-SIX

"Okay, one more thing." In the living room at Aunt Millie's house, Natalie adjusted Lilah's shawl on Brooke's shoulders and then pulled a box from her pocket. Inside was a gold-toned spiral shawl pin with pearls at the top. "Colin gave this to me, but you can use it tonight."

Brooke took a deep breath. "Thank you. That's beautiful."

"You're beautiful." Natalie hugged her. "Are you ready?"

She'd been ready since the middle of April.

Lilah popped into the room. "Oh, gosh, you're gorgeous." She came up to Brooke and adjusted one of the flowers she'd woven into her hair. "Jonathan is going to pass out on the spot."

"I hope not." Brooke's nose wrinkled. "Then we'll have to try all over again next Monday."

They drove to Saint Lucy's as the sun went down.

Brooke wrung her hands. In the twelve days since the Town Meeting, everything had gone topsy-turvy. Natalie had crocheted like the wind to finish Lilah's wedding shawl so Brooke could wear it. Lilah had hunted half of Maine with Brooke to find a pretty dress.

Jonathan had moved out of Aunt Millie's house because he said it would be too tempting, and in hindsight, Brooke had to agree. They still had dinner together and spent time reading or playing piano, but even at that, they kept getting distracted from their respective books.

She'd kiss him goodbye at the door, and he'd linger. Last night, holding her, he'd said, "Tomorrow night, I'm coming home, and I'm not going to leave."

Cars dotted St. Lucy's parking lot, including Jonathan's truck—which was good because without him, nothing was happening.

Natalie said, "None of your family."

Brooke hadn't invited her parents or her brother. She and Jonathan had picked Monday so Colin and Austin could be here. "You guys are my family."

They entered the church, and Jonathan turned. The moment he caught sight of Brooke, he beamed. His father pushed him on the shoulder, and Jonathan met Brooke halfway up the aisle.

Natalie went to sit with Colin, and Lilah waited at the back door for Emerson. That left Brooke and Jonathan alone, and she took both his hands in hers. "You ready for this, most fascinating husband?"

He squeezed her hands. "I am entirely ready for this, most esteemed wife."

They'd put out the word rather than issuing invitations. People arrived from the BCG, from Jonathan's grief support group, and from the yarn store. Austin showed up, pleased that for once there was an event he didn't have to cater. Gemma had driven from Burlington. Afterward, there would be little sandwiches and a cake in the church hall, with no angry church ladies to deny Brooke the half and half.

Father Tim started the Mass the same way he always did, and in place of the homily, he called Jonathan and Brooke to the front. "Jonathan and Brooke, have you come here to enter into marriage without coercion, freely and wholeheartedly?"

"We have."

Freely and wholeheartedly. Jonathan had made his heart whole for her. He couldn't have given it before, but now that it was healed, it was all hers.

"Since it is your intention to enter into the covenant of Holy Matrimony, join your right hands, and declare your consent before God and his Church."

Facing Brooke, Jonathan met her eyes. "I, Jonathan Levesque, take you, Brooke, to be my lawfully wedded wife. To have and to hold from this day forth, for richer, for poorer, in sickness and in health, until death do us part."

She'd spent every day this week rehearsing their vows. "I, Brooke Evart, take you, Jonathan, to be my lawfully wedded husband. To have and to hold from this day forth, for richer, for poorer, in sickness and in health, until death do us part."

Father Tim finished the prayer for them, then said, "Do you have a ring?"

Jonathan's sister brought him a box, and he opened it. In a low voice, he said, "I'm not following the script. I wanted you to have something more."

In the box was not only her gold band, but also a ruby solitaire. Brooke gasped as Jonathan slipped the ruby onto her hand. The band was etched with leaves winding all around. Then Father blessed the wedding ring, and Jonathan put Brooke's band onto her finger. "Receive this ring as a sign of my love and fidelity."

Father said, "May the Lord in His kindness strengthen the consent you have declared before the Church and graciously bring to fulfillment His blessings within you." He put one hand on Brooke's hand and the other on Jonathan's, and then he placed them together. "What God has joined, let no one put asunder."

Brooke stretched toward him, and Jonathan kissed her. They were really married.

EPILOGUE

Brooke navigated the crowd to find Jonathan on the lawn, talking to Adrian. She slipped her hand through his arm. To Adrian, she said, "I hope you don't mind, but I need to steal this endlessly fascinating man in the tuxedo."

Adrian went to join another group of wedding guests while Jonathan said, "Do you need me to cover for you while you a make an escape?"

The Sky Ridge yard thronged with people, and Brooke gazed around, thinking that yes, a little quiet might not be out of place. "I'm okay for now, but the caterers want to know when we should bring out the cake. I don't want to bug Lilah about yet another thing."

"We are hosting, theoretically." Jonathan glanced at his watch. "People are still dancing, I don't want to pull them off the dance floor. I'd say another ten minutes."

"I'll let the DJ know." Even so, she didn't leave Jonathan's side. "Isn't Lilah beautiful?"

Jonathan side-eyed Brooke. "Second most beautiful woman at this wedding."

"Rude." She giggled. "Also, Natalie is here, so if anything, I'm a distant third."

"I disagree." He fingered a stray hair that had escaped her updo. "But it would be unfitting for you to upstage the bride, so I'll play along."

She smoothed out her gown. "At least I didn't *unfit* into my dress. That would have been embarrassing. As well as distracting from the bride and my fellow bridesmaid."

"You look fine." He kissed her. "You update the caterers, and I'll have a word with the DJ."

Brooke picked her way back through the crowd, and after she gave the ten minute warning, she joined Lilah and Emerson at the head table. Lilah was wearing the wedding shawl, and she looked stunning. "I hope you've got room for cake," Brooke teased.

Lilah sprang up from her chair and hugged Brooke. "This reception is amazing. I didn't even know you could do half this stuff with a back yard wedding."

"Good thing you stood up for back yard weddings at the town meeting." Brooke stepped back. "Besides, you helped arrange it."

"I didn't really. I was hoping you and Natalie had it all under control." Lilah made a worried face. "Thank you for putting up with me."

Brooke hugged her again. "Thank you for being my best friend." She turned back to Emerson. "No thanks to you for taking her away from me, you terrible man."

Emerson inclined his head. "I saw her and couldn't resist."

Jonathan rejoined them as Brooke was saying, "As soon as the current set ends, the caterers will bring out the cake, and DJ will call for the champagne toast."

Jonathan said, "And sparkling cider?"

He looked concerned, so Brooke added, "Yes, plus sparkling cider. Think of the children."

Jonathan extended his hand. "Would you care to dance during the final song before the speeches? They promised it would be slow."

"As it turns out, I would." She took his arm. "Lead on, endlessly fascinating husband."

The song did change to a slower tune, and Brooke was just as glad for that. She'd ditched her heels for flats as soon as they got into the back yard, but she'd been exhausted lately, and gyrating on a crowded dance floor had never had much appeal.

Jonathan pulled her close, and she rested her arms over his shoulders. "You're a schemer. You asked for a slow song to end the set."

"I'm even worse than you know. I asked for a slow *Paxley* song to end the set, but they didn't have one." He kissed her neck. "But I can't be blamed for wanting to dance with you, so here we are, shamelessly swaying on the dance floor."

Brooke fingered the hair at the back of his neck. "What will the church ladies say?"

Jonathan said, "I'm sure they suspect we do more than dancing."

Brooke snickered. "Soon enough, they'll *know* we do more than dancing."

The song ended, and the DJ said, "Everyone, if you could please return to your tables, we're going to take a break for the cake cutting. But first, a toast!" And then he handed it over.

Brooke would have rather spun iron filings into aluminum foil than give a speech. She carried the mic to Natalie.

Natalie, on the other hand, sounded like a natural. "Thank you, everyone! Hasn't this afternoon been just the best wedding?"

The guests applauded. Brooke slipped into her seat at the head table. The servers had placed glasses of sparkling wine all around.

Natalie continued, "Back in school, Lilah was this loud kid who always got into trouble, and soon she was the loud kid who was getting my cousin in trouble. My cousin taught her to knit, and the rest is history."

Jonathan hadn't gotten back yet. On Brooke's other side sat Colin, who watched Natalie with intensity.

"Lilah's always been a dynamo. Three years ago, she started an indie dyeing business. A year after that, she got elected to the Economic Development Board. Another six months, and she started the Brighthead Crafters Guild. She also met one Emerson Charles, a painter and former park ranger and, as it turns out, a guy with the extraordinarily good sense to fall in love with her."

Jonathan joined Brooke at the table, holding a glass of sparkling something. He set that glass in front of Brooke and, without making a big deal of it, removed the other glass from in front of her. She rested her hand on his leg.

"You could say it's fate," Natalie said, "but I'm going to

credit art. All three of us who work at Bright Stitches have found the love of our lives in the past two years. Brooke got married last year, I got engaged six months ago, and Lilah got married today. That's because creativity doesn't stop at creating a *thing*. Yes, we create a scarf or a hand-dyed skein of yarn, but creativity insists on spending itself on others. People create art, but then art creates community, and community creates friends, and friendship creates love."

And love creates people. Brooke wove her fingers through Jonathan's, and Jonathan squeezed.

"Therefore, please join me in acknowledging that art and creativity brought this couple together, and today, they've created their family." Natalie picked up her glass. "To the bride and groom!"

Jonathan and Brooke raised their glasses and toasted. Lilah kissed Emerson, and everyone applauded. Then Lilah and Emerson went to cut the cake.

Brooke leaned against Jonathan. "Thanks for swapping out my drink."

He put his arm around her. "Are you ever sad that you didn't have a wedding like this?"

"I'd rather be married to you than have all the fantastic weddings in the world."

Lilah and Emerson stood together, and with his hand on hers, they cut the first slice. More applause, and lots of pictures.

Jonathan said, "Sometimes I regret that we got married in stages."

Brooke rested her head against his shoulder. "And the rest of the time, you know for a fact this was the only way it could have happened."

At the dessert table, Lilah picked up a morsel of cake on a fork and fed it to Emerson. Again, pictures and applause.

Brooke said, "Do you regret not becoming a priest after all?"

"And miss out on all the meetings and fund-raising? No. I'm glad I never had a vocation if it means I get to be here with you. Besides, the world didn't need Father Jonathan."

Brooke freed his hand from hers and rested it on her abdomen. "Not that kind of father Jonathan."

He kissed her temple. "You're a treasure."

Brooke leaned against him. "And you're amazing. I love you so much."

Lilah and Emerson returned to the table. "Go, grab some cake, you lovebirds!"

Jonathan took her hand as they went. What had begun with bright stitches would, after all, end in a bright future.

THANK YOU!

Thank you for reading the yarn shop romances! I hope you've had a great time getting to know Natalie and Colin, Lilah and Emerson, and Brooke and Jonathan. Also, I hope you paused the last time you passed a skein of yarn and thought to yourself, "What if...?"

Please-please-please consider leaving a review at Goodreads or wherever you picked up my stories. Reviews help authors and other readers so much. It doesn't have to be complicated, just a star rating and a couple of sentences, but that's usually enough to let a reader know whether they will or won't like a story. Everyone wants happy readers, right?

Please join us for "Maddie Mondays," where I share weird stories about life in the swamps of New England. I also share recommendations of books I've enjoyed, sales, and interesting craft projects. You can sign up for that here: https://stats.sender.net/forms/erBXBe/view

Again, thank you so much for reading, and I hope you'll stick around for more.

-Maddie

Something else you might like!

If you've enjoyed knitting, crocheting, and falling in love, then please check out my string quartet series: **The Castleton String Quartet Romances.**

The Castleton String Quartet has had a terrible year. After being diagnosed with a terminal illness, the first violinist stepped down. Now his daughter, Lindsey Castleton, struggles to preserve his legacy, and his quartet.

Heart of the Violist
Violist Ashlyn learned to express herself only after she was adopted into a family of musicians—but now a handsome man has come along claiming he's also a member of the family, himself given up for adoption.

Soul of the Cellist
Hannah, the cellist, reaches out to Enrique, vocalist and longtime friend, for help when a stalker upends her life, only to discover falling in love can upend it even more.

Spirit of the Violinists
And the first and second violinists are forced to work together despite their longtime feud, only to discover they have far more in common than they ever anticipated.

Life, love, and loss intermingle as the quartet players learn to blend heart and harmony in this sweet small-town romance series.

"Love is friendship set to music."

The Castleton String Quartet

HEART OF THE *Violist*
maddie evans

SOUL OF THE *Cellist*
maddie evans

SPIRIT OF THE *Violinists*